SAGEBRUSH

SAGEBRUSH

A Novel

William Wayne Dicksion

iUniverse, Inc.

New York Lincoln Shanghai

SAGEBRUSH

iUniverse books may be ordered through booksellers or by contacting:

iUniverse
2021 Pine Lake Road, Suite 100
Lincoln, NE 68512
www.iuniverse.com
1-800-Authors (1-800-288-4677)

Because of the dynamic nature of the Internet, any Web addresses or links contained in this book may have changed since publication and may no longer be valid.

This is a work of fiction. All of the characters, names, incidents, organizations, and dialogue in this novel are either the products of the author's imagination or are used fictitiously.

ISBN: 978-0-595-48625-0 (pbk)
ISBN: 978-0-595-60719-8 (ebk)

Printed in the United States of America

ACNOWLEDGMENTS

This novel would not have been possible without the tireless encouragements and patience of my wife Millie. She provided counsel and guidance in story content and continuity. She traveled with me and assisted in doing research. Her editing and advice on subject matter was indispensable.

Thank you to my daughters, Sue Brooks and Peggy Toelken, for reading the manuscript and offering valuable critique. To my son, William Donald Dicksion, for giving me an empty book and suggesting that I should fill the pages.

To my niece, Geri Tsuzuki, who encouraged me to write my stories for others to read.

To my sister, Dr. Naomi Watrous. Your believing in me helped me to believe in myself.

To the many others who made contributions. Some didn't even know that they were making contributions.

To my editor, Caron Wilberts. I want to extend special thanks for her careful and capable work.

THANK YOU!

CHAPTER 1

▼

THE INDIAN ATTACK

Wheels turning through the virgin sod of the Great Plains, and the prairie grass brushing against the bottom of the wagon, had lulled Michael to sleep. When he awoke, he saw his mother and father sitting on the buckboard and heard them talking about the vastness of the open space. The wagon bumped and jostled as the horses pulled it over clumps of grass. He laid back and again fell asleep.

Suddenly, horses running and people yelling awakened him. He looked up and saw an arrow penetrate his father's chest and then watched his mother being dragged from the wagon by two Indians. She was fighting them with all her might until one of them struck her with his tomahawk. She fell from the fast-moving wagon and disappeared from his sight and his life forever.

Robert McBain, Michael's father, fell backward on the floor of the wagon, the arrow still protruding from his chest. His eyes were open, but he was seeing nothing. He had died instantly. He was a skilled frontiersman and an excellent marksman, but he didn't even get a chance to fire his gun.

The attack happened so fast that the horror of what Michael had witnessed had not yet registered in his young mind. Fear, combined with the desire to go to his mother's aid, filled his heart. The faces of the two Indians fighting his mother were seared in his mind forever. One of them was a big man with a strong, muscular body, wearing only a loincloth. His stringy, black hair hung over his face, and he had a long, purple scar on his right cheek. The other man had a high-beak nose, with black scowling eyes under a craggy brow. His mouth was just a thin purple slit across his face. His vicious smile showed that he was enjoying the killing. Michael would never forget those faces.

The horses pulling their wagon were running frantically, and the wagon was bouncing over the heavy clumps of grass, making it impossible for Michael to stand. The Indians were in full pursuit, yelling and making whooping sounds. In panic, the horses ran across a small gully, flipping the wagon over on its back, pinning Michael and his dead father beneath it. When the wagon flipped over, the frightened horses broke free from their hitch, and ran off, dragging their harness. The Indians, wanting those horses, continued in full pursuit.

When Michael regained consciousness, he had a large lump on his head and felt sick. He had no way of knowing how long he had been unconscious, but he remembered that the attack had occurred in the late afternoon—now it was morning. He listened. It was quiet. His father lay dead only a few feet away. At first, he was too stunned to cry. He had seen his mother and father killed. He was only twelve years old and completely alone. They were gone and he didn't know what to do. *They can't be gone*, he thought. But he knew they were. He would never go into the woods again with his father, or hear the sound of his mother's voice reading to him. It was more than he could bear. Michael cried for what seemed an eternity till his body had nothing else to give.

The silence was so complete that it was overwhelming. The heat was building up inside the overturned wagon. He was hungry and thirsty, but the water barrel, which had been tied to the side of the wagon, lay in splinters. The wagon had fallen astride the small gully, leaving just enough space for Michael to squeeze through. He wiggled out, stood up, and looked around, hoping the Indians were gone. A vast landscape of grass and rolling hills, extended to the horizon in every direction. In the distance, a line of trees ran through the middle of a small valley. Michael thought, *There must be water. Maybe I can get a drink.*

He began walking. The grass was waist high and so thick that it tangled around his legs, forcing him to struggle. The day was hot. He was lost, thirsty, hungry, and frightened. It took a long time to reach the center of the valley, but he had guessed right—a stream ran along the center. On either side, giant trees grew, with their branches hanging over the water. The stream was only a few feet wide, but it had deep pools in places. Where it ran across sand and gravel, sunlight glistened in the rippling, clear water.

The water was cool, and he drank until he couldn't drink anymore. He saw fish in the water. *If I could catch those fish, and had a way to cook them, I would have something to eat. But I have no way to catch them, and no fire to cook them.*

Wild plums grew on low-hanging branches. He tasted one; it was delicious. He picked and ate plums until he felt sick. He didn't know all of the different animals that lived in this lonely place, but he knew there were wolves, bears, and mountain lions. He had no idea what else might be out there. The plains seemed to be an endless sea of grass. Incessant wind created waves in the long, thin blades causing them to move like grasping fingers gathering the wind.

A herd of buffalo grazed in the distance; their shaggy humps stood out against the steel-gray sky. They snorted as they grazed. He didn't know if they would harm him, and he wasn't going near them to find out. He didn't know what to do, and he had no one to help him, so again he began to cry. Then he realized it would do him no good to cry; his mother and father were both dead.

Michael didn't know how far along the trail the wagon train had traveled when they were attacked, but he knew that they had started from St Louis more than two months ago, and their destination was Santa Fe, New Mexico . . . . Originally, there had been nine wagons in the train. The people were reluctant to make the journey because nine wagons was too small a train to be traveling through hostile territory.

They had been following the Santa Fe Trail, which followed the Arkansas River. Michael remembered the men saying that when they reached the headwaters of the Arkansas, the trail would then take them through Raton Pass, and down the west slope of the Sangre de Cristo Mountains to Santa Fe. Michael also remembered hearing the men discussing a shortcut that was supposed to be an easier route.

The man telling of the shortcut said, "We could cross the Sangre de Cristos farther south and, by going that way, we won't have to go through the pass at Raton. The shorter trail is called the Cimarron Trail. I've been told that the Cimarron River runs dry at times, but this is springtime, and there's been plenty of rain. There are also stories of others who have taken the Cimarron Trail and had to fight off raiding Indians. So far, all of the Indians we've met along the Santa Fe Trail have been friendly, and I think that the Indians along the Cimarron will be friendly, also."

Michael's father, mother, and two other families decided to take the shortcut and get to Santa Fe early. The people in the six remaining wagons were not happy about them splitting up the train. They felt that a smaller number of wagons were more vulnerable to Indian attacks, and the new trail was just too risky. The people in the six wagons decided to continue on the Santa Fe Trail.

*   *   *   *

The three wagons had been following the Cimarron for about two weeks when they came to a spot where it was flowing out of the northwest . . . . The direction they wanted to go was west. They looked again at their crude maps and noticed another river only a few days farther south that was bigger. It flowed from the west with its headwaters beginning just northeast of the town of Santa Fe.

One of the others said, "Why don't we follow that river, since it goes right to our destination? It's bigger, and it probably has better water."

"Have you heard of other wagons taking that route?" a second man asked.

"No, but I've heard of mountain men taking that route, and they said it was good water all the way, with easy terrain for wagons."

"We could save about two weeks by not taking that big loop to the north following the Cimarron," the first man explained.

"Well, let's give it a try," the second man said. "Perhaps we'll start a new trail."

The three wagons turned south to intercept the new river and were en route when the Indian attack occurred. The attack had happened so suddenly that they were caught off guard. There were so many Indians and so few people, that they didn't have a chance. It was all over in a matter of minutes.

*   *   *   *

Michael continued climbing the hill wondering what had happened to the other two wagons. A mother and father, with a boy and a girl, were in the second wagon; in the third wagon, there were two men and one woman. It had sounded like a large group of Indians in the raid, so they were probably also dead. It didn't matter, because he had no way to find them, and they would have no way of knowing he was still alive. He probably wouldn't be alive if the wagon had not hid him when it overturned.

He had to hurry. The sun was already halfway down, and he had to get back. There might be something left in the wagon that he could use, and he had to think about where he was going to sleep tonight. He dreaded going back. His father was still lying under the wagon; he would have to drag him out into the open and bury him. Then, he would have to look for his mother. He didn't know how he could bear looking at his dead mother, but it had to be done.

He hadn't thought to mark his trail while walking into the valley, so he was having difficulty finding his way back. Everywhere he looked, tall grass waved in the wind. Animals and birds scurried away as he passed. The land was alive!

Trees grew in the low spots with crows, blue jays, and meadowlarks sitting on their branches. Red-tailed hawks circled, watching for rodents. A large bull snake crawled through the grass right at his feet. It startled him, and he jumped. His father had told him that bull snakes were harmless, but any snake eight feet long and four inches in diameter, was frightening. *They may be harmless,* Michael thought, *but it sure gives you a start when a snake that big crawls right by your feet.* Life was everywhere—in the air, on the ground, and in the water.

Climbing through the tall grass was tiring. He wanted to sit down and rest, but he couldn't because there were snakes, scorpions, spiders, and no telling what else in that grass. He found a gully that made the walking easier and followed it. Just before reaching the top of the hill, he found the wagon. Its wheels sticking up in the air reminded him of a tortoise lying on its back unable to right itself.

The opening through which he had crawled wasn't large enough to drag his father through. A board had broken from the side of the wagon, and Michael tried to dig with it, but it didn't work very well. His father was a big man, tall, and heavy through the shoulders. Moving him was difficult, but Michael was finally able to drag him to a suitable place to bury. First, he had to remove the grass to get to the dirt to dig the grave.

He couldn't dig with the board, so he crawled back under the wagon to find a better tool. His father's pistol and rifle were still lying where they had fallen, but he couldn't dig with a gun, so he kept looking. Michael's father hadn't known how long it would take to accomplish his mission. He came prepared to stay a long time. When the wagon overturned, it scattered pots, pans, clothes, and dishes, breaking most of the dishes on to what had been the canvas top of the wagon. Michael found his father's toolbox, and in it were woodworking tools, a pick, an ax, and a shovel!

He also found a box of fishhooks and a roll of line. The food locker still contained hardtack and beef jerky. He was hungry, but he didn't have time to eat. Eating would have to wait until after he had buried his father. He crawled from beneath the wagon and began digging. He wanted to give his father a proper burial, so that the animals couldn't dig him up. As the hole got wider and deeper, he had to climb into the grave to throw the dirt out. By the time he got the grave dug, the sun was setting. He wrapped his father's head in one of his shirts. Then, because he was so heavy, Michael had to roll him into the grave.

He felt that he should do something more than just bury him, but he didn't know what to do. He loved his father. They had camped together many times and explored the mountains of Virginia. He sat with tears running down his face, remembering those wonderful times.

He remained kneeling, crying, and praying, until the sun was just a red ball slowly moving below the horizon. The fading light colored the high, thin clouds, and the final rays glowed across the empty sky. Confused and bewildered, he looked around. A vast plain lay before him. It was hundreds of miles to the nearest settlement. Thousands of Indians, many of them hostile, stood between him and the settlement. He didn't even know in which direction to go. His only hope was to survive long enough that perhaps another wagon train might travel through, and he could join them. He was beginning to understand the hopelessness of his situation. For now, he had to put it out of his mind because it was so overwhelming.

He filled the grave with dirt and knelt, as his mother had taught him to do when he was saying his prayers. He asked God to take care of his father and his mother, and to let them be together in heaven. Then he asked God to help him because he was stranded and didn't know what to do.

He crawled back under the wagon and ate beef jerky. He needed water, but it was too far to the creek, and he wouldn't be able to get back before dark. Night was coming on, and it was getting cold. He found a couple of blankets to roll in, used his extra clothes for a pillow, then lay down and tried to sleep. The day had been silent, but the night was filled with sounds. In the distance coyotes were howling and wolves yelping down by the creek. Night birds were calling. Mentally and physically exhausted, he fell asleep. Later in the night, he was awakened by an animal moving around outside. He had no way of knowing what kind of animal it might be or why it was prowling around the wagon. He wedged a box into the opening, hoping it would prevent whatever it was, from getting to him. He sat with his feet holding the box in place; after a time, the sound went away, and he went back to sleep.

Morning light awakened him. He was desperately hungry and thirsty. It was a long walk to the creek, but he had no choice; he had to have water. His father's canteen was lying nearby. He would take it with him to bring water back. It was too far to keep going back and forth each time he needed a drink. He followed the gully and had gone only a short way when he noticed that the grass was wet. There was no standing water, but it was very wet. He turned around and walked back, looking for the source of the water. After only a short distance, he saw water coming from a draw that entered the gully. He followed the draw and saw water was seeping from between two layers of rocks. It was just a trickle, but after digging a hole at the base of the rock, a small pool formed.

The hole was taking a long time to fill, and he couldn't wait. He had to have water! He knelt and drank like an animal. The water was a little dirty, but it was nice and cold. The pool wasn't deep enough to fill the canteen, so he made it deeper. Enlarging the hole muddied the water. He had to wait for the dirt to settle. The second drink was better, no dirt this time. As soon as there was enough water in the pool, he filled the canteen.

Now, he had to have something to eat.

After returning to the wagon, he found the barrel of salt pork that had been tied to the wagon. Plenty of pork was buried in the salt, and by cooking the pork, he would have oil for cooking other stuff. He had camped with his father many times and had learned survival methods. He had meat, seasoning, and water. He found flour and meal in other containers. He had watched his mother cook, but he had never really paid attention to what she was doing. Now, he wished he had.

He had to make a fire. But how could he make a fire? He had no wood, no flint, and no tinder. His father had taught him many things, but he had never taught him how to make a fire without a flint stone and striker.

Thinking of his father and mother brought tears, which he quickly brushed away . . . . It would do no good to cry. He had to get a fire built, but where are the tools for making fire? Where would Father have kept them? They weren't in his toolbox, and they weren't in the food locker. Maybe he had them in his pockets. *Oh, no, I can't dig Father up to find out if he has them in his pockets.* Then he remembered the secret compartment, hidden under the floorboards. After searching for a while, he found the compartment and removed the covering. The contents fell around him.

The compartment contained his mother's books, papers, and a big leather pouch, filled with gold coins! He didn't have time to count the coins or read the papers—he'd do that later. He needed a fire, so he continued looking for the flint stone. In another pouch, he found the stone and striker. The compartment also held an ornate knife in a scabbard. The beautiful knife was about 10 inches long, with a grip inlaid with silver. As Michael held it, he remembered his father liked to collect knives, and this one was his prized possession. The blade was made of the finest steel and shimmered as he held it. His father once said, "Who knows, Michael, maybe a pirate owned this knife before me. Imagine the stories it could tell."

*   *   *   *

Michael's father was the owner of a shipbuilding business and frequently took Michael with him on his cruises. Michael learned navigation, so he wasn't completely lost—he knew where they had come from, and where they were going, but he had no way of knowing the distance either way, other than that they had been traveling for more than a month when the Indians attacked.

He needed a fire, but the grass was still wet from the dew. Dew hadn't formed on the grass under the wagon—it was dry. He gathered some of the dry grass, picked up the flint stone, and then crawled out. First, he had to clear an area to build the fire. If the prairie caught fire, everything around him would burn. Using the shovel, he cleared an area. Now he had to have wood. A cottonwood tree was just over a little rise. He found plenty of deadwoods beneath it, but it was too wet from the night dew. He was hungry and didn't want to wait for the wood to dry; he needed a fire right now.

The board that had broken from the wagon would have to do. He used the hand ax to cut it into slivers, to use as kindling. He placed the kindling over the pile of dry grass, held the flint, and struck it with the metal striker. Sparks flew, but they didn't land in the dry grass. He had to get the sparks to land in just the right place. It took several tries, but at last a spark landed on the dry grass, and he saw a tendril of smoke. He blew gently, and all of a sudden there was a flame! He fed more dry grass into the flame until it grew larger. He then placed pieces of the dry board into the flame, and soon they, too, were burning. He had a fire! After the fire was well established, he placed pieces of cottonwood into the fire so it would dry. It worked just as he hoped, and soon the fire was hot enough to cook.

He cut pieces of salt pork and placed them in the kettle with a handful of flour, then poured water into the mixture, and set it on the fire. It took a long time to cook, but it turned into a kind of thick gruel. It didn't look good, but he was so hungry it tasted wonderful. After eating, he armed himself. He rigged a sling to carry the hand ax under his left arm, where he could reach it quickly. The knife and scabbard he placed on his belt. The knife and the ax would have to do—that was all he had. The guns were good, but he had no gunpowder so they were useless.

He lay under the wagon trying to figure out how to find people who would help him. He could think of nothing. The only people he knew about were Indians, and they wanted to kill him. He was going to have to make it on his own. He would have to survive, until another wagon train, or some other settlers came by.

CHAPTER 2

▼

THE SEARCH FOR HIS MOTHER

Michael had to know what had happened to his mother, and the only way he was going to find that out was to go looking for her. He hoped he might find her alive, but in his heart he knew she had been killed when that evil-looking Indian hit her with his tomahawk. Michael dreaded seeing what he felt sure he was going to see when he found her.

He put some beef jerky and hardtack in his pockets, refilled the canteen, and began tracing the tracks of the wagon. The tracks were easy to follow because the wagon had been pulled through previously undisturbed grass. The distance was greater than he thought. He felt sure that if he kept following the tracks, he would find his mother. When he came to where the tracks of horses combined with that of the wagon, he believed he had located the spot where the attack had occurred. If his mother had been killed when she was hit with the stone ax, she should be lying nearby.

A little farther along, he saw a piece of cloth and recognized it as his mother's bonnet. It brought back memories of the last moment he had seen her, and he was overcome with grief. Seeing her bonnet made him realize just how great his loss had been. The attack had happened so suddenly that at the time he couldn't grasp the tragedy that had unfolded before his eyes. He dropped to his knees in the tall grass, held his mother's bonnet to his chest, and sobbed uncontrollably . . . . Then something warned him that he was not alone.

He stopped crying and looked around. On a ridge just across a valley, he saw four Indians on horseback following the tracks of one of the other two wagons. Michael dropped into the tall grass knowing that he must not move or make a sound or he would die. The Indians were talking in a language he couldn't understand. Two were riding the horses they had stolen from his father's wagon! He waited until after the sounds had passed then chanced another look. They were gone—at least he couldn't see or hear them.

He had to control his fear and not cry, if he were going to survive long enough to avenge the killing of his parents. Right now, he had no place to run, no place to hide, and no one to go to for help. Seeing the men who had killed his parents caused anger to well up in his throat. He had to find a way to avenge the wrong they had done. He didn't know how, but he would find a way. At that moment, he promised himself he would not cry again, until he had destroyed the men who killed his parents. He didn't want to harm innocent people, so he had to make sure he knew what they looked like. They had no way of knowing he existed. He had been asleep when they attacked, so they couldn't have seen him.

He followed, staying low in the grass, with his ears tuned for the slightest sound. He saw a spot of dried blood. One of his mother's shoes and a piece of torn clothing lay nearby. His mother's body wasn't there. An overpowering anger consumed him, but he wouldn't cry. The Indians might hear him. He was just a boy and had no chance against even one full-grown man, and he would certainly have no chance against four armed Indians on horseback. It would take time to find a way to avenge this terrible wrong, but he was determined to survive and prepare for that day. He vowed that he would not let them go unpunished.

He crawled to the top of a knoll and, by peering through the grass, he saw them in a low spot just a stone's throw ahead. They were pillaging one of the other two wagons. There had been a family of four in that wagon. Four dead bodies were lying in the grass, so he knew he could expect no help from them.

He looked at the Indians carefully. One was big and powerful with a long scar on his right cheek. The scar pulled his right eye down leaving a dark purple streak across his face. Another was tall and thin who moved quick and sure. He was intent on what he was doing and reminded Michael of a vulture picking at the remains of a dead animal. This man's identifying mark was a missing finger on his right hand. The third man was short and stocky with strong, heavy arms. He pushed his way past the other men trying to get to the spoils. He would be easy to identify—he limped, favoring his left leg. The fourth Indian had a face Michael would never forget. Everything about his face was cruel and mean. He had a high-beak-like nose with two piercing black eyes, set too close to his nose, giving him the look of a huge rat. He was the one who had struck his mother. Their horses were loaded with plunder, but they continued looking for the other wagon.

Michael followed even more carefully now. He took care not to move the grass as he worked his way through it. It didn't take long for the Indians to come upon the other wagon. It was still standing, but it had been partly burned. He counted the bodies of the three people. Their bodies had been too long in the sun, and the stench was terrible. The smell didn't bother the Indians; they were scavenging without hesitation. Soon they had all they could carry. They climbed on the horses and rode over the hill southbound.

After watching them pillaging the wagons, Michael was sure his mother was dead. He hadn't seen her body, but there was a lot of blood on the grass where she had fallen. He would like to have buried her, but he was not sure he would have had the strength to do it. He was relieved that he didn't have to endure something so painful.

He had to get back to his wagon and salvage all he could before the Indians came back. It wouldn't be hard to find—the tracks were easy to follow.

CHAPTER 3

▼

THE SEARCH FOR A NEW HOME

It was still early afternoon when Michael got back to his wagon. He hadn't eaten since morning, and he was hungry. He thought he should save the hardtack and beef jerky, so he ate the remainder of the food that was still in the black kettle. It wasn't what he would have liked, but it helped to satisfy his hunger.

He began salvaging the things his parents had brought along. He had never lived alone, and he had no one to help or guide him. He didn't know what to take. He would have to leave some of the stuff behind, and hoped he would be able to pick it up later. He had no gunpowder, so the guns were useless. He had looked for the gunpowder, but all he found was the broken keg. Some day the guns would come in handy, so he would try to save them. If they were to remain usable, he would have to keep them oiled and dry. He wrapped them in canvas and covered the canvas with grease from the bucket his father used to grease the axles of the wagon.

He would need the hand ax, the knife, and also the flint stone and striker. He was lucky to have the iron skillet and pot in which to cook his food. There was too much stuff for him to carry. It would probably be best to bury the things he couldn't take with him, as he didn't want the Indians to get them. He selected just the things he would need right away, and rolled the rest in the canvas and dragged the loaded canvas to the top of a hill. He covered it with grease and buried it, hoping that by so doing, it would give him enough time to recover the things later. He took the ax, knife, flint, striker, gold coins, iron pot, skillet, fishhooks, and line. He also brought extra clothes and two wool blankets. That was all he could carry. There was no way he could hide the evidence of his having been at the wagon. He felt sure the Indians would come hunting him when they found that someone had survived. His new hiding place would have to be good . . . .

He followed the draw to the creek, waded in the creek to prevent leaving tracks, and followed it downstream for about an hour to a spot where there was a wide tree-covered meadow on the left and a tall limestone cliff on the right. At this point, the creek made a right turn around the cliff and continued through a limestone canyon. A small, clear stream was running into the creek from the limestone cliff. He placed his load on a dry, rocky ledge, and followed the small stream. It ran from under some willow trees, their branches sweeping the water. He had to crawl, to keep his head low enough to pass under the branches. He pushed the branches aside and continued to follow the stream. It was about three feet wide and a foot deep—the bed of the stream consisted of soft, white sand. Michael was pleased to see that the water flowing over the sand filled his tracks leaving leaving no trace of his passing. After crawling past the willows, the stream made a sharp left turn, and there he found the source of the water. It was running from a small crevice in the wall of the canyon. The small cave-like opening was hidden by the willows and by the rock formation.

Perhaps inside of that opening would be a place where I can hide, Michael thought.

He entered the cave. It looked like a perfect hiding place. He had to turn his body sideways to squeeze through the small opening, which was too small for a full-grown man. Once he got inside, he found a cavern that opened into a room about twenty feet long and ten feet wide. The top of the cave was so high that he couldn't reach the arched ceiling. The floor was a rock ledge covered with dry sand. The cave was dry, other than where the water ran along one side. He heard a waterfall farther back, but it was so dark he could not see it. Michael thought, *This is a perfect spot! I can come and go without leaving tracks.* The opening was almost impossible to find; he didn't really *find* it, he just *stumbled* onto it. This would be his new home! It seemed his prayers had been answered. He would have to live in semi-darkness, but he had all the water he would need for drinking and bathing. He could make his bed and store his things on the dry ledge. He'd find a way to provide light when he needed it. He would go back to the wagon and get the pork that was in the barrel that would provide salt for his food and oil for cooking. He was lucky to have stumbled onto such a place, or had he been blessed?

Crawling back through the small opening, he went outside to where he had left his things, brought them into the cave, being careful to step only in the water and leave no footprints. He had to return to the wagon and get the rest of his stuff, but he knew exactly what he had to do. It required several trips and took him most of the day, but by the end of the day, he had nearly all of his belongings stored in the cave. The rest he re-wrapped in the canvas and again buried it on the hill. After completing this vital task, he sat down to rest. He was tired and hungry, but for the first time since he regained consciousness, he felt safe.

He bathed in the stream, washed his clothes, and laid them on the limestone ledge to dry. He gathered dry grass and wood, carried them into the cave, and built a fire, hoping the Indians wouldn't return until tomorrow. Again, he made gruel from the meat and cornmeal. It eased his hunger, but he would have to find a way to supplement it, because he was running out of the beef jerky his mother had made.

After eating the gruel, he sat watching the fire and thinking about the last two days and wondered how long he could survive. The sadness, fear, and loneliness were almost more than he could bear.

The fire gave off enough light to enable him to see a waterfall about twenty paces back. The floor of the cave was nearly flat all the way back to the waterfall. The waterfall would provide a good place to bathe.

He noticed a strange thing—the smoke from the fire wasn't gathering in the cave. It was disappearing back into the cave, in the direction from which the stream was coming. That meant there was a draft of air coming in the opening he had crawled through, and the draft was blowing the smoke toward the back. There had to be another opening back there. He'd have to check that out tomorrow. Daylight wouldn't light the cave, but it would help him to see the opening the smoke was escaping through. He was too tired to think about it now, so he rolled in one of the blankets, used the other blanket for a pillow, and went to asleep.

When he awoke, a faint light was coming in through the opening of the cave. It was morning. He dressed, and cautiously ventured out. He had to find food. He had enjoyed the wild plums and hoped to find more. He was in luck. After only a short search, he found an abundance of wild plums, and he also found ripe blackberries. He removed his hat and filled it with the delicious fruit.

On his way back, a cottontail rabbit jumped up from where it was hiding and ran to a new hiding place under a bush just ahead. The rabbit had been well hidden and Michael wouldn't have seen it at all if it had not moved. He laid his hat down, quietly picked up a rock, took careful aim, and threw the stone with all his might. Again, luck was with him. The rock hit the rabbit and knocked it unconscious. He picked it up, held its hind legs in one hand, and struck a blow behind the ears with the edge of his other hand, breaking its neck. He had been taught to do that by his father. Now all he had to do was skin and clean the rabbit.

He was elated. He had fresh meat. He would fry the rabbit, using the oil and salt from the pork. He would also fry some bread by making a mixture of cornmeal and flour. He cooked a good meal of fried rabbit and cornbread, and then ate plums and berries for dessert. He felt much better about his chances of survival. After eating, he cleaned his pans with sand and rinsed them in the clear running water.

Last night he had a bath and slept well, and this morning he wore fresh, dry clothes. He was not so frightened anymore and ready for the new day. First, he had to explore his cave and find out where the smoke was going. He wanted to make sure his cave was secure and that he was not going to be found by the Indians should they locate another opening to his hiding place.

Wrapping dry grass around a stick and tying it together with cloth, he made a torch. Then he soaked it in grease and lit it from the fire that he had used to cook his meal. He followed the smoke into the dark cave. The waterfall was only about fifty feet back from the main room. The cave was high enough that he could walk upright. He passed the waterfall and noticed that the water was running over a white limestone ledge creating a perfect pond. As he proceeded farther back, he found places where the water tumbled over other ledges of limestone. While following the stream, he saw several small rooms. *One of these rooms would be a good place to store the things I had wrapped in the canvas and buried on the hill. They would be close, should I ever need them.*

After traveling about two hundred feet, the cave was still large enough for him to walk upright with plenty of room to spare. He was concerned about getting lost and was just about ready to turn back when he noticed where the smoke was escaping. He saw light coming through a crevice at the top of the cave. A portion of the cave had fallen in, leaving boulders he could climb to reach the small opening. Michael noticed that the stream continued on beneath the surface, and the water was too clear to be contaminated by surface water. It had to be an underground stream, possibly continuing underground for many miles, but he had found what he was looking for and felt no need to follow the stream any farther.

He had to climb over limestone rocks and ledges to get to the opening. It was too small to squeeze through, so he used his knife and ax to increase the size, making it just large enough for him to wiggle through. He made his way outside and found himself on top of the limestone that formed the canyon. The top of the cave was rough with many layers of limestone in tumbled confusion. Large boulders were scattered around, making it possible for him to remain concealed should anyone be looking. From this vantage point, he could see for miles. He spread wide his arms and felt he had the whole world to himself.

The water that drained from the rolling hills surrounding the vicinity, where the Indian attack had occurred, had made the creek he followed to his cave. After the stream passed the opening to his cave, it had cut its way through the limestone and eroded a canyon that wandered on through the deep valley to the southeast. The terrain on both sides was rough, with many smaller canyons and gullies leading off to either side. Large trees grew in the canyons. It would be difficult to ride a horse through it.

Michael was enjoying the scenery when he realized that at this position he was silhouetted against the sky to anyone in the valley below. He dropped to his knees and crawled to the edge of the cliff, taking care to remain concealed among the boulders. Looking over the edge, he saw the canyon where the opening to his cave was located. It was about a hundred feet below and two hundred feet away. He could see up the creek to where he had entered the water, when he was carrying his belongings to his new home.

After he had watched for a while, he saw four Indians riding horses, coming down the hill from the direction of the wagon. When they reached the spot where he had entered the creek, they paused. They were tracking him, and they were taking no chances of losing his trail. After examining the spot where he had entered the stream, two of them rode up the creek and two rode down. They realized that the person they were following had hidden his tracks by wading in the water, but they didn't know if he had gone up or downstream. The Indians had had a lifetime of practice tracking animals, and they were good at what they were doing.

Michael was concealed on the ledge, and he had a good view of the valley. He watched the two Indians who had come down the stream getting closer and closer. If they found the opening to his cave, they still wouldn't be able to enter, because they were too big to squeeze through. But if they found a way, they would see his things and continue hunting him. If they found him, he would have no chance at all. His fate would be determined by what happened in the next few minutes. He was frightened and wanted to run, but there was no place to run to. He was almost afraid to breathe. The men rode right on by. He heaved a big sigh as he watched them ride down the canyon, still looking for signs of where he left the water.

The riders who had gone upstream returned to where Michael had entered the water. Apparently, they decided he had not gone that way. They stopped where they had separated from the two, who had gone downstream. Michael felt sure that that meant that the other two would be returning.

Afraid to move, he waited for what seemed a very long time. Then, just when he turned to re-enter the hole, he saw the two Indians who had gone downstream riding up the hill only a few hundred yards away. He lay still until they all disappeared. Needing something to conceal the opening, he found small sagebrush, and then wiggled into the hole, feet first, pulling and wedging the sagebrush into the hole, thus concealing the opening. It would be mere chance should anyone find the back entrance to his cave. From the outside, it would look like sagebrush was growing in the crevice. Moreover, the sagebrush would not block the flow of air needed to vent the smoke from his fires. The smoke would not be visible after traveling the long distance through the cave, and then the sagebrush would scatter the smoke even more, making it nearly impossible to detect from the outside. When he opened the hole to get out, all of his diggings had fallen inside, leaving nothing disturbed that could be seen from the outside.

His eyes had been exposed to the outside light and the cave seemed even darker. His torch had gone out. Slowly, his eyes adjusted to the darkness and the shapes in the cavern were becoming visible. He started working his way back through the cave. Deeper into the cave, the darkness was so complete that he had to feel, crawling to prevent stumbling into a crevasse, as he followed the flow of the water. Before long, he heard water running over the rock ledges. He was careful to stay on the same side of the stream, remembering the way he had climbed. But it seemed as though he had been following the stream a long way, and he was getting concerned. *What if I should get lost?* His heart was pounding and realized that there was no choice but to continue. At last, a light appeared below him. He was less frightened now that he was getting close to his destination.

A feeling of triumph came over him when he reached the room chosen for his new home. The Indians won't come looking for him here again. He had seen them returning to their camp, carrying the plunder from ransacking his family's wagon. *I hope they haven't found the things I buried.*

Michael spent the remainder of the day gathering fruits and nuts. He made torches from pitch from the pine trees. The torch he had made to search for the second opening had worked all right, but torches made from pitch would burn longer and give off more light. Other than for the small amount of light that filtered in through the opening to his cave during daylight, the torches and his campfire were his only light. He formed the pitch into balls, placed the balls on the ends of sticks, then pushed the sticks into the ground, forming standing torches. He could have all the light he wanted; plenty of pitch-bearing trees were available near his cave.

Night came, and Michael wished he had someone to talk to. He heard the night animals and wondered if any of them used his cave for a den. What would he do if an animal challenged him for the right to use it? He would have to learn what kinds of animals made what kinds of sounds, and then he would recognize danger.

He bathed in the waterfall, had something to eat, and then looked through his mother's books by torch light. One was a book of instructions on how to tan leather, another on how to preserve meat and fruit by drying it in the sun, or over a fire. These books contained knowledge that he was going to need if it became necessary for him to live a long time in this wild land. After reading for a while, he rolled up in his blankets and went to sleep. He had spent his first day in his new home. How many more would he have to spend before he could find a way to escape from the people hunting him, and find his way back to civilization?

Fear was his constant companion. Michael kept busy and tried not to think about being alone.

At first light, he took the shovel back to the wagon and dug up the things he had buried. Fortunately, the Indians hadn't found it. It required several trips to carry all the things he had stored.

He worked all day recovering the trove, carrying it to his cave and storing it. By the time he had completed the task, it was getting dark. He again prepared a meal of fried bread, salt pork, fruits, and nuts. Then he crawled outside and sat on the rock ledge in front of his cave, enjoying the sunset and watching the little animals playing in the meadow across the stream from his cave.

The large trees in the meadow created a park-like appearance. Under the trees, the ground was nearly bare. The shade of the giant trees covered the ground so completely that no sunlight could get through and no vegetation could grow. Off to the northeast, he saw a smaller creek running into and joining the one that ran in front of his cave. These streams ran together only a short distance below the opening to his cave, and they met at the beginning of the limestone canyon. It was a beautiful place; the evening was warm, with a soft breeze blowing. High, thin clouds reflected the rays of the setting sun, and the pink light reflecting from the clouds illuminated the trees in the meadow, giving it a magical glow. Under any other circumstance, it would have been a wonderful thing to see, but now it only made him more aware of how alone he really was. He wished he had someone to share it with, someone to talk to, someone to tell him what to do. He had no one with whom to share his thoughts, his hopes, and his concerns. There was no one, just the animals, and they couldn't talk.

The next morning he began going through the things he had recovered. He didn't know the value of the gold coins—they were of Spanish mint. They were heavy, and there were more than a hundred of them. At least, when he found his way out of his predicament, he would have money.

Among the papers was his mother's Bible and nine other books. One was the book of instructions he had started to read last night, on how to do the things a person might need to do while living on the frontier. Where he and his family had lived, on the coast of Virginia, people made their living doing the tasks mentioned in the book. The book gave instructions on how to make gunpowder and how to make the lead shots for the guns.

How to make gunpowder—a lot of good that would do me. I don't have the material for making gunpowder. The ingredients are charcoal, potassium nitrate, and sulfur. I could make the charcoal, but how do I get potassium nitrate, or sulfur? I have no way to make these now, but maybe someday I'll have a use for it.

In the collection were books about history, mathematics, geography, and English literature. There would be plenty of time to read the books, and there was information in them that might help him to survive. At least, they would help pass the time. These books were his mother's treasures, and he would cherish them always.

He read his father's papers. One of them explained the reason they were going to Santa Fe. It was a document of title to 50 percent ownership of a ranch in New Mexico. The other paper was a letter written by a man named Don Diego to his granddaughter Señorita Juanita Diego, explaining who Robert McBain was, and why he was coming to her aid. Don Diego explained that he had been on his way to Santa Fe to help her when privateers sank the Spanish galleon he was a passenger on.

The letter also explained how he had been floating for days in the ocean clinging to debris. Robert McBain rescued him and took him into his home. He and his wife cared for him and tried to restore him to health, but he had been in the water too long. Realizing he could not recover, he asked Robert to act in his behalf and help his granddaughter save the land. The papers and the letter were signed: Don Antonio Fernando Hidalgo Diego. There was also a letter signed by Robert McBain, swearing a solemn pledge, that he would do everything in his power to prevent Juanita from losing her right to the land.

Father is dead now, so this obligation has fallen upon my shoulders, and I'll try to keep the pledge. I know that is what Father would want me to do. First, though, I've got to survive, and my chances of surviving don't look too good right now . . . But if I do survive, the first thing I've got to do is to avenge the killing of my mother and father.

Continuing looking through the things, he found an eight-place setting of silver knives, forks, and spoons. He also came across a box of family pictures, a book of family records, two unbroken crockery containers with lids, and a few other kitchen tools. He stored them away in a dry chamber deeper in his cave.

CHAPTER 4

▼

LEARNING THE WAY

Michael made a pledge to himself that each day he would gather food and store it for when he might not be able to obtain food. He knew that if he didn't do everything possible, he would never survive long enough to fulfill his father's pledge.

He developed a routine, so that everything that needed to be done would get done. He began each day by cleaning his cave and making sure there was nothing left on the outside to indicate that his cave was occupied. When his morning chores were completed, he went out to explore his surroundings and gather whatever he needed.

There was no shortage of food. The creek abounded with fish, so he learned different methods for catching them. He used the fishhooks and line he had recovered from the wagon. For bait, he placed grass-hoppers and night crawlers on fishhooks and tied a small rock onto the line. The rock caused the bait to sink into the water. He then used a piece of dry wood as a float and tied it to the line, to allow the bait to sink into the water to the depth he wanted. When a fish was caught on the hook, the floating wood would bob up and down, letting him know that he had a fish on the line. He cleaned the fish with his knife, then took them to his cave and fried them.

As time went by, Michael learned by trial and error the best way to cook fish. On most days, he did things simply and just roasted the fish over the fire. Sometimes he baked the fish by wrapping it in a leaf, then packing the whole thing in wet clay and laying it in the fire until it was cooked. After the fish was cooked, he peeled away the layers of leaf and dried clay, and he had a delicious baked fish.

He watched to see where the prairie chickens and wild turkeys would go to roost at night. Then it was easy to go to their roosting place, and catch the ones he wanted, while they were sleeping.

He caught animals, and prepared them for cooking, before he brought them back to his cave, to prevent leaving evidence that some-one was living in the cave. He left the remains of the cleaned animals for the scavengers. In that way, none of the animal went to waste, and he kept the forest clean. To an Indian who might see where he had cleaned the animal, it would look like a predator had caught and eaten the catch.

When he chased a rabbit, it would usually run into a hollow log or a hole in the ground. By cutting a green stick that had a forked tip, he could reach into the hole, and by pressing the stick against the rabbit's hide, give the stick a twist. It would catch in the rabbit's hide, and he could pull the rabbit out. Then all he had to do was clean and cook it, and he had his meal for the day.

Herds of elk, deer, antelope, and buffalo roamed the plains. These animals were more difficult to catch, but just one of them provided a lot of meat, so he didn't have to catch many. He used a similar tech-nique for catching and killing the larger animals that he used for catch-ing the birds. He watched to see where the herd would lie down to sleep, then creep into the herd, cut the jugular vein of the yearling he wanted, and then wait until morning. When the other animals moved away, he would go to the animal he had slain and claim his prize. He would then remove its hide, take only the portions he wanted, wrap them in the hide, and carry his hard-earned prize back to his cave.

Sometimes, he had to compete with predators for the animal he had killed. The smell of fresh blood sometimes attracted wolves or coyotes. He had to frighten them away to prevent them from taking what he had worked so hard to earn. After taking his kill back to the cave, he cooked a meal from the fresh meat. The rest, he cut into long, thin strips, and smoke-dried it over a fire, so the meat wouldn't spoil. This was called jerking. Making jerky was a slow process, but if he did it right, and stored in a dry place, it would remain good for a long time. In this way, he was able to store a supply of meat for winter.

He tracked wild pigs and found ways to catch them. He had to learn to catch, prepare, and cook them. He got the oil he needed by rendering the fat, but catching wild pigs was dangerous. His father had told him that a wild boar is as dangerous as a bear. It took Michael a long time to learn how to catch the pigs, while avoiding the dangerous boars. He had to be wary of other dangerous animals, such as coyotes, wolves, bears, bobcats, and mountain lions.

He collected the skins of fur-bearing animals, such as fox, possum, muskrat, beaver, wolverine, and raccoon, and made excellent clothes and blankets. The Great Plains was a land of abundance, but poisonous snakes, spiders, centipedes, and scorpions had to be contended with also. Most of the big animals were not dangerous unless they believed their offspring were being threatened. He avoided most of them and learned to defend against those he couldn't avoid. Watching from a distance, Michael observed their habits and methods of hunting. He learned the art of stealth, how to be invisible, and how to catch the food he needed. Little did he know that not only would it save his life someday, but the lives of others as well.

In spring and summer, he gathered seeds and green succulent leaves, and learned which plants he could eat by watching what the grazing animals ate. Some of the things the animals ate were coarse and bitter, but some of it was good, and gave him fiber in his diet. His favorites were the things his father had shown him how to gather, such as squaw cabbage and wild onions. The fruits consisted of strawberries, blackberries, crab apples, grapes, plums, persimmons, mulberries, and hack-berries. He also found gooseberries and currants. He harvested the fruit in season, sliced it thin, and placed it in the sun to dry. If he kept the dried fruit stored in a dry place, it would remain good, so he had an abundance of fruit and seeds to use in the winter.

He retrieved honey from the bee hives that he found in hollow trees. He knew how to use smoke to prevent being stung too badly, as his father had taught him. Unfortunately, bee stings hurt, but other than the sugar in the fruit, it was his only source of sugar, and well worth the pain. He kept honey in the crockery jars he had saved from the wrecked wagon or in hollow logs. He placed the logs on end, sealed the ends with wedges of wood, and kept the honey fresh for a long time. He made candy in his spare time. He mixed chopped nuts, honey, and flour, formed them into patties, then fried them until they were crisp. They were delicious. It was a simple and nutritious food that could be stored easily or taken with him on his trips.

He gathered acorns, walnuts, hickory nuts, and pecans in the autumn when they were plentiful, and stored them; he had nuts all year round. There was no shortage of food, and no shortage of danger. He learned to live by using what nature provided. At times, he had to place himself in danger. *Should I fall from a tree while gathering fruit or nuts, I might break a leg,* Michael worried. *If I hurt myself, with no one to help, I would be in serious trouble. How could I set a broken leg and provide for myself while the injury healed? I have to be cautious, but caution has to be tempered by my need.*

His father had taught him many things, including the art of boxing and the skill of wrestling. He also taught him to use tools for working wood and metal. He had learned to smoke meat and tan hides. Michael learned other things by reading his mother's books. He smoked and cured enough meat to last through the cold winters. He used hides to make clothing to replace those he wore out or outgrew. He hadn't thought to bring his father's extra clothes from the wagon. When he went back to get them, the Indians had taken them. But fortunately, they had not taken the tools. They had left a good set of files, wood-working tools, and a set of tongs for working hot metal. He would need these things if he were going to have tools for hunting and weapons to defend himself. He gathered all of the metal he could find. He even removed the springs from under the wagon. He took the metal hinges from the boxes, and stored them in a dry place.

He fashioned a spearhead from one of the hinges and fastened it to the end of a long, straight pole with rawhide, making a very effective spear. He practiced for hours every day, until he could throw the spear with enough force and accuracy to impale a large animal. He had no one to teach him, so he had to learn from nature's greatest experts— the animals themselves.

He spent hours watching the animals so he could learn from them. They had learned to blend with their surroundings. If the animals remained still and hidden, they were difficult to notice. Only when they moved could he see them. He practiced sitting completely still for long periods of time. When he dressed in skins that blended with his surroundings and sat completely still, the animals didn't see him. The predators had to find him by their sense of smell, which gave him time to defend himself. When the predators had to face the point of his spear, they moved away.

It was important not to look directly at the animals. If he looked directly at them, they could sense his presence. Placing branches before his eyes helped him to remain unnoticed.

He practiced using *all* of his five senses . . . seeing, hearing, smelling, feeling, and tasting. He learned to identify the sounds of the day, and the sounds of the night. After observing them for a long time, he could identify plants, trees, and everything else around him, by the way they looked, felt, and smelled. He knew the seasons by watching the plants and animals.

In the spring, the earth renewed itself. Bright new plants sprang up, flowers bloomed, bees and other insects came to harvest the pollen, and cross-pollinating allowed them to reproduce. In the summer, the seeds then grew to maturity. In the autumn, they ripened, and bore their seeds, then grew old and died. Their seeds fell to the ground, beginning the process all over again next spring. The winters were brutal and cold; the days were short and the nights were long. Some animals made dens and hibernated through the cold winters. Others, like Michael, had to struggle to survive.

Each season brought its rewards, and each made demands on both him and the animals. In the autumn, he gathered dry wood, and stored it in his cave. He had to be sure to gather enough to provide the fuel to cook and warm his cave. He cured hides and used them for shelter and bedding. A pile of dry grass with a buffalo hide over it made a good bed; it was warm and comfortable, even on cold winter nights.

He hung buffalo hides to form enclosures to contain the heat from his fires. The stream provided water for cooking, drinking, bathing, and washing his clothes. It was an underground stream, so it didn't freeze in the winter. It remained about the same temperature all year round. Since it was fed by springs, it was unaffected by flooding.

Surviving kept him busy most of the time. However, sometimes in the hot summer afternoons, he liked to lie on his back under one of the trees and watch the clouds drifting past the openings of the branches, giving dimensions to the cloud's movements.

The clouds gathered into towering thunderheads and produced flashes of lightning. The rumbling of thunder reverberated across the plains, sounding like the wheels of wagons rolling across wooden bridges. At times, the thunder was like the cracking of a coachman's whip echoing through the canyon.

From the clouds rain would come, slowly at first, leaving the smell of raindrops on the dry ground. Soon, the rain would fall in torrents, flooding the creek with turbulent cascades of brown water. The animals would scurry for cover. Squirrels hid in hollow branches, rabbits hid in hollow logs or under overhanging rocks. Grazing animals sought shelter under the large trees, then waited patiently for the rain to pass.

When it passed, they shook the water from their coats and went on about their business of living, as though nothing had happened. After the rain, the air smelled clean, and everything was refreshed. Mother Nature had given the world a bath.

On long summer evenings, Michael sat on the rock ledge in front of his cave listening to the night sounds and learning what kind of animal, or thing, caused each sound. Many creatures and things created sounds, such as the creaking of tree branches moving in the wind, fish splashing in the ponds, and the mating calls of the animals, birds, and even insects. Everything made sounds; each sound was distinct to whatever made them. After really listening carefully and noting who or what made the sound, he could identify each one. Babies and adult animals made different sounds. Mother animals called to their babies, and the babies replied. Michael learned that animals talk to one another. They didn't use words, of course, but they had ways to express fear, anger, pain, and love. They warned one another of pending danger, and when they had found enough food to be shared. During mating season, the males and the females would call out with different sounds, each letting the other know of its needs. Michael learned about life by watching them mating, giving birth, and caring for their young. He watched them grow old and die.

Plants live in a world most people never notice. In certain environments the plants are happy, and when they are happy they thrive. If plants are unhappy, they don't do well. Plants must fight for their right to live, and they must fight for their place in the sun, or their place in the shade, whichever the plant needs to live out its life and fulfill its destiny. Plants fight for moisture, space, nutrients, and sunlight. They fight against being destroyed by grazing animals, by growing new branches, when they are cropped off and eaten. Michael noticed how the plants fought to live and reproduce. He learned to revere all life and respect each and everything, because each thing has its place and fulfills a need in the larger scheme of things.

He learned to determine when there was a predator in the area by listening to the sounds, or the lack of the animals being preyed upon. For instance, when a wolf or a mountain lion was preying upon them, they remained quiet and still.

In the evenings, he read his mother's books, until he could recite some from memory. He learned math, history, and language from the books. He read his mother's Bible. He didn't understand it, but he felt his mother would have wanted him to read it, so in her memory he read it.

He spent days exploring the countryside, looking for signs of other white men. He knew he was far south of both the Santa Fe and the Cimarron trails, but he had no way of knowing how far.

Occasionally, he saw Indian women gathering fruit, roots, nuts, and vegetables, and placing what they gathered in baskets, woven from branches or vines. Some of them used bags made from the hides of animals. They wore clothing made from the skins of animals. Some wore their hair braided or tied back from their faces. Others wore their long, shiny hair hanging around their faces and shoulders. They chattered and laughed as they worked. Michael wasn't afraid of the women, but he knew they were a source of danger, so he remained hidden. If they knew he were there, they would tell the men, and the men would come hunting him. Sometimes he followed them to their villages, remaining well back so as not to be detected.

His highly honed senses of seeing, hearing, smelling, and feeling, and his practiced awareness of the presence of danger, enabled him to remain undetected. On occasions, he saw bands of Indian men on horseback, but he didn't see his old enemies. He watched them from a distance; their villages were to the north or east. His enemies had gone south after they plundered the wagons.

Michael wanted to know where they lived, so he could avoid meeting them accidentally. As far as he was concerned, all Indians were dangerous. After the experience he had with Indians, he didn't trust any of them.

*   *   *   *

One day, while searching near his cave, he found a narrow opening to a blind canyon that would make a perfect corral for animals. The canyon's opening was only a few feet wide. Until after you entered it, then it opened to about one hundred feet wide and several hundred feet long. The enclosure had an abundance of grass with a small stream running through it. It looked like it had been an underground stream at one time, and the top of the cave had fallen in, forming a hidden valley with vertical walls. Like his cave, you had to stumble onto it to find it. It couldn't be seen from a distance. *This would be a perfect place to keep animals,* Michael thought, *if I could catch wild horses and train them, I would have horses to ride. Having horses would help when I'm ready to leave my cave in search of white settlers.*

Years passed, and Michael became adept at living in the wild. He grew too big to get through the opening of his cave, so he carefully enlarged it, just enough to squeeze through. He concealed the opening by planting more willows. He never stepped on bare ground, or left a track. Stealth was his way of life.

In winter, when the ground was covered with snow, he didn't venture out. He couldn't prevent leaving tracks, so he waited for the snow to melt. He spent these times making tools and practicing with the ones he had, honing his ability to throw his knife, spear, and ax with deadly accuracy. He was far enough south that the snow would seldom last more than a few days.

He had enough food stored to last him for extended periods. He spent hours exercising, to build up his strength and agility, always preparing for the time when he would go against his enemies. He made clothes and fashioned covers for his feet by taking long strips of buffalo hide, putting his feet in the middle, and pulling the ends up around his feet and legs, then lacing the sides together with thin strips of the hide.

He made thick soles by placing extra layers of buffalo hide in the bottom. The coverings gave him both protection and warmth.

The cold wind howled through the canyon, leaving snowdrifts and covering everything. The tree branches were free of leaves, and everything was stark and bare. The nights were long and lonely. He watched animals burrow into the snow to get out of the cold wind, lining their dens with grass and twigs to prevent sleeping on the cold ground. Animals taught him how to survive in the bad weather, and they taught him how to stay hidden, even in winter.

After the long cold winter passed, the sun returned and warmed the land, then rains came, and life sprang forth. In summer, violent storms passed through the area, and at times the wind would be so strong that it would knock down even the largest trees. The creek would flood and wipe out all traces of anyone having ever traveled through the area.

Six years passed. Michael became a full-grown man. His hair was the color of sand. He had wide-set blue-green eyes, and he was more than six feet tall, with a strong, muscular body, wide shoulders, narrow hips, and waist. He moved with the fluid movements of a cat. His strength and agility were exceptional. He no longer feared anything that moved. Nature provided everything he needed, except human companionship.

He practiced telling the time of day, by watching his shadow move around him like the shadow on a sundial. The sun crossed the sky by rising in the East, and setting in the West telling him directions. He didn't remember the names of all the stars, but he knew about them and could tell the time of night by watching the other stars rotate about the North Star. His father taught him this when he took Michael with him on shakedown cruises. Michael was no longer afraid of getting lost. It was time for him to find the men who had killed his mother and father and settle the score.

*   *   *   *

The night before he was to leave, he was awakened by an animal growling. It was too dark to see, but he knew by smell that it was a mountain lion trying to get into his cave! He grabbed his ax and spear and moved near the opening. In the faint light, he could see only the head and part of the shoulders of a huge lion. If the lion were having difficulties working its way into the cave, that meant it was larger than Michael! Like his father, Michael was strong, but no man is a match for a full-grown mountain lion. He didn't dare allow this beast to enter his cave, and he knew that he had to deal with it in the narrow confines of the opening, or he would lose his home and his life to this animal.

The lion had the advantage. Its eyesight was better in the dim light, and its sense of smell was probably better also. Michael held the spear in one hand and the ax in the other. He faced the formidable adversary and knew he was in a fight to the death. The lion hissed and snarled as it made swipes with his long claws. One swipe with those claws would kill him or leave him damaged for life. He poked and gouged with his spear, yelling and screaming, trying to scare it away. The lion only hissed and growled louder.

Michael realized that he was not going to be able to frighten the lion away, so he knew he must kill it, or the lion would kill him. He readied his spear, aimed at a spot just below the jaw of the lion, and made one powerful lunge. If he were successful, the lion would be killed, but if he missed, *he* would die. The point of the spear struck true, penetrating the throat of the huge animal and going all the way into its body, slicing its heart. In one quick and decisive move, Michael had won the battle! The lion's body lay half in and half out of the cave; its blood was being carried away by the stream.

Michael sat with his feet in the water. The seriousness of the fight and the flow of adrenalin left him shaken. It took a while to regain his composure . . . . To be awakened from a deep sleep and have to fight for his life was not something he wanted to do every night. Now that the lion's body was limp, Michael was able to drag it into the cave. He would deal with the disposal of the carcass tomorrow. He spent a troubled night, almost afraid to go back to sleep. Each time he fell asleep, he was startled to wakefulness by the slightest sound. He was glad when morning finally came.

When the first light entered his cave, he was eager to begin the day. He took one look at the dead lion and realized that its skin would make a perfect garment. By preparing it just right, he could wear it in a way that he would make him look like a lion. It would take a few days, but it would be worth the effort. After the hide was cleaned, scraped, and tanned, he shaped it to fit his body. The skin that had covered the head of the lion he left attached, so he could wear it over his head, or push it back. The color of Michael's hair and beard matched the color of the lion; the effect was startling. When Michael lay crouched in tall grass, he looked like a lion.

CHAPTER 5

▼

EVENING STAR

Before going after the men who killed his parents, he wanted to make sure he was ready, so he made a test run. He departed early, traveling in a direction he had never before explored. After walking for hours, he heard a commotion. It sounded like a pack of wolves attacking a human. He moved toward the sound, careful not to be seen. After passing a knoll, he saw what appeared to be two Indian women.

One was a girl; the other was a mature woman who was old enough to be the girl's mother. The terrified woman was sitting on the ground with her back against the wall of the canyon and seemed to be unable to get up. The girl was trying to fight off the wolves with a heavy stick.

The wolves were circling, snarling, and slowly moving forward, knowing that soon there would be an opportunity to close in for the kill. The women were frightened, and well they should be. Without help, it was just a matter of time before they would be killed. A single wolf would never attack an uninjured human, but this was a pack of wolves, and one of the women was injured. These hungry beasts were intent on the kill.

What should I do? For years, I've been avoiding Indians. If I don't go to the aid of these women, they'll be killed. If I do go to their aid, everyone in the Indian village will know that I'm here and I'll be in danger. They won't know about my cave, but they'll know that I'm in the area, and they'll hunt me like an animal.

Michael couldn't just leave the women to be killed by that vicious pack, so he drew his ax and readied his spear, then approached the pack from behind. The wolves were so intent on their victims that the women saw him before the wolves did. When the women saw him, their faces showed sheer terror. They saw a mountain lion with a human face, carrying what they believed to be a tomahawk and a spear. This was even more frightening than the wolves! They believed the lion to be some kind of an aberration, that it was helping the wolves! They expected to be killed by this terrible beast at any moment.

The wolves became aware of Michael and turned as one, to face him. Wolves would never attack a mountain lion. This looked like a mountain lion, but the wolves knew by their ability to smell, that it was not. They moved forward, against him in a compact force. Some circled him, while others approached in a crouched position, prepared to leap. Michael knew that if he could kill one of them, the others would run away. He took careful aim with his ax. He had practiced this throw many times; now he would see if he had acquired the skill he believed he had. If he missed, he would have only his spear and his knife to fight off the entire pack. He had better be right; if he missed he would be just another victim of that snarling pack.

He threw the ax at leader of the pack with all his strength. The razor-sharp blade struck its target with a reassuring thud, severing the wolf's head. The rest of the pack turned and ran off into the trees. The fight with the wolves was over, but now he had to decide what to do about the women.

Their faces showed sheer astonishment. What they had just seen was something that none of their tribe would believe.

Michael retrieved his ax and placed it with his spear on the ground, so the women wouldn't be afraid of him, then moved forward slowly. The women were still frightened, but they were beginning to realize that he had saved their lives, and that he meant them no harm. They could see that it was not a lion with a human head. He was a yellow-haired young man with a golden beard, dressed in the skin of a lion. They dared to believe that their lives had been saved. Holding his hands up with the palms out in an effort to show his peaceful intentions and using sign language, he indicated to the girl his willingness to help her carry her mother back to their village. He cut two poles and placed his buffalo robe between them making a travois, then helped the injured woman onto the rack. The girl saw what he was doing, walked in the direction of their village, and beckoned him to follow.

They walked for hours. Michael had to ease the travois over, and around, logs and boulders. It was a long and tiring journey, but he proved worthy of the task. As it was starting to get dark, he smelled campfires. He couldn't see the village because of the trees, but he knew it was close. He placed the travois against a log, being careful not to injure the woman, then picked up his spear, and started walking away. He indicated to the girl that he didn't want to go any farther. She saw that he was concerned and knew he didn't know what to expect from her people; however, she knew they would want to thank him. She took his hand to lead him. He drew back and again walked away. The girl ran after him.

By this time, the people of the village had learned of their presence and came to see what was going on. When they saw the strange man, they were as startled as the women had been. But when the women explained what had happened, they helped the girl with the injured woman. Indians had attacked the wagon train, and Michael expected to be attacked by these Indians, also. He grabbed his spear and stood ready to fight to the death. There were so many of them, he was sure he would be killed, but he wouldn't go down without a fight.

The girl again took his hand, and for the first time, he looked closely at her. She was beautiful. Her eyes were black and expressive; her shiny black hair hung almost to her waist. She stirred fires in him he didn't know were there. The others were looking at him and talking excitedly.

They had never seen anything like him. They had never seen a man with so much hair on his face. To add to the confusion, he was dressed in the skin of a lion. They had heard of white men, but they had never seen one before. The girls were all looking at him and giggling. He was on display, and he didn't like it.

The young men watched him cautiously. They didn't know what to make of him. He was big and powerful, and he was obviously brave. He had stood off a whole pack of hungry wolves. They saw the strength in his body, and they didn't like the attention the girls were giving him.

When they got to their village, they all sat beside a fire and indicated they wanted Michael to sit, also. They brought food and drink. The food tasted strange, but he ate it anyway, feeling it would be impolite not to. The people were looking at him and talking. They seemed harmless, but he still didn't know what to expect, and he wanted to be back in his cave. The village was in the valley of a stream with lots of trees. *What will happen tomorrow?* Michael thought. *Will they let me leave? If an opportunity presents itself, I can slip away into those trees.*

The women wanted to see and touch his hair. His beard fascinated them. The two he rescued told the others how he had killed the wolf with his ax, so everyone wanted to see his ax. They had never seen metal before, and they were astonished by its sharpness. With many gestures, they made Michael realize that they wanted to see him throw the ax, so they could see how he had killed the wolf. He placed a stick, about six feet long and about two inches in diameter, against a tree. Then, from thirty paces, he threw his spear pinning the stick to the tree and in a continual movement, drew his knife and split the stick. Then he threw his ax and cut the stick in half. A sound of astonishment came from the crowd.

The chief sat quietly watching this strange young man. When he saw this remarkable display, he stepped forward to examine the spear. He looked closely at the steel blade, then contemptuously picked up a rock and struck the side of it. The rock broke, but the blade was undamaged. A look, close to fear, crossed the chief's face. He knew that this was a weapon, far superior to anything he and his warriors had. Michael, seeing an opportunity to convert a potentially dangerous enemy into a friend, stepped forward and, in a gesture of giving, handed the spear to the chief. A look of amazement appeared on the chief's face. Was this young man offering him this priceless weapon? Of course, he could just take it, but that would be an unthinkable act, after this stranger had risked his life to save two women of the tribe. The chief had to give a comparable gift, or he would lose face, but what could he give?

He noticed that Michael didn't have a bow or arrows. The chief picked up his own bow and quiver of arrows and handed them to the young man. This was an appropriate exchange—a weapon for a weapon. *I can make another spear, and with the bow and arrows as models, I can make my own.*

To celebrate the safe return of White Bird and Evening Star, the Arapaho were eating, drinking, talking. They danced into the night. Soon the people started to leave the party. The chief asked the young woman Michael had saved, if she and her mother would accommodate Michael in their lodge. Evening Star—that was the girl's name—was pleased. There was no man in their teepee. A Comanche warrior known as Scarface had killed both her father and brother. Michael was pleased, also, because he had gotten to know the women, and there was nothing about them to fear. In addition, the young woman was very pretty, and he wanted to spend more time with her. It had never occurred to him that an Indian girl could be pretty. She had a trim, shapely body with round, firm hips and breasts that stood out against her tunic. She moved with the fluid grace of a doe. There was a trace of a smile on her face; her lips were full, and her eyes glowed when she looked at him. Michael had grown up alone and knew nothing about girls.

Evening Star led him to their lodge. He could tell, as he entered, that they were poor. They made him a bed of skins on one side of the lodge. White Bird and Evening Star's bed was on the other side. They offered a gourd of water and a piece of dried meat. He had been eating and drinking at the party, and he wasn't hungry; they were just being kind to a guest. He accepted the water but declined the meat.

Michael removed the lion skin, but he kept his loincloth on and placed his buffalo robe beside his bed should it get cold during the night. The women disrobed without the slightest concern for his presence. The sight of the beautiful young woman's nude body aroused him, and he didn't know what to do about it. He had been without human companionship for more than six years. Now to be exposed to such a tempting display of feminine beauty was more than his undisciplined young mind could come to grips with. He had no way of knowing what was expected of him, so he lay in his bed, with no chance of going to sleep. His keenly honed senses told him that the young woman was also awake.

Michael needed time to consider his situation, so he got up, placed the buffalo robe around his shoulders, and went outside and sat beside the lodge. Right away, he heard movement inside the teepee. Evening Star came and sat beside him. He wanted to touch her, but the intensity of his need was so great that his hands were shaking. She sat still and quiet, then placed her hand in his and caressed his arm. He didn't dare speak. She wouldn't understand what he said anyway, but there was an unspoken understanding between them. She seemed to be aware of his need and was not frightened or disappointed by it. They sat in silence for a long time, just looking at the stars and listening to the muffled sounds of the sleeping village. The forest was dark, and the sounds of animals were coming from it. Michael at last regained his composure. Evening Star touched her face against his, got up, and went back into the teepee. He sensed her mother was awake and didn't seem to mind that her daughter had been alone with him. He returned to his bed and was soon asleep.

He was awakened by the stirring sounds of the village. He dressed quickly, went to the stream to bathe and wash his hair. After bathing, he walked into the forest and soon found what he was looking for and returned with wild chicken eggs, persimmons, and nuts.

The women were up and concerned about where their guest had gone. Since there was very little food in their lodge, they were wondering what they could serve him. When he returned, both questions were answered—he had returned with the morning meal. While the women prepared the food, Michael went for a stroll, taking care to notice where everything was located. He wanted to know the shortest distance to cover. He wanted to know the location of the trees, and what kind of trees were they? Where were the people going to get their drinking water? He was trying to determine how many men were in the village. It was a large village, and he estimated there were more than fifty warriors. Everywhere he went, people watched; he would have no chance of escaping unnoticed. He would have to find another way to leave the camp.

Evening Star and her mother had the food ready when he returned. As they ate, he tried to learn a few words of their language. By the end of the meal, he had learned about twenty words that he could use in a limited way.

Michael tried to tell Evening Star that, in his language, the evening star was called Venus. She seemed to understand and was pleased. He explained that his name was Michael McBain, and asked them to call him Michael. The older woman's name was White Bird. She was Evening Star's mother. Because of her broken leg, she couldn't walk without someone helping her. The medicine man had set the broken bone, but she had no crutches. Michael cut two strong branches with his ax, formed them into crutches, and then showed White bird how to use them. White Bird and some of the other women watched him make the crutches. They were amazed at how quickly he fashioned what they called "walking sticks."

The women didn't talk much and their language consisted mostly of gestures and facial expressions, but he was rapidly learning to communicate.

CHAPTER 6

▼

THE ARAPAHO CHIEF

Time passed in the village. Michael spent his days listening and watching. He paid attention to how the people talked and how they lived. He had learned enough so far that the men of the village used a combination of words and sign language to explain to Michael that he was in the village of the Arapaho. For as long as anyone could remember, the Arapaho had been sharing hunting grounds with the Cheyenne and the Pawnee, but that was starting to change. The Comanche and the Kiowa, whose hunting grounds were traditionally to the southwest, were now encroaching upon their area. They were both powerful tribes, feared by everyone. They also possessed more horses, had more warriors, and apparently made war on their neighbors and took what they wanted.

Michael now had an understanding about what he would be up against when he went against his enemy the Comanche. Michael went to the chief's lodge to show him how to sharpen the blade of his spear by rubbing it against a sandstone. The chief was so impressed that he willingly showed Michael how to use the bow and arrow. The chief was amazed that Michael's arms were so strong that he could pull the heaviest bow and send the arrow farther than most of the men who had been using the bow all their lives. The chief told Michael that with practice he could become very skilled.

The chief wanted to trade for the ax and the knife. When Michael shook his head indicating that he couldn't part with these tools, the chief's eyes told him that he was considering taking the ax and knife by force.

I'll have to watch this man, Michael thought. *He's not to be trusted. I have something he wants, and I don't know how far he'll go to get it.*

The young men wanted to wrestle with Michael to test their skills against his. Michael's father had taught him wrestling, and he was stronger than the Indian men and could have beaten them easily, but he pretended to be untrained. He wanted the advantage of surprise should he ever need it.

Michael went back to Evening Star's lodge. He wanted to teach her some of the things he had learned about survival, so that she could provide for herself and her mother. He wanted to learn her language, so she helped him to learn.

He started by telling Evening Star and her mother, "When I found you being attacked by the wolves, I was on a mission to avenge the killing of my mother and father, who were killed by four men in the raiding party that attacked our wagon train. These men killed everyone but me, and they would have killed me, too, if I had not been hidden under the wagon. When they killed my mother and father, they left me to die. I was just a child then, but I am a man now, and I must avenge my parents. I can identify the killers. One is a tall, thin man, who makes quick movements, and he is missing a finger on his right hand. The second is shorter, but he is heavily built and limps from an injury to his left leg. The third is big and strong with a long scar on his right cheek. The fourth has an evil grin, a high beak nose, a thin and cruel mouth, with scowling black eyes, set too close to his nose. Out of respect for my mother and father, I've sworn to kill these terrible men."

"Oh, Michael!" Evening Star exclaimed. "We know those terrible men. They are skillful fighters, and they are the strongest warriors of the Comanche tribe. They have killed many men from our village, including my father and my brother. You can't go against these men alone. I'm frightened for you."

"Don't worry. I've trained for six years for this mission, and I won't fail."

"I'll be happy when these terrible men are dead," Evening Star said. "Our people will owe you a great debt for eliminating our common enemy, and everyone will be grateful when these men are no longer a threat to our village."

"Thank you for sharing that information. Could you get someone to stay with your mother while you and I gather food? Bring two large baskets."

Evening Star and her mother had been gathering food when her mother fell from a tree. They were gathering wild grapes from vines growing in a tree. The grapes were small, but they were sweet and juicy, and could be stored for winter by drying them and making raisins.

Michael had gathered lots of grapes and recognized the vines from a great distance. He used his ax to show Evening Star how to make a tool for harvesting the grapes, and then explained that she could harvest nuts the same way.

"I'll make you a knife, so you can make tools for yourself. Cut a long pole with a hook at the end, and you'll be able to pull the branches down and pick the grapes without climbing trees."

He showed her how to cut and use a long pole to thresh nuts from the trees so she wouldn't have to compete with the animals and insects by picking the nuts that had fallen on the ground. In only a short time, they had their baskets full. In one day, they gathered enough grapes and nuts to last all winter.

Evening Star was amazed at how easy it was for Michael to gather food. She couldn't understand how he could make a knife, but he said he would, and she believed him. This remarkable young man had skills that she had never seen before. He was handsome, and she had fallen in love. She was still young, but the chief was urging her to marry. Since there was no man in her lodge, the chief had the right to choose her husband. Many men had asked for her, but there was none she wanted. Now, her body told her she was ready, and her heart cried out for Michael to hold her. She knew he was the man she wanted.

Any time he was near her, Michael was keenly aware of how pretty she was. He accidentally rubbed against her, as they were gathering fruit. Each time he touched her, excitement ran through him. He was glad he was wearing a heavy garment to hide his arousal. When their baskets were full, they took them back to Evening Star's lodge. He asked her to come with him again tonight. He wanted to show her how to find roosting birds, so she could have all she needed. He told her not to tell anyone the secret. If she told others how to catch the birds, they would soon be gone, and she would have to go farther and farther into the woods to catch them. Evening Star told her mother what they were planning to do.

"Mother," she said, "Michael wants to teach me how to catch birds and gather their eggs, so that we won't have to worry about going hungry."

White Bird was skeptical. She had noticed Michael's interest in Evening Star. But she also saw the food they brought back and was inclined to allow Evening Star to go. She, being an older woman, understood the young man's need and envied her daughter.

"Evening Star," White Bird said, "I'm concerned."

"I know that Michael wants me, but I can handle him," Evening Star said, trying to reassure her mother.

"Yes, that's what has me concerned. We need a man in our lodge, and this one would be a good provider, but I don't think the chief will approve of your marrying him. Black Crow is a friend of the chief's, and he has been asking for you. He is a sub-chief, and you would be lucky to get such a husband."

"I don't want Black Crow; he already has three wives."

"As a chief, he can have all the wives he wants," White Bird said. "Besides, it's not so bad having other women to help you with the work and help meet the needs of your husband."

"I don't want Black Crow," she repeated. "I want Michael!"

"All right, go with him, but everyone in the village will know that you are alone with him. He has a strong desire for you, and you must remember that the chief will want a high marriage price for you. If the men in the tribe think you have given yourself to Michael, they will not be willing to pay a high price for you. The chief will be angry."

White Bird watched them walk into the darkening forest. The evening was warm, and the last rays of the sun were filtering through the thinning leaves of the giant trees. Michael and Evening Star walked side by side into the privacy of the forest. Only nature could have produced such a magnificent setting.

After walking a while, Michael said, "We will find where the birds go to roost."

He showed her how to make a hook from a branch of a tree, so she could hook the leg of a turkey, pull it down, then grab its head to keep it from crying out and frightening the other birds. They watched a flock settle down in an oak tree

"Sit still and remain very quiet," Michael said.

They sat so still that Evening Star could hear her heart beating. She was wondering if Michael could hear it, too. Was it beating hard because she was sitting so quietly, or was it because she was sitting so close to Michael? They waited until the turkeys were asleep . . . . They took only one turkey. One turkey provides a lot of meat, and that is all they needed for now.

He showed her how to use the knife to dress the turkey. They dressed it in the forest, leaving the remains as food for the foraging animals. They wasted nothing, and left no mess to be cleaned up. The turkey was ready to be cooked when they got it to the lodge.

"Tomorrow," Michael said, "I'll show you how to find the chickens' nests, so you can gather the eggs."

And then he showed her how to locate the chicken's roost, so they could have a chicken dinner anytime they wanted. Evening Star was amazed. She and her mother would have food in abundance, and it was stored by nature, ready for their use. This young man, by living alone in the wild, had learned things that her tribe had not learned in all their generations of living off the land. Her admiration and love knew no bounds.

On their way back to the lodge, they found a grassy knoll and sat for a time listening to the night. Sitting very closely, Michael put his arm around Evening Star's shoulders to keep off the evening chill. He could feel her firm breasts, and she sensed his need, and was warmed by it. She wanted desperately to fill his need and, at the same time, fill her own, but he was shy and inexperienced—she did nothing to encourage him because she was afraid it would frighten him away. They both knew what they wanted, but each was afraid to make the first move.

As they walked back to the lodge, Michael said, "After we finish our evening meal, I'll return to my world." He wanted to go back to his cave but was reluctant to leave Evening Star . . . . He explained how and when they would meet again. "When the sun is overhead, at the time of the next full moon, I wish to meet you at the big bend of the river. The bend is halfway between your village and where I live. The time is only ten days from today. At that time, I will give you the knife I will be making for you."

"How will I know when ten days have passed?" Evening Star asked. "We do not mark the passing of days."

Michael drew a line in the sand and said, "Make a mark on the ground inside of your lodge each morning when the sun comes up. When the marks are the same as the fingers on both your hands, ten days will have passed . . . . That is when I will meet you."

"I will bring my girlfriend with me, so I won't have to travel alone."

"That is good. Come prepared to spend the night, so you and your friend won't have to travel back in the dark."

White Bird was pleased to see them return. It was getting late, and she was getting worried. When she saw them returning with a full-grown, fully-dressed turkey, she hoped her daughter would get this young man as a mate. He would make a good provider. His obvious strength would enable him to protect their lodge and defend their village from the marauding Comanche.

After the evening meal, Michael bade them goodbye. They watched him walk into the forest just as the moon was rising, and Evening Star wondered if she would ever see him again.

The woods held no fear for Michael. He had given the chief his spear, so he cut a long pole and sharpened the end to use as a lance. If he needed to, he could climb a tree to avoid ground predators, or he could fend off a mountain lion with his sharp lance. As he walked through the dark woods, his mind was filled with conflicting thoughts.

I made a vow to kill the men who killed my parents. When that is done, I have to fulfill Father's obligation to Señor Diego and try to save the land for his granddaughter. To get to Santa Fe, I will follow the river my parents were planning to follow. I have no idea how far it is, or what dangers I might encounter, but I must try.

∗   ∗   ∗   ∗

He arrived back at his cave just as the sun was rising. The light was cascading across the pale-blue dome of his world that had changed forever because of the events of the last few days. Evening Star had come into his life, and his life would never again be the same. There were others to think of now, and he had to consider their feelings and needs. What happened to him now mattered to someone other than himself. He felt responsible for the welfare of Evening Star and her mother, and they would forever be a part of his life.

He went into his cave, fixed something to eat, and lay down for a good sleep. Tomorrow, he would begin fashioning a knife for Evening Star. He had to get it done, and get it to her before he could go to find the Indians who killed his parents. At least, he knew a little more about the evil men he was hunting, and he had a better understanding of how the Indians lived.

The next morning, he started making the knife by using a spring that he had taken off the seat of the wagon. He fashioned a crude bellows from hides, then built a fire, using the hardest wood he could find. The fire had to be very hot. He increased the heat by using the bellows to blow air into it. Then he placed the spring into the fire, and heated it super hot to take the spring out of the steel. He straightened it by using a hammer, and then tempered the steel so it could be sharpened. This is another thing he learned while working with his father in his shipbuilding business.

Michael had to make another spear to replace the one he had given to the chief. This time, he made the blade a little longer to give it more cutting surface. He filed it to form a finely-honed blade. This spear was much better than his previous one.

He wanted the knife for Evening Star to have just the right weight so she could swing it with enough force to cut through a piece of wood. This knife would enable her to make the tools she would need for harvesting fruit and nuts. He made it strong enough to cut through wood but light enough to use for skinning animals and preparing their meat for food. When it was completed, it was twenty inches long and sharp like a machete . . . a fine weapon, as well as an effective tool. He thought, *With this knife, if she can prevent the chief from stealing it, she can gather all the food she and her mother will need.* He wanted to make sure she would be well fed and free to care for herself until he returned.

Some nights, he could think of nothing but Evening Star. On the day they were to meet, he arrived at the bend of the river early. He didn't want to take a chance of missing her.

When Evening Star arrived, she and her girlfriend, Little Calf, had a young man with them. The young man's name was Gray Elk. Gray Elk was nervous. He had heard of the wonders Michael could work, and was a little afraid of him. Gray Elk was likable, and it was obvious that he and Little Calf were in love.

Michael couldn't take his eyes off Evening Star. She was even more beautiful than he remembered. After the excitement of their meeting was over, he gave her the knife. She held it and looked at it with wonder. To her, it was a gift beyond the words she had to express her appreciation. With this tool, she would be the envy of the entire village. Michael took Gray Elk aside and told him that he would return to the village one day, and he wanted to see the knife still in the possession of Evening Star. No one must take it from her. He knew Grey Elk would spread that message, and he hoped it would prevent someone from taking the knife from Evening Star.

Michael demonstrated the use of the knife. He threw it and stuck it into the trunk of a small tree. Then he removed the knife and, in a few strokes, chopped the tree down. After cautioning her about the danger of cutting herself, he gave the knife to Evening Star and showed her how to make a hooking pole to catch birds and another pole for threshing nuts. He cut another branch and showed her how to sharpen the end to fashion a spear. He had made a scabbard so she could carry the knife around to her waist. She was pleased with the gift, but she was more interested in the giver.

Evening Star asked Gray Elk and Little Calf to walk on ahead when they were returning to the village. She wanted to be alone with Michael. She knew they had only a little time, and she wanted to treasure every moment. If she were to be given in marriage to a man she didn't love, she wanted this moment with the man she *did* love.

After her friends had gone on ahead, Michael asked Evening Star to spend the night with him. He wanted to show her his lodge and train her to use the knife. Evening Star ran ahead, caught her friends and asked them to continue on to the village without her.

"Tell Mother not to worry," she said. "I will be home tomorrow."

She ran back to Michael, happier than she had ever been. Michael took her hand, and while walking to his cave, told her that she must never tell anyone of what he was going to show her. They might need the secret to save their lives. She made a solemn oath to never reveal what he would show her. He instructed her on how to enter and depart the cave without leaving footprints. He explained that they must never leave a trace of having been there.

Evening Star said, "The chief has had warriors searching for your lodge ever since you left. They couldn't find it, and now I know why."

His cave fascinated her. It had everything that was needed for a comfortable lodge. She had never seen many of the things Michael had, such as an iron kettle or an iron pan. The crockery jars, the knives, forks, and spoons amazed her. He had so many things she had never seen, or even knew existed. She was breathless. She imagined herself keeping this lodge for Michael as her husband. She would be proud to be his squaw.

Michael told her to oil, sharpen, keep the knife dry, and always keep it sharp and ready. He fried rabbit and seasoned it with salt, and served it with honey-sweetened fruit and nuts on a plate with a knife, fork, and spoon. She had never eaten fried food, nor had she ever tasted food seasoned with salt. Everything was so new to her that she was overwhelmed.

After the meal, they sat on the rock ledge and watched the animals playing in the meadow until the sun set in a golden display of colors. The sky was an arch of iridescent blue, with streams of pink, red, and gold. It was a scene of such beauty that only the power that created the universe could have arranged it. They listened to the night birds and watched the wind swaying the branches of the giant trees. They were in heaven as they sat holding one another.

When darkness came, they went into the cave and bathed together in the waterfall. She was so beautiful that he was embarrassed by his arousal. They lay down on the soft bed of skins. Their appetite for one another was insatiable, and their lovemaking lasted long into the night. At last, in a wonderful feeling of exhaustion, they fell asleep in each other's arms.

They awoke, still in the embrace and made love again, and then bathed in the waterfall. They had a wonderful breakfast of broiled meat and caramel nuts, and dipped cold water from the stream right by their breakfast table. After breakfast, he lit a torch and showed her the back of the cave. He told her that if she ever needed to hide, she could use the cave, but he cautioned her again, to never tell anyone about what he had shown her. She reassured him that she would never divulge their secret.

With a heavy heart, he told her he had to take her back to her village. She grabbed him and held him tight while she told him of her fear that he might not prevail against four seasoned fighting men. He assured her that he would proceed with extreme caution, and repeated that he had been preparing for six years, and he didn't think he would fail.

✳   ✳   ✳   ✳

The journey to her village took all day. When they arrived, they went directly to White Bird, who had been apprehensive. She took one look and knew they were in love. In her heart she was glad. She embraced her daughter and held out her hand. He took her hand and looked into her eyes; he knew he was seeing a mother's love.

Gray Elk and Little Calf came to the lodge. They, too, were worried until they saw the glowing faces of their friends, and then they were happy.

Michael told them he must go. He took Evening Star in his arms once more and grasped the hands of the other three . . . . Indians almost never cry, but before he walked away, Evening Star clung to him, tears running down her cheeks. The parting was too painful. He turned and walked into the forested valley again, just as the fading light confirmed the end of an event he would never forget.

He was troubled. He had no way to know when he would see Evening Star again. If he survived his mission to slay the men who killed him mother and father, he would then be going to Santa Fe. Destroying the four evil men would also avenge the deaths of Evening Star's father and brother, and help to end the threat to her tribe. Michael felt sure he would return some day. He said a silent prayer and asked God to keep Evening Star well, and then hurried to his cave.

After Michael left, Evening Star showed her mother the knife. She was expecting her mother to be pleased, but instead, she gasped. "Surely you know the chief will never allow you to keep that weapon. Women are not allowed to carry weapons. Hide it! Don't tell anyone you have it!"

"Gray Elk and Little Calf already know. They saw it before they returned to the village. They were there when Michael gave it to me."

White Bird said, "Call them back quickly; maybe they haven't told anyone."

Evening Star called. "Have you told anyone about the knife?"

"Yes, I told some of the girls," Little Calf said. "They wanted to know why you didn't return with me and Gray Elk."

"I told some of my friends," Gray Elk added, "and told them about the remarkable things Michael could do with the knife."

"This will bring trouble," White Bird wrung her hands. "We must decide what to do. I know . . . you can give the knife to the chief!"

"I can't!" Evening Star replied. "This is a gift to me from Michael."

Gray Elk and Little Calf realized the seriousness of the situation, and they were also expressing concern. They heard a commotion outside.

"The chief is coming!" Little Calf said in an excited voice.

The chief entered the lodge and demanded, "Let me see that knife!"

Evening Star reluctantly handed the knife to the chief. He examined it and demanded, "This weapon has strong medicine. Give it to me!"

Evening Star tried to explain, "This is not a weapon; it's a tool for gathering food."

"There is no stronger weapon in all the villages," the angry chief replied. "A warrior could sever an enemy's head in one stroke with this knife."

"It is not meant to be a weapon," cried Evening Star. "It's mine!" she said, holding the knife to her bosom.

The chief couldn't force her to give the knife to him without losing face, and he couldn't just take it from her. Other members of the tribe would criticize him. He turned and strode angrily from the lodge. He had to have that knife, and he would find a way. She was his to give in marriage. When she married, her husband would own all her property. He would give her to the man who would give him the knife in trade.

White Bird knew this was not the end of the disagreement. She was worried. She didn't know what the chief would do, but she knew he would do whatever it took, to gain possession of the knife.

"Evening Star," White Bird said, "the chief must never find out that you made love to Michael. It would reduce the price men would be willing to pay, even with your great beauty."

Evening Star knew that she must take a husband soon. The people were aware that she was three summers past her first time of the moon. It was the duty of every woman to marry and bring warriors into the village. Their tribe was getting smaller, and they needed all the man-children the women could provide, to keep the tribe strong.

When Evening Star told her mother of the mission Michael was on, White Bird's despair was enormous.

"There's no hope that one young man," White Bird said, "regardless of how strong, could kill the four most seasoned warriors of the Comanche tribe. The Arapaho know these men well. "Scarface" is the man who killed both your father and your brother, and they both were great warriors. The man Michael called "Limpy" is the man who held your father's arm when Scarface plunged a knife into him. His limp is result of a wound your father inflicted on him. "Three Fingers" is the man who helped Scarface kill your brother. Then the one he called "Evil Eye" is the one we call Black Cloud. Black Cloud is a mean and heartless killer. Michael won't have a chance against these terrible men."

"Forget Michael," White Bird cried, "and take your pick of the men bidding for your hand. That will settle the problem about the knife."

Evening Star explained, "Michael has great skills with his special weapons, and I believe he will prevail. I love Michael, and I am going to wait for him."

"He'd better hurry back to claim you. The chief won't wait much longer."

Evening Star spent a restless night. Conflicting emotions flowed through her head. She thought of the wonderful night she had spent with Michael. She was worried about him going against such over-whelming odds. She thought about the knife and knew her mother was right about the chief forcing her to accept a husband. It was the chief's right to give her in marriage to any man he chose, and she must do as the chief commanded. That had been the way of their people for as long as anyone could remember. It was a good way; it had kept the tribe strong. It was a woman's duty to bear children and to keep her husband's lodge. The man she wanted was not the man the chief would choose for her.

CHAPTER 7

▼

THE SEARCH FOR
HIS ENEMIES

Michael spent the evening preparing for his journey. He used a length of his fishing line to mark the path back through the dark tunnel to the opening at the top. He picked fresh sagebrush and wedged it into the small opening and tied it to a rock inside of the cave, making sure it wouldn't blow away and reveal his home.

He wore the garment he had made from the hide of the lion. His long, sandy-colored hair and full-flowing beard made him look like a lion. While wearing the lion's skin, it would be easy to remain obscured in the daylight, and it would be almost impossible to see him at night. He would use the same methods of concealment the lions used when they lay in wait to pounce upon their prey. Michael's feet were covered with double layers of buffalo hide—the inner layer had hair on the inside to protect his feet; the outer layer had the hair on the outside to give him better traction and help conceal his tracks. He carried an extra pair of moccasins tied to his waist. Should he leave a track, only the most trained tracker would recognize the tracks as one left by a human.

He carried his ax slung under his left arm and carried his father's knife at his waist. With his father's knife, he would settle the score by taking the life of the man who had killed him. He would use the ax to kill the man who had killed his mother with an ax. A deep anger welled in his heart when he remembered how his mother and father had been wantonly slain.

He carried a canteen of water, and for food, he had smoke-dried meat. With these supplies he could hide for days.

✳   ✳   ✳   ✳

He left his cave while it was still dark, and proceeded to the spot where he had seen the Indians plundering the last wagon. He continued southbound, in the direction they had gone. For hours, he traveled south across rolling grassland. He crossed creeks and gullies lined with trees and continued steadily southbound until, just as night was coming, he came to a river. The river was shallow. The water was only about thirty feet across, and it had a wide bed of fine yellow sand. Crossing that sand without leaving tracks would require all the skill he had. He decided to sleep hidden in the trees and cross the stream in the daylight.

He was hungry, but he didn't dare use his reserve, so he gathered berries and nuts. He couldn't build a fire; he was sure the Indians could smell fire for miles. He wrapped himself in his buffalo robe and went to sleep in a thicket beside the stream. The night was dark, and he heard animals all around him. He knew that the smell of the lion's skin would keep predators away, so he slept soundly.

As the sun was breaking the horizon, light reflected off the clouds bathing everything in gold. He followed the river for several miles looking for a place to cross. He found a collection of bones. He could recognize bones of every kind of animal he had ever seen, but these bones were different. They were human bones, too small to be the bones of a man. They were mature, so they had to be the bones of a woman.

Previously, when he had hunted for his mother, he had not found her. There was a good chance that she had been dragged to this spot, and this was where she had died. How she had died, he dared not think. He wasn't sure that these were his mother's remains, but he had a strange feeling that they were. He carried the bones to a lovely spot near a giant oak tree and buried them. Then he planted sunflowers; the golden color of the flowers matched his mother's hair. He sat remembering his mother, and how much he had lost when the Indians took her from him. His resolve became even deeper and he was more committed to settling with the evil men who had done this great wrong. He would not let them go unpunished.

He walked downstream looking for a place to cross without leaving tracks. He found just the place. He came to a place where the water crossed the sandy bed and flowed to the other side. He followed the water across the sandbar leaving no tracks. Just before he reached the other side, he came upon a bed of quicksand. He had seen quicksand before, and he had learned how to cross it by watching a water snake slither cross it. The snake's weight was distributed over the full length of its body. Michael had tried crossing the quicksand with his body flat on the sand, and he, too, could wiggle across without sinking. Using this method, he crossed the river and found a place on the other side where he could step out of the water onto a log. The log was lying half submerged with half of it extending out onto dry land. He had succeeded in crossing without leaving tracks. He would remember this spot; it might come in handy.

After crossing, he walked for hours in the direction he had seen the Indians going. He climbed to the top of a hill where he could see in all directions. He remained hidden and sat quietly, with all of his senses tuned to the task of finding the Indian village. Nothing was evident.

He continued southbound, trekking in the creeks and valleys, avoiding placing himself on a hill where he could be seen. He continued until well into the afternoon, then, as he rounded the crest of a hill, he saw another stream in the distance. This stream was different. It didn't have a wide sandy bottom; it flowed through a deeper channel. He would have to cross a wide valley before he could get to the stream.

He climbed to the top of another knoll on the rim of a deep canyon. His senses told him there was danger ahead. Although he saw nothing, he remained hidden, watching and listening. Just as the sun was going down, he heard a dog barking. He had heard that many Indians had dogs. He waited for the sun to set.

Darkness came slowly, with a long and lingering twilight. The setting sun lit the high clouds with an array of brilliant colors.

A herd of buffalo grazed on a hillside; deer grazed in the valley. Michael understood why the Indians had built their village here. It was protected from the cold north wind in the winter, with trees to provide wood for their campfires. The river provided water for drinking, bathing, and fishing. They could hunt animals for food, and the animals would also provide skins for their lodgings and clothes.

This is a land of plenty, Michael thought. *Why then did they need to plunder and kill? If the Indians did not attack the wagon trains, and if the people in the wagons would respect the Indians' territorial rights, perhaps everyone could live in peace.*

Night came, and Michael moved slowly into the valley. To be seen was to be killed, but he had to see into the village if he were going to find the men who had killed his mother and father. He saw the light of the campfires and heard them preparing their evening meal. The men ate first, then the children, and then the women.

After everyone had eaten, the men sat around talking while the women put the children to bed. Michael moved cautiously along a draw leading past the village to the river. After getting into position to identify the men who killed his parents, he heard a disturbance. He looked for the source of the disturbance, and saw a man beating a woman with leather thongs. She was crying and trying to protect herself. The man had a long scar on his cheek! *That* was one of the men he had come to find! He hid in the hollow of a burned-out tree at the edge of the village, and watched to see where that man would go to sleep. He waited silently, not moving a muscle. He didn't think anyone would find him, but he was worried about the dogs. Dogs would smell the skin of the lion. After a time, the village was quiet. Still he waited. Then slowly, he moved to the opening of the lodge where the man with the scarred face lay sleeping. He crawled into the tepee until he was beside the killer. He couldn't see clearly, and he didn't want to kill an innocent man. Not wanting to make a mistake, he rubbed his hand across his enemy's cheek. When he touched the scar, the big man jumped. It was too late; the long blade of the knife, which had belonged to Michael's father, had already penetrated the evil man's heart. A grunt was the only sound the Indian made.

Michael silently made his way back to his hiding place in the hollow tree, but before he could get away, the woman who had been beaten by Scarface came to the opening of the lodge and cried out. Men came running, gathering their weapons and putting on their garments as they ran. This was no time for Michael to move. He remembered the lesson of the rabbit . . . he had not seen it until it became frightened and started to run. He wouldn't make that same mistake. He remained still as a stone and silent as the dark itself. From his vantage point, he could see clearly. Everyone was running around excitedly—someone had slain one of their most fearsome warriors!

The village was in chaos. Scarface was dead in his own lodge! That frightened them, but what frightened them even more was that they couldn't figure out what had happened. How had this fearsome warrior been killed, and who did it? No one saw or heard anything unusual. It seemed to some that Scarface had enemies in the camp. They thought that perhaps, one of his own people had killed him. They suspected his wife; he had been beating her that evening, and it was not unusual for him to beat his wife and kids. But he would not be doing it again.

After searching the camp without finding an intruder, most of the people went back to their lodges. But three still looked. One of them limped, and one was the man with the evil face. Michael wasn't sure but suspected the other had only three fingers on his left hand. Michael waited, hidden in the hollow tree.

Soon he heard a searcher coming near. With his ax poised, Michael waited. A hand grasped the opening to the hollow tree—the hand had only three fingers! Still Michael waited. Three Fingers made the mistake of looking into the hollow tree. It was the last mistake he ever made. One quick and silent blow eliminated this killer forever—he would never kill again. Michael, the avenger, moved silently into the night. He didn't stop moving until he reached the crest of the canyon where he had first gotten warning that the enemy camp was near. The two searchers found the second of their cohorts dead in the hollow tree, but there was no sign of who had done it. They would wait until morning, gather more men, and go in search of the silent raider. They knew this was someone different, someone very deadly, and someone they must contend with or none of them would ever sleep peacefully again.

Michael ate and drank sparingly, then continued in the direction of the sandy river. He had to get distance between him and his pursuers. They would be riding horses and could travel faster. Michael had to give himself every advantage, and distance was one of those advantages. He would wait for another opportunity to deal with the other two men.

Now that I know where they live, I can bide my time, and systematically eliminate them one by one. I won't stop until I have completed what I came to do.

Michael ran all night and all next day. When he reached the sandy river, it was too dark to cross the dangerous quicksand. He decided to rest and cross it next morning. To wait could be fatal, but it could also be a fatal to wander into that treacherous quicksand in the dark. Once a victim sinks into the grasp of quicksand, there's no escape. The opening to its trap closes suddenly, and there's no doubt about the outcome.

The extreme activity of the last two days left Michael needing rest. He went to sleep almost immediately.

*   *   *   *

A sense of danger aroused him just as the first rays of the sun lit the landscape. He looked back and saw two riders coming at a gallop. Michael had no doubt who they were. A quick look confirmed that they were Evil Eye and Limpy, pursuing him with determination. He was pleased and surprised that there weren't more of them. He had expected the whole village to be following him. But this was no time to be wondering about that. He had to cross the stream, and there was no way to do it without being seen. He ran into the treacherous water, not worrying about leaving tracks, went around the quicksand, and continued across. If he could reach the other side and make his stand in the trees, he might have a chance. The trees would limit the movement of their horses. They would have to get off their horses to get to him. If he could confront them one at a time, he could beat them, but if he had to face them both on horseback, he would be at a disadvantage, and the outcome was far from certain.

When he looked back, Evil Eye, whom the Arapaho called Black Cloud, was crossing the river upstream. Limpy followed the stream. *Surely, he's not going to ride his horse into that quicksand.* Then he heard a yell and watched in amazement as Limpy and his horse disappeared beneath the treacherous quicksand.

That left only one enemy to contend with. Michael had waited a long time for this opportunity. This was the man he had seen kill his mother with a stone ax.

Michael went directly to the spot where he had buried his mother, and stood on the knoll near her grave, waiting for Black Cloud. He didn't have to wait long before Black Cloud rode into view. The evil-faced man just sat on his horse staring at Michael, not sure what to make of him. Black Cloud saw a boy dressed in the skin of an animal, standing on the hill with his hands on his hips daring him to come. That was more than his cruel mind could stand. Black Cloud dismounted. His dismounting pleased Michael. His mother's killer was climbing the hill on foot, to kill what he believed to be a foolish boy, waiting for his executioner. Black Cloud was thinking, *I killed his mother with my ax. Now I will kill him, with the same ax.*

The evil man ran up the hill, his cruel face getting closer and closer. He took a wide and powerful swing with his ax sure of a quick kill. Michael sidestepped the swinging blow, moved inside the arc and, in one smooth movement, drew his knife and drove it with all his might into the stomach of the attacker. Then, just as smoothly, he drew his ax and split the evil face like a block of wood. Without a sound, Black Cloud dropped to the ground. The world was forever free of a very bad man.

Michael dragged the body away, so the blood would not soil his mother's grave, then knelt beside her grave. Now, he could cry. His pent-up sorrow drained from his heart through the tears; he had fulfilled his promise by removing forever the four men who had killed his mother and father. A great burden had been lifted from his shoulders. He removed his head cover, bowed his head, and thanked the Creator for the delivery of his enemies.

He put his head cover back on, said his final goodbye to his mother, and walked away, leaving that tragedy behind him. He would always remember his mother and father. He had settled the score with those who had killed them and left him to die at the age of twelve. He had refused to die, and now he was a man. In honor of his father he would fulfill the pledge his father had made to Don Diego.

As he left his mother's grave, he looked back and noticed the horse Black Cloud had been riding. It was the Arabian stallion that had belonged to his father. Michael went to the horse. It was frightened at first, but after a while, the horse allowed Michael to catch and pet him.

While holding the reins in one hand, Michael grasped the horse's mane with the other and swung onto its back.

By the time he reached his father's grave, it was getting late. He knelt and told his father what had happened. He felt deep in his heart that his father had approved. He still felt a heavy sorrow for the loss of his parents, but his mind was now at peace; it was time to go back to his cave and prepare for the task of finding Santa Fe.

CHAPTER 8

▼

THE MOUNTAIN
MEN

For the first time, since the Indian attack, Michael didn't hide his tracks. He was riding the horse the Indians had stolen from his father, and he couldn't prevent the horse from leaving hoof prints. But he could prevent hoof prints from leading to his cave, so he took the horse to the blind canyon. The canyon had water and grass, with trees to provide shade. He rode the horse into the canyon, petted him, rubbed him down with dry grass, removed the headgear and set the horse free. Michael placed a dead tree across the mouth of the canyon, so the horse could not wander off.

As he was walking back to his cave, he heard gunfire! It had been a long time since he had heard gunfire. He moved forward with the caution of the mountain lion he resembled. As he got closer, he saw what appeared to be at least a dozen Indians who had two white men cornered on the limestone above his cave. One of the men was wounded. It was just a matter of time before the Indians would overwhelm them.

These were the Indians Michael had expected to be chasing him. They had split up when they came upon the tracks of these two men.

That unlikely event had probably saved his life. He had to help these men who were trapped. He made his way into his cave, then quickly followed the line he had arranged for just such a purpose, to the top opening. He untied the sagebrush and lifted it just enough to see what was going on out on the ledge.

Two white men were only a few paces away. He called out softly to the man nearest. Startled, the man turned to look in the direction of the call. What he saw was the blond head of a young man with long hair and a flowing beard beckoning to him from under a sagebrush. At first, he couldn't believe what he was seeing. Was that a man's face on a lion? Michael pushed the sagebrush farther away, exposing the opening, and again beckoned to the man.

The man called out to his companion, "Hey, Joe, there's a sagebrush over here waving to us to come and crawl under it!"

"We'd better find something to crawl under. We can't hold out much longer here!"

The men crawled through the opening head first. The opening was almost too small for the bigger one. Michael caught them as they came through, preventing them from falling to the stream below.

One of the men asked, "Where in the sam hill did you come from?"

Michael made no reply. He was too busy pulling the stem of the sagebrush back into the hole and securing it inside the cave. He put his hand to his mouth, indicating silence.

They could hear the Indians moving around outside on the limestone. The men in the cave couldn't understand their words, but they recognized the astonishment in their voices. The Indians couldn't figure out how the white men could have disappeared. They looked and looked, but to no avail; not a trace of their escape route could be found.

Pat, the larger of the two, was standing with his rifle pointed at the bottom of the sagebrush covering the hole. He blurted, "It will cost them dearly to find that hole."

Michael looked at him, shook his head, and put his hand to his mouth, indicating they should remain silent. The older man recognized his rescuer's concern and nodded.

After a time, there was silence outside. Michael's keen sense of smell told him the Indians were gone. The Indians thought they were chasing the ones who had slipped into their village and killed two of their warriors.

Michael indicated with the movement of his head for the men to follow him. Holding the line, they descended into the darkness. As they got deeper into the cave, it got darker and darker.

The younger man said in a quiet voice, "This is even scarier than fighting them damn Indians."

Michael, remembering his own fears the first time he descended into the cave, spoke the first words he had spoken to another white man in six years and said, in halting words, "We're almost there."

Pat, with a little laugh, said, "That's the second-best news I've heard in a long time."

Soon they saw light coming from the mouth of the cave. Even though the opening was not visible, it gave off light, and after the long trek through the dark cave the light seemed bright.

When they reached Michael's room, he motioned for them to sit and indicated by gesture that they should remain quiet. He knew the Indians would continue searching, knowing that the white men had to have gone somewhere. It was a puzzling thing. How could they have slipped through all of their warriors without being seen?

Michael gave the men water, dried fruit, and jerky, and then cleaned Joe's wound and stopped the bleeding with clean, dry ashes from his last fire. Michael looked at his guests carefully. One was about forty, six feet tall, a big man with a growth of whiskers. His calm brown eyes showed that fighting Indians wasn't new to him. Michael knew instantly that this was a man he could trust.

He said, "My name is Pat Connors, and this is my partner Joe Martin."

The other man was young, Michael guessed about twenty. He was also about six feet tall, but he was clean-shaven for a frontiersman. His hair was light brown, and he had blue eyes. His movements were quick and smooth. He had a sense of humor, and he smiled easily. There was something hidden about this man, but Michael liked him.

After the sun had set and the light was no longer coming through the opening, Michael followed the stream outside, then knelt under the willows and listened, waited, and watched, making sure the Indians had gone somewhere else. Then he went back into the cave.

He looked at the men, nodded his head, and said, "We can talk now; the Indians are gone."

Joe was the first to speak. "Where in the world did you come from? How'd you get here? What's your name?"

When Michael didn't respond right away, Pat said, "Every time I look at him I'll see the sagebrush that saved my life. Let's call him Sage."

Michael only smiled. The name stuck, and after that, his new companions called him "Sage."

After starting a fire to provide light, Michael, the man they called Sage started to speak. He told them the whole story. They sat in silent amazement listening to his remarkable story.

Michael told them: "I'm the sole survivor of an Indian raid on a wagon train that consisted of only three wagons. I managed to survive and lived alone for the past six years. I made a commitment to kill the men responsible for killing my parents, and I have, just today, fulfilled that promise. That's why the Indians were chasing you. They were looking for the killer of their warriors. Now that I have settled that score, I must fulfill a commitment that my father made to a man named Don Diego."

"Where was the wagon train going?" Pat asked.

Sage said, "We were going to Santa Fe."

"Why were you going to Santa Fe?" Joe asked.

Sage explained: "My father owned a shipbuilding business in Virginia. It was his custom to take his ships for a shakedown cruise before he turned them over to the people he had built them for. While returning from his last cruise, he found a man floating on debris in the Gulf of Mexico. The man was the only survivor of a raid by privateers on a richly laden ship. The ship was en route from Spain to Mexico. Father brought the sick man home and tried to nurse him back to health. In spite of all he could do, the old gentleman's health continued to deteriorate. When it became apparent that he was dying, Señor Diego divulged his story.

"His name was Antonio Fernando Hidalgo Diego. He was a man of wealth and political influence in Spain. He was the descendant of people who were part of the aristocracy of Spain. The old man's grandfather had been a personal friend of the king, and the king bestowed a land grant to Antonio Diego's grandfather. The tract of land is in New Mexico, near the town of Santa Fe. It has been in the Diego family for five generations. Antonio Diego inherited the land from his father, then passed it on to his son, who, with his wife, was killed by Apache while on a journey from Santa Fe to Mexico City. So the land then passed on to Don Diego's granddaughter.

"When Señor Diego was called to Spain, his granddaughter was too young to manage the affairs of such a large ranch. So he left it in the care of someone he trusted. While he was in Spain, he received news that his granddaughter was in danger of losing the land. The Don sent a messenger telling her that he would be sending someone to help her.

"When Don Diego realized he was dying, he begged my father to go in his stead, and save his granddaughter's land. Father was reluctant, and told Don Diego he had a shipbuilding business to run and a son to raise. Antonio Diego explained that after he had saved the land for his granddaughter, he could return to his shipbuilding business by going down the Rio Grande to Matamoras, and there, board a ship back to Virginia.

"As an inducement to get my father to undertake the responsibility, Don Diego drew up a paper assigning half ownership of the land to my father. Of course, the ownership was valid only if his granddaughter had not lost the land.

"After much consideration, Dad decided to grant the dying man's wish. He felt this would be an opportunity to continue my training, and enable us to learn about the new land that President Thomas Jefferson had purchased. Father decided to leave the shipbuilding business in the care of my grandfather until he returned. Father drew up a will leaving the business to me should anything happen to him and my mother while we were on the trip.

"Dad grew up on his father's land in the Appalachian Mountains. Appalachia was still unsettled then, so he had a good knowledge of how to survive in the wilderness. When he got time away from his shipbuilding business, he and I visited Grandfather. Dad took me into the mountains and taught me how to live off the land. He taught me how to hunt and fish, how to kill animals, and to prepare the meat so it wouldn't spoil. We skinned the animals, tanned their hides, and made clothes. As part of my training, father also took me on some of his shakedown cruises.

"He taught me to use the sextant to locate our position on the globe. I learned to tell time by the sun during the day, and by the stars at night. That training helped me to survive here.

"Dad taught me to stand alone, never depend upon other men. He told me to trust all men until they prove themselves untrustworthy; then never trust them again. He said, 'If they do you wrong once, they'll do it again, if you give them a chance.'"

Pat Connors and Joe Martin were mountain men, and they realized what a remarkable thing this young man had done. After Michael finished telling his story, they then told their story.

"I came west when I was just a boy," Pat said: "My family lived on a farm on the Ohio River. Both Mother and Father got sick one winter and died. I tried to run the farm, but it was too much for me. A group of men traveling down the river came by. They were going west to trap beaver. I gave them food and asked if I could go along as one of their party. I had a horse and a gun, and I could provide for myself, so they let me tag along. There were no trails; we just followed the rivers. We went into the Colorado Mountains, where we trapped beaver and sold their pelts to fur traders in Taos. Most of the Indians were friendly in those days. We gave them knives and blankets for pelts; then we sold the pelts to the traders in Santa Fe or Taos.

"Sometimes we spent the winters in Taos or Santa Fe, and sometimes we spent them with the Indians. That's how I learned to speak five Indian languages. Being able to speak their language sure helps. I took a partner, and we did some mining for a time. My partner married a Mexican woman, who runs a cantina in Santa Fe. He was killed in a mineshaft cave-in, and I went back to trapping furs.

"I lived part of the time with the Cheyenne, and part of the time with the Arapaho. I married a beautiful Arapaho woman, and she bore me two sons. While I was away selling my furs, a band of Blackfoot Indians raided the village and killed my family. I searched for the ones who had killed them. I became a recluse and lived only for the purpose of killing Blackfoot. One day, the Blackfoot had me trapped in a canyon and were closing in on me, when a young man came to my rescue. That's where I met Joe. Together we fought them off. We've been trapping partners ever since."

Sage looked at Joe Martin and said, "Now, may I know who you are?"

Joe replied: "Well, there really isn't much to tell, and most of it I would like to forget. My family went to Texas when Steven Austin was recruiting people to settle in Texas. The Mexican government gave land to settlers who would live on the land and become Mexican citizens. My family moved to Texas only to find that the right of ownership to the land was in question. The Comanche thought the land belonged to them; Mexican settlers thought the land belonged to them. Anyone who wanted to keep the land had to fight for it. Being good with a gun was a requirement. I found I had a talent with a gun. My reputation spread, and other gunmen came to challenge me. I was forced to kill several of the men, and my reputation spread.

"I could find no peace, so I ran away into the mountains, hoping my reputation would die down and someday, somewhere, I would be able to return to society and live a normal life. While I was in the mountains, I came upon this mountain man who was in conflict with a band of very determined Indians. I decided I had little to lose, so I joined in the fight. You know the rest, all except how we happened to be on top of your cave.

"Pat and I decided to sell our pelts in Saint Louis. After we sold them, we went down the Mississippi to spend some of our money in New Orleans. After a few weeks of drinking, dining, and dancing, we decided to go back to the mountains. We were following the Canadian River, since its headwaters is in the Sangre de Cristo Mountains near Santa Fe. We followed the Red River to the Washita, and then we were following the Washita to join the Canadian when we were jumped by a hornet's nest of angry Indians. We had no idea what they were so mad about, but they were sure stirred up. You came just in time and showed us a way out. Thank you very much. Say, Sage, since you want to go to Santa Fe, and that's where we're going, why don't you join us?"

"The Indians who attacked your wagon train and killed your family are Comanche," Pat said. "They're the most hostile of all the tribes in the west. You're either very lucky, or very skilled, to have survived this long in this part of the west."

Pat had to remove the arrowhead buried in Joe's shoulder. He boiled water and sterilized some old clothes that Sage had saved to use as bandages to wrap the wound. Sage watched carefully, so he could learn how to remove arrowheads.

The mountain men needed food.

"You men wait here," Sage said, "and I'll get us some prairie chickens for dinner."

"How are you going to do that?" Pat asked.

"I know where they roost. I'll just pick up one for each of us," Sage replied.

"I'm beginning to understand how you've survived this long," Pat murmured.

Sage disappeared through the opening, and in a short time returned with three prairie chickens, cleaned and ready to be roasted.

"I'm insisting that Sage comes along with us," Pat smiled. "Joe, he'll be a handy man to have along."

"The first thing we've got to do is get our horses back," Joe remarked.

"No, the first thing we've got to do is to get your shoulder healed," Pat corrected, "and then we'll get our horses. We couldn't ask for a better place to hole up and get you well enough to travel."

Sage added to the conversation. "I have enough food to last all of us for quite a while, and I have a horse."

"You have a horse!" they both exclaimed in surprise.

"It's one of my father's horses that the Indians stole when they attacked the wagon train. I took it back when I killed the last of the Comanche. It's a good horse. I call him "Midnight" and I have him penned in a blind canyon only a short walk from here."

"Well, let's go get him!" Pat said excitedly.

"No, you can look at him, but I don't want him near the cave. He might expose its location, and this cave must be guarded at all costs. When Joe is ready to travel, we'll figure out a way to get more horses from the Comanche."

Joe agreed. "That sounds like a damn good plan to me. Let's sleep on it. I am a little tuckered out." He crawled into a pile of hides and was asleep in seconds.

Sage looked at Pat. "Come, let's check on the horse. I want to make sure he's all right."

Sage coached Pat on how to leave no tracks as they left the cave. The walk required about half an hour, and found the horse in good condition. The hidden canyon had plenty of room for the horse to move about to evade a mountain lion, should one threaten him.

"That's a fine animal," Pat said. "Your father was a good judge of horses."

"Yes, he believed in buying only the best. The Indians stole three more of equal quality when they raided the wagon train. They were yearlings when they were stolen. They'd be in their prime after six years. We could pen the other horses here when we get them, but only for a short time. The Indians will find them if we leave them here."

"Well, this horse is doing just fine. Let's go back to the cave and get some sleep. This has been an eventful day for all of us, and we have a lot to do, to get ready."

After rubbing the horse down, they returned to the cave and went to sleep.

*   *   *   *

They awoke early, bathed in the waterfall, and Sage prepared a good breakfast. While they ate, they discussed their plans for recovering the horses.

"I have a pistol and a rifle," Sage volunteered, "but I have no powder or shot."

"We have powder," Joe replied, "but we're running low on shot. Do you have lead? We have bullet molds but no lead. Our lead was in our saddlebags, but the Indians have them now."

"I don't have lead here," Sage replied, "but there was lead in the wagon. I had no molds and no powder, so it was of no value to me. Perhaps we can find it. I doubt the Indians would have taken it; they wouldn't know what to do with it."

"Let's see if we can find it," Pat said. "Lead doesn't spoil no matter how long it lays around, and we can make all the bullets we'll need."

"Joe," Sage asked, "can you hold the cave against invaders while we're gone?"

"Oh yeah, I'm feeling better this morning. There's no fever in this wound, and I can hold off a whole tribe of Indians trying to crawl through that small opening. You guys do whatever you need to do; I'll be just fine. Be careful crawling back in, though, I might mistake you for an Indian."

"Okay, let's go, Pat," Sage said. "We've got a lot of work to do to get ready."

They went to what was left of the wagon. Decaying boards and rusting iron was all that was left. The wagon was almost completely overgrown with grass. If you didn't know it was there, you could walk right by it and never see it.

Before beginning the search for the lead, Michael went to where he had buried his father. He had left no marker, but he remembered where he had buried him. He gathered white quartz rocks and formed a cross to mark his father's grave. He removed his lion-skin cap, knelt beside the grave, and said a silent prayer. This might be the last time he would ever see his father's grave. He then went to his mother's grave, formed a cross, and placed wildflowers at the site. With a heavy heart, he and Pat returned to the wagon to search for the lead.

Sage remembered where the toolbox was lying the last time he saw it six years ago. They probed the grass for quite a time before they found the remains of the old toolbox. They found other tools, but they were rusted beyond use. At last, they found two bars of lead. They each had a bar to carry.

"The other two wagons may have lead, also," Sage said.

"This is more than we'll need for now. Let's get it back to the cave and get the bullets molded."

They gathered fresh persimmons on the way, and Sage killed a rabbit for lunch. Pat was astonished at the skill Sage displayed when he threw his knife to kill the rabbit.

"One day you're going to have to show us what you can do with those weapons of yours. That was a remarkable throw you just made."

"I'll be glad to," Sage replied.

Sage cleaned the rabbit and washed it in the stream. It was ready for cooking when they got to the cave.

They had lunch, and Joe said, "Now, let's see those guns of yours."

Sage went into the cave and returned with the guns. He had kept them oiled and wrapped, so they were in perfect condition.

"These are fine guns," Joe remarked. "We'll have to teach you to use them."

"He may not need them," Pat said. "You should see him throw a knife." He turned to Sage and asked, "How about showing us what you can do with your spear and ax?"

"Let's go outside, and I'll show you." Sage hung the skin of the rabbit on the trunk of a tree and, from thirty paces, threw his spear, ax, and knife. It was done so fast that the sound was: clunk, clunk, clunk. All three weapons hit the skin in a pattern that could be covered with the palm of your hand.

The men were astonished. Then Joe said, "I sure don't want him for an enemy."

Pat said, "Joe here is the best man with a gun I've ever seen. If he teaches you, you'll have been taught by the very best, and with the talent we've just witnessed, I think you're going to be good with those guns, very good indeed. Sage, I'm proud to have you as a friend. You have a good head on your shoulders, and you'll be a great asset to the West. Let me shake your hand." He turned to Joe and said, "Now, Joe, get busy and teach this young man the fine art of handling a gun, both pistol and rifle."

While Pat was making shot, Joe taught Sage to fire his guns.

When Sage was out of earshot, Joe told Pat, "He'll soon be as good as I am, and maybe better."

Pat joked, "Don't tell him that, or you'll give him a big head."

"I don't think so," Joe replied. "Not that young man."

"I think you like him," Pat commented.

"What's not to like? He obviously has good bloodlines; he's strong, agile, and he's smart."

When Sage returned, Joe said, "I'll be ready to travel in a couple of days. Let's figure out how we're going to get those horses from them damn Indians."

"I have an idea," Sage suggested. "Pat and I can take the horse we have, to carry the supplies, then go in at night and get your saddles and bridles. We'll get the saddlebags, and whatever else they may have that belongs to you, and stash them on a ridge above a canyon I know of. The canyon is about an hour's run west of their village. You and Pat can wait on the ridge while I go to their village and stir them up. They'll chase me on horseback, and I'll lead them into that canyon, and you pick them off. While you're keeping them busy, I'll pick up the horses and meet you on the ridge. We'll load up and be off to Santa Fe. They'd never catch us. And if they do, they'll be sorry. With three of us to do them damage, I doubt that they'll want to catch us. They may be savages, but they're not stupid."

"Sounds pretty damn risky to me, but I think it might work," Joe agreed. "Let's give it some thought—it'll take some planning."

"All right, Pat," Sage said, "tomorrow you and I will scout the area, then lay out our final plans."

"Okay, let's take a look. We may as well get our saddlebags and as much of our other stuff as we can while we're at it."

"I was thinking it would be good if we planned this so everything will work smoothly. We don't want them to know that we're there until we hit them. We could take them completely by surprise and do it all at once," Sage said.

"See," Pat marveled, "I told you he has a good head on his shoulders."

Sage said, "I want to practice with the guns, and I want to develop proficiency with the bow and arrows. Also, I want to show you my trove of hidden treasure. It's the stuff I recovered from the wagon. Most of it I'll have to leave here—it's too bulky to take it with us."

He brought out his mother's Bible, pictures, and the papers concerning the ownership of the ranch.

"You'll be a very rich young man. The Don Diego ranch is one of the largest and best ranches in the upper Rio Grande valley. I've heard they're having trouble with rustlers. You've got your work cut out for you, if you're going to straighten out that wild bunch," advised Joe.

"Can I count on you to help me?" Sage asked.

"He saved our lives, and he wants to know if he can count on us to help? You're damn right you can," exclaimed Pat.

Then Sage showed them the bag of gold coins. Again, they were astonished.

"There's a lot of money!" Joe said. "This is Spanish gold! It's going to be heavy to carry, but it's worth carrying. Your father must have been a wealthy man."

"He owned a shipbuilding business in Virginia. I guess I own it now, if I ever get back to Virginia to claim it." Sage was just beginning to realize how great his inherited responsibilities were. Along with the responsibility of saving the ranch for Don Diego's granddaughter, he had a shipbuilding business to run. He would have to deal with each problem one at a time, when and if he got an opportunity.

The mountain men helped him go through the things he had stored and helped him to decide which ones he should take, and which he had to leave behind. He told Joe and Pat that he would some day return to recover the things he couldn't take with him. He hoped he would some day be able to share them with Evening Star. He told them about Evening Star and that he must go to see her once more before they left.

Pat knew the sorrow of having to leave an Indian woman behind, and his eyes showed it. He remembered his own wife and his two sons. He carried the sorrow of their death wherever he went.

"Do you want me to go with you?" Pat asked. "I speak their language."

"No, I'll go alone," Sage said. "I'll go tomorrow and be back in a couple of days."

Pat nodded. "I understand why you would want to go alone. We'll be ready to go when you get back."

CHAPTER 9

▼

SECOND TRIP TO THE INDIAN VILLAGE

Sage left when there was just a trace of light. He had a long way to go, and he wanted to arrive at the Arapaho village by mid-afternoon. He was hoping to spend the night with Evening Star, and tell her he would come back for her when he had completed doing the things he had to do. The journey to Santa Fe was too dangerous for her to go with him. He hoped she would understand, that she would be better off with her own people. He was also concerned about how she would feel about leaving her mother and her village when he returned.

Long before he reached the village, a feeling warned him that something had changed. He slowed his stride and moved cautiously. When he neared the village, he saw a group of young men playing a game. Gray Elk was among them. Michael remained hidden and waited for an opportunity to beckon to Gray Elk. When Michael attracted Gray Elk's attention, Gray Elk looked around to make sure no one was watching, then slipped away, and went to Michael. Grey Elk and Michael walked farther into the thicket, where they couldn't be seen.

Michael asked, "Is everything all right with Evening Star and her mother?"

"No, things have changed."

"Can you get word to her that I'm here and ask her to meet me?"

"Evening Star and her mother are being held in the lodge of Black Crow. They're not allowed out of his sight. The chief wanted the knife you made for Evening Star, and she wouldn't give it to him. Black Crow has taken Evening Star as his wife. He already has three wives, but since he is a sub-chief he can have more than one wife. He made a trade with the chief. If the chief would give him Evening Star, he would give the knife to the chief in exchange. That was exactly what the chief was looking for, so the bargain was made."

Michael was furious. "I'll go get her."

"No, you mustn't. Black Crow has sworn to kill both Evening Star and her mother if you are seen near the village. She asked me to find you, and ask you to not try to rescue her. She's carrying your child and wants it to be born. Many men have tried to find your lodge and couldn't. She wouldn't reveal the cave's location even to save her life. You must go now. You can return, after the baby is born. She asked me to tell you that this is the best way."

"I can't leave her. I've got to rescue her."

"No! She belongs to Black Crow, and he is a man of high standing. He'll kill her and her mother before he'll let her come to you. He's expecting you to come for her, and she's guarded night and day."

"Can you get word to her that I'm here? Ask her what she wants me to do. I'll be waiting. No one will see me."

"I'll return tomorrow," Gray Elk said, and hurried back to join his friends before they began to wonder what had happened to him.

Michael withdrew into the woods and waited. The night was long. He had a canteen of water and dried food, but it seemed that tomorrow would never come. His tortured mind kept thinking of Evening

Star in the lodge of another man. Repeatedly in his mind, he heard the words, "She is carrying your child."

What can I do? If I try to save her, I'll be putting both her and her mother's lives at risk. If I don't save her, she'll be living as the woman of another man. He wasn't prepared to deal with this. He needed the council of his friends. Pat would know the right thing to do. He had to hear it from Evening Star before he left. She had to know that he was waiting, and that he had kept his promise. Michael was going mad with anxiety. It was midmorning before Gray Elk returned. Michael approached Gray Elk cautiously, and appeared to him so quickly that it startled Gray Elk.

"What did she say?"

"She said she knew you would come, and she asked me to tell you that her heart aches for you, but you must not try to rescue her. She wants to bear your child, and she will not be able to do that, if you try to rescue her. She said to tell you that after time has passed, you can return. She also said to tell you that her spirit will travel with you wherever you go."

"Tell her the men I went to kill are no more, and they will not trouble the village again; then tell her I'll return."

Michael grasped Gray Elk's arm in a gesture of thanks and farewell, then turned and silently disappeared into the woods. Gray Elk knew he had been in the presence of a great warrior. He walked to the village to relay the message to Evening Star. She was pleased that the terrible men were dead, and she wasn't surprised that Michael had settled the score. They had heard talk of a brave warrior who had entered the Comanche village and killed their four braves. Her village knew of the debt they owed this young warrior. Her heart was heavy, but she was glad. Evening Star had the greatest of rewards—she was carrying Michael's baby.

It was late when Michael returned to the cave. He gave a low whistle and then entered. He told Pat and Joe what had happened.

Pat said, "You've done the right thing. Black Crow would have killed both Evening Star and her mother if you had tried to rescue her. She's not too bad off. She'll be with her mother and her friends. The Arapaho are her people, and in time, she'll take her place in the village. Her husband will know that the child is not a product of his loins, but it will make no difference. In an Indian village, the child will be treated well."

Michael vowed, "One day I'll return to see the child and make sure Evening Star is doing all right. I will sleep tonight, and tomorrow we will go to get horses."

CHAPTER 10

▼

GETTING THE HORSES

"Pat, can you walk in moccasins? Those boots will leave a trail a blind man could follow."

"Yes," Pat laughed. "When I lived among the Cheyenne, my woman made moccasins for me, and I wore them often. I also learned to ride bareback like the Indians. I've spent my life on the frontier, and I'm not without skills. Don't worry about me; I'll keep up."

"I meant no disrespect. I've noticed your skills, and I hope to learn from you."

"And so you shall, Sage. There's much I can teach you about being a mountain man."

Joe explained to Sage, "Pat can track a cat across a rock pile, and drive a nail in a tree with a rifle bullet from a hundred yards away. He is highly respected among both mountain men and Indians."

Pat muttered, embarrassed by Joe's praise, "I'll make myself a pair of moccasins while you sleep. You say it's a two-day journey, so we'll leave early in the morning."

They ate, discussed the task, and went to sleep. They were going to need all the sleep they could get. They had five days of traveling ahead of them, and it would take two days just to reach the Comanche village. They would need one day to scout the area and to locate their horses and saddlebags. Then it would take another two days to get back to the cave.

Sage lay down on his bed of hides and was instantly asleep. He awoke after only a couple of hours, and began preparing for the scouting trip. He checked and sharpened his weapons, packed dried food, and made a backpack for the horse from a buffalo hide.

Joe fashioned a bridle. His wound was healing nicely, so they didn't have to worry about him. Pat and Sage were ready, and left before sunrise. It was a glorious sunrise. The sun rays reflected off the high clouds long before it appeared on the horizon. They picked up the horse Pat would ride. Sage felt more comfortable on the ground. He ran for hours, while Pat rode at a gallop. They wanted to arrive at the Comanche village before dark of the second day, so they could get the lay of the land while they still had light.

Middle of the afternoon on the second day, they saw a flock of birds fly up in the distance. Pat immediately dismounted and hid the horse, and said in a low voice, "Let's check this out. Something frightened those birds, and we'd better find out what it was."

They moved cautiously, until they topped a little rise and saw three Indians riding southwest in the direction of the Comanche village. Sage watched them while Pat went back for the horse. Two of the horses the Indians were riding looked like the ones that had belonged to Sage's father. Seeing them brought back memories of his father's death, and anger boiled in his chest.

Pat noticed the look of anger and said, "Sage, never let anger override caution; it can get you killed. We'll have our revenge when we take those horses."

Sage realized he had been given some wise counsel. He nodded, keeping an eye on the men.

Pat smiled and thought to himself, *This young man is an adept student. He'll make a great frontiersman.*

They followed the horsemen for about an hour, being careful not to be seen. Sage recognized the terrain and knew the Comanche village was near. He signaled for Pat to stop.

"The village is only a short distance ahead," Sage said. "Let's work our way around the village and scout out the canyon I was telling you about. I want to find a good place for you and Joe to lie in wait while I bring the Indians to you. You've got to be secure and have a good view of the Indians riding up the canyon. There are only three of us, so we have no room for error."

It took about an hour to work their way to the canyon. They found a spot where the canyon made a turn to the left. From this spot, Joe and Pat could hide on the rim and fire on the Indians who would be chasing Sage. The mountain men's rifles would be effective, long before the Indians were within bow-and-arrow range. Sage could hide behind the rocks until the Indians retreated, and then he pick up the stray horses that had been left by the fallen Indians. Sage would ride one of the horses and lead the others while he rode farther up the canyon to where the horses could climb out. The Indians who had not been shot would have to ride back down the canyon before they could get out of it to pursue the mountain men. Before the Indians could get back, Sage and his companions would be long gone.

Pat was pleased. "It's perfect. Now let's see where they've put our gear."

"Let's wait until dark," Sage replied, "then work our way to the river. By floating down it, we'll leave no tracks, and we'll have a good view of the village from the riverbank."

"Won't they be coming to the river for water?"

"Yes, I'm sure they will, but there's plenty of brush. It'll be easy for us to remain hidden, and after we spot your things, we'll return to the cave."

"All right, let's take a look."

The Indians were settling down for the night when Pat and Sage got to a place where they could see, although it was almost too dark. At first, they couldn't make out the saddles.

Then Pat said, "I think I see them behind that tepee . . . over there at the edge of the village. I can't be sure, but I think that's our gear."

"Come, we'll check it out."

"You mean you want to go into the village?"

"We have to, unless you want to wait until morning when the light gets better."

"No, let's do it now," agreed Pat.

They waited until the village was asleep. Then they worked their way to where Pat thought he spotted the saddles.

"Yep, those are our saddles, all right. The saddlebags and most of our things are still in them, but the bedrolls are gone."

Pat began dragging one of the saddles back to the river and signaled to Sage to bring the other. Sage hesitated—this wasn't the plan. There was no way they could discuss it where they were, so Sage dragged the other saddle.

Sage heard a noise coming from inside one of the lodges. He stopped and lay completely still. An Indian came out, looked around, and after seeing nothing, returned to his tepee. Sage lay still until he heard the sound of the man's deep breathing, then continued dragging the saddle to the river.

"That's the damnedest thing I've ever seen," Pat marveled. "You must have ice water in your veins."

"I learned that from a rabbit," Sage explained. "What made you change your mind about taking the saddles?"

"You'll have to tell me about that rabbit someday," Pat said, and then answered, "We were there, so I thought why not just take them. We can hide them in a ravine near where we're going to stage the ambush. That way, we can do it all in one quick move . . . . You wait here. I'll get the horse to help carry this stuff back to the canyon."

"Okay, I'll wait, but hurry, we've got to get out of here before daylight. This place is going to get downright unhealthy after the people wake up."

They pulled the saddles farther into the thick brush where Sage could wait, and Pat disappeared. When Pat returned, they loaded the saddles and bedrolls onto the horse and returned to the rim of the canyon. They were on their way back to the cave just as it was getting daylight. They rode double for a while to put distance between them and the Indians. They were both big men, and too heavy for the horse, so Sage got off and asked Pat to continue on alone.

Sage said, "I can get away from the Indians better on foot, and your horse's tracks will lead them away from me. You can get back to the cave quicker by riding alone. You'll be safe when you reach the cave, and I'll be there tomorrow."

Pat had seen this young man's skill at eluding the Indians and knew he would be safe. When Pat looked back, Sage had already melted into the prairie—he was invisible. Pat was amazed that Sage could conceal himself where there was so little cover.

When the Indians discovered that the saddles were missing, they began looking for the persons who had taken them. Pat lost the Indians long before he arrived back at the cave. He put the horse in the blind canyon and placed the dead tree across the opening. He gave a low whistle before entering the cave to warn Joe that he was coming. He didn't want to surprise Joe and get shot. He told him what they had done and explained the plan of the ambush.

"I'm ready to go," Joe said. "I'm feeling great and the wound has nearly healed."

*   *   *   *

About four hours later, Sage crawled into the cave with a big smile on his face. "The Indians are still looking for us," Sage said, "but they've gone off in another direction. They have no idea what happened. Won't they be surprised when we turn up at their village again in a couple of days?"

"That will work to our advantage," Pat said. "They'll be so frustrated that they'll chase you right up that canyon to where Joe and I will be waiting."

"I made a pot of buffalo stew," Joe commented. "Help yourself, and then get some sleep. I've got everything packed and ready to go. We're going to need a horse to carry our supplies, and we can take three horses just as easily as we can take two. That way, we'll each have a horse to ride, and one to carry our stuff."

"I'll be ready for that sleep just as soon as we get something to eat," agreed Pat.

Sage and Pat ate and then went to sleep. Joe cleaned the place and made ready to leave. The next two days were going to be very busy. Everything had to go just right if they were going to survive, and they had to have those horses.

$$* \qquad * \qquad * \qquad *$$

Each man checked his guns and made sure he had plenty of shot and powder, a canteen of water, jerky, dried fruit, and a pouch containing salt. Pat told Sage that salt was a real luxury on the frontier. The iron skillet and pot were too heavy and cumbersome to carry. Sage oiled and wrapped them in a skin to keep them dry, and stored them in his cave thinking that he might want to return someday . . . . Evening Star might want to use the cave while he was gone. He longed to hold her once more, but there was no chance.

They walked out into a beautiful autumn morning, each man carrying a load. They would all have to walk until they could get more horses. They went straight to the hidden canyon, loaded Midnight, and ate their breakfast as they walked. It would require two days to reach the Comanche village, which gave them plenty of time to plan their strategy for getting additional horses. Both Pat and Joe wanted their own horses. However, there was no guarantee that their horses would be the ones abandoned during the ambush. They would recognize their horses and try to pick off the Indians riding them, leaving their horses unattended for Sage to pick up. They described their horses to Sage.

Sage wanted an Arabian mare to match his stallion so he could start a new herd. The Arabian stallion would sire a better grade of riding animals and it would be helpful to have a pair. Their colts would be in high demand. Sage was wondering how Juanita Diego was going to feel about being only half-owner of a ranch that had been in her family for five generations.

On the second morning, they arrived at the canyon. The spot was ideal. It provided good cover, with an open field of fire on the Indians that would be coming up the canyon. Sage would hide in the rocks until the Indians riding the horses they wanted were eliminated, and the horses left unattended. Not wanting to be encumbered, he would carry only his knife and ax. He would have to outrun the Indians long enough to lead them into the ambush.

Joe figured about two hours before sunset was the ideal time to start the action. The Indians would have the sun in their eyes, and he and Pat would have the sun at their backs. They would have the extra firepower of the two guns that belonged to Sage. The Indians would have no way of knowing how many attackers they were facing. They wouldn't think that only three men would attack their whole village. If they were lucky, the Indians wouldn't continue chasing them after losing eight or ten men in the assault. The Comanche had already lost six of their best warriors.

"All right," Sage said. "I'm ready. I'll start a commotion about a quarter of a mile from the village. That'll give me enough lead-time to outrun them to the canyon. When you start picking them off, that'll slow them down and give me enough time to pick up their stranded horses. Try to knock off the riders of the horses you want. Make sure to get the rider of one of the Arabian mares."

"We're ready, too," Joe said. "Start the show."

Sage ran down the canyon. He had no need for caution; the earlier the Indians saw him, the better. He was in luck. Someone shouted an alarm while he was still about a mile from the village. He paused long enough to make sure there would be plenty of Indians chasing him and then started running up the canyon. The Comanche knew the canyon had steep sides and it would be difficult for this intruder to climb out. They would catch him long before he could escape. It never occurred to them that they were being led into an ambush.

Sage had a good head start. The mountain men waited until they couldn't miss, and then started shooting. They recognized their horses, so they picked off those riders first. They saw one of the Arabian mares—she was pure white.

Joe said, "You can't miss her; she stands out like a light, and she has a saddle on her."

Both men fired at the rider, and he dropped like a rock. While they were concentrating on that rider, two others got through the line of fire. They had dismounted and were chasing Sage on foot. The mountain men realized that Sage was in real danger.

Joe exclaimed, "I'm going down to help!"

Pat restrained him, and said, "No! With that bad arm you can provide more help right where you are. Use your skills with that rifle and keep those two ducking. Sage can handle them."

Sage crouched behind a boulder. Joe and Pat watched the first attacker moving forward, creeping from rock to rock, and never giving them a good shot at him. The other attacker was approaching from another direction, making it impossible for Sage to remain hidden from both of them. Sage waited with his ax ready. When the first Comanche got into range, Sage stood up, exposing himself to the second attacker. An arrow from the second attacker cut a crease in his neck. Without flinching, Sage hurled his ax at the first Comanche with swift and final accuracy, and then turned his attention to the Indian who had shot the arrow. The second Indian didn't know what had happened to his helper, so he continued forward. Sage stepped out of sight behind a boulder and waited. When the second attacker was close, Sage grappled with him, using wrestling techniques his father had taught him, threw the Indian to the ground, and ended the fight with his knife.

"Now do you see what I mean?" Pat said.

Joe replied, "I sure do, and again I tell you, I wouldn't want him for an enemy."

The mountain men continued laying down a volley of rifle fire, Sage gathered the reins of the horses, and ran up the canyon to a place where he could climb out. The Indians were confused. None of them wanted to chase Sage and encounter that terrible line of fire that was being laid down from the rim of the canyon. Eight warriors still on their horses turned and retreated down the canyon leaving their dead and wounded where they lay. The riders that had been shot abandoned the horses just as Sage had hoped. Sage selected the horses and found a way out of the canyon.

CHAPTER 11

▼

TO THE GREAT MOUNTAINS

When Sage arrived, Joe said. "Good work, Sage; you've got them all. Now let's get 'em loaded and get the hell outta here!"

They saddled the horses and changed the pack from the stallion to the mare. Sage wanted to ride the stallion.

They mounted and rode into the setting sun. They didn't know if the Comanche were following, so they rode until midnight, and then stopped by a small stream, giving the horses a chance to rest. They each took turns standing guard while the others bathed. It had been two days since they had a bath.

After refreshing themselves, they remounted and rode all night and all the next day. By the end of the following day, the land was becoming flatter. The big sandy river still had water, but it was shallow. The summer had been drier than usual, and the flow was diminishing. They passed great herds of buffalo and many smaller herds of elk and antelope. Meat was plentiful. They stopped at a spring with a stand of willows.

Pat said, "We'd better camp here and rest for a while. We'd be in poor shape to withstand an attack, and we're in Kiowa territory. They're not as bad as the Comanche, but when they're attacking, it's hard to tell the difference."

Pat shot a buffalo. They took only the meat they needed and buried the remains. Scavengers might draw the attention of a band of hunting Indians. They built a fire of dry wood under the trees. The branches dispersed the smoke. A column of smoke was like a beacon of light to anyone trained in the ways of the west, and Indians were surely trained.

After a meal of the fresh buffalo meat, they smoked and dried the rest. On the third morning, while traveling across land that was flat, they saw hills in the far distance. The hills were still several days' ride away, and shimmered in the midday sun, seeming to move farther away as they rode toward them.

A cloud of dust appeared. Buffalo could be causing the dust, but Pat didn't think so. There was not enough wind to stir up that much dust, so it probably meant trouble. But what kind of trouble?

They increased their pace, but moved carefully. They wanted to see what was happening before whatever, or whoever, causing the cloud of dust saw them. From a high point, they saw a wagon train being attacked by about thirty Indians. The train had eight wagons, which meant there would be about twelve fighting men, and the rest would be women and children. The defenders were outnumbered and needed help badly.

"By riding down that little draw we can remain concealed until we get within a hundred yards to the wagon train," Pat uttered. "We can jump the tongue of the last wagon and get into the circle before the Indians realize we're there. Let's go!"

Down the hill they rode at a full run. When they broke into the open, the Indians were confused, but by the time they realized what was happening, the three men were already inside the circle of wagons.

They bounded off their horses, firing as they ran for cover. Both Joe and Pat were dropping an Indian with every shot. Sage fired the charges he had in his guns, and two Indians dropped, but he had not yet become proficient at reloading. He grabbed his bow, and when an Indian fired an arrow, he would pick up the arrow and kill the startled Indian with his own arrow.

The wagon master ran to them up and said, "I'm sure glad to see you. I was afraid we were goners. I don't know where you learned to shoot like that, but you're damn good at it."

Sage turned just in time to see two Indians attacking a young woman with long blond hair. It brought back memories of the Indians attacking his mother. In a blind rage, he rushed in, slashing with his ax and knife. He sank the ax in the skull of one, and buried the knife to the hilt in the heart of the other. He must have looked like a madman, dressed in an animal skin with long flowing hair and beard, his eyes wild with fury.

When the girl looked up, she was astonished. She saw a frightening thing: a wild-eyed young animal with a bloody ax in one hand and a bloody knife in the other, pure fire coming from his eyes. She didn't know whether to run to him and hug him for saving his life, or shrink from him in horror. After eliminating the Indians, Sage turned and dashed back into the fray, dropping Indians as he went.

With Pat and Joe firing, and each dropping an Indian with nearly every shot, they were decimating the attackers rapidly. Quickly, the Indians realized that the advantage had changed, so they broke off and rode away. The travelers gathered around the three men expressing their gratitude.

"We'd better attend to the wounded," the wagon master said. "Boil some water. We've got to remove these arrowheads before the wounds get infected."

Two of the men were dead, four were seriously injured, two suffered lesser wounds, and only four were unscathed. Four women had been wounded, two more were scuffed up a bit, and the girl the Indians were attacking showed signs of shock. The people couldn't have held out much longer—the mountain men had arrived just in time.

"There's a river about an hour's ride from here," the wagon master advised. "As soon as we get these wounds treated, let's move there and set up a defense. Then we'll get these wagons ready to finish the journey." The wagon master said to the mountain men, "We're going to Santa Fe to spend the winter, then we'll be going on to California by the way of the Old Spanish Trail." He looked at Pat and asked, "Are you Pat Connors, the mountain man?"

"Yes," Pat replied. "Pat Connors is my name."

The wagon master said as he shook his hand, "It's an honor to meet you. Men talk of you all over the frontier. My name is Grant Davis." He turned to Joe and asked, "And who are you?"

"My name is Joe Martin."

"Joe Martin, the gunfighter?"

"Some say that," Joe said, showing embarrassment.

"No need to be embarrassed; I've heard a lot of stories about your ability with a gun, but I've never heard a bad word said about you. Not many gunfighters have that good a reputation. I'm pleased to meet you, Joe Martin," Grant Davis said, shaking his hand. "Now I understand why there was an Indian falling every time I heard a shot. Thank you, all three of you, for saving our scalps. And who is this magnificent young wild man?"

Pat spoke, "His name is Michael McBaine, but we call him "Sage." He saved our scalps back in Indian Territory. You don't want him for an enemy, but he's a damn good man to have on your side in a fight."

"Yeah, I saw him dispatch the two Indians who were attacking Sally, and you're right, I wouldn't want him after me." He turned to the young woman and said, "Sally, I'd like to introduce you to the young man who just saved your life. Sally, this is Michael McBain; they call him Sage. Sage, this is Sally Taylor."

"There's just not enough words for me to express my gratitude," Sally smiled. "All I can say is 'thank you,' and I'd like to see what you look like."

"What would it take for you to do that?" asked Sage.

"I'd have to remove some of that hair."

"Would you cut it for me?"

"I sure would, just as soon as we get to the river and get our defense set up," Sally replied.

Sage looked at Pat and said, "Well, let's get moving."

"Help me get these wounded folks into one of the wagons," Grant said. "We can have camp set up before dark. Graves must be dug, funeral services held, and loved ones comforted. We lost two good men today. They're going to be sorely missed."

The wagon people were pleased to have been rescued, and the wounded would recover. However, they were saddened by the loss of two men. One was the father of two children. The other was the eldest son of a middle-aged couple with two other teenaged sons and a daughter.

The wives and children of the men who had been killed were crying. The other families were trying to console them. Sage understood their sorrow and assured them that he would stay with the wagon train until it reached Santa Fe.

"I'll provide all the meat you'll need," Sage said.

"I'll scout for you," Pat volunteered.

"And I'll ride guard," Joe promised. "You won't get surprised again."

After the wagon train was located by the river, the burying done, and the train secured, the travelers went to sleep. It had been a difficult day, and they were exhausted. The mountain men pitched their camp nearby, then took turns standing guard. The Indians returned during the night and retrieved their dead. They had taken heavy losses in the last five minutes of the fight, and there was little chance they would attack again.

Before daylight, the men tended to the animals, made sure the wagon wheels were greased, and the loads secured. Then they sat down to a meal of fresh buffalo meat that Sage had provided. They talked of the battle and of the journey left to be made. Pat and Joe told them what to expect when they reached Santa Fe. Everyone felt better having the mountain men along.

Sage went to Sally and said, "Now, about that haircut."

Sally got a pair of scissors, a comb, and a mirror from their wagon, then pulled a cloth around Sage's shoulders and began removing a six-year growth of hair. The people gathered around watching. They, too, wanted to see what this tawny-haired young man would look like without all that hair. Sally's mother and father watched closely. Sally was old enough to marry, and this young man appeared to be a likely catch. He was strong, considerate, and resourceful.

Other young women watched, also. One of them said to her friends, "I wish it had been me the Indians were attacking."

Another of the girls said, "Yeah, me, too."

Bonnie, one of Sally's girlfriends, had already set her cap for Joe. They were a couple right away. She was beautiful in a petite way, and Joe had a reckless charm that was attractive to most women.

Sage was ill at ease with all the attention. This was the first time, in a long time, that he had seen himself in a mirror. He had seen his reflection in the water, but this was different . . . . Sally was pretty, but when he looked at her, it only reminded him of Evening Star. Sally saw that she was not getting the response she was accustomed to getting. When she finished cutting Sage's hair, there was enough hair piled around the chair to make a saddle blanket. The difference in his appearance was striking. He had the fine-honed features of his Scottish blood, firm and sharply defined. His expressive blue-green eyes looked out from under well-shaped eyebrows. When he stood in his buckskin, tall and strong, he looked like the warrior of the plains he truly was.

One of the older women murmured to her friend, "Now that's a fine figure of a man."

The attention was too much for Sage. He felt naked without his beard and hair. Going without it would take a little getting used to. He thanked Sally and shook the hair from the cloth she had placed around his neck. Sally smiled and he smiled back. He then walked to the river to wash away the loose hair. The wild boy of the plains was no more. He was now a frontiersman, a man of the West. When he returned to the wagons, Sally, Bonnie, and Joe were talking. Joe was telling the girls the remarkable story of how Sage had survived alone on the prairie, and of his skills with the weapons he carried. The girls were wide-eyed with wonder. Sally had a hundred questions she wanted to ask. She took Sage's hand and asked him to walk with her beside the river.

Sally was beautiful. Her beauty and her nearness stirred in him a hunger and a longing to which he dared not respond. Sally sensed his need and his frustration. She thought, *This man carries a hurt in his heart that will take time to heal. I'll give it some time. He's worth it.* Later, she told one of the other girls, "I think I can bring him around in time, and we have a lot of time before we get to Santa Fe."

*   *   *   *

Morning came, and the wagons moved west, leaving behind the graves of two good men, and the last remnants of a wild boyhood. The young man riding his father's horse was now a man of destiny.

Day after day, they saw a horizon of hills in the distance. When they arrived at that horizon, all they saw was another horizon and more hills still farther in the distance. The Great Plains seemed to go on and on forever. At times, they traveled through areas that were barren and dry. But at other times, the land was wild and beautiful. Great herds of buffalo, deer, elk, and antelope grazed the endless grass. Sage saw tracks of wolves, bear, and puma.

This land was wild, and it could be cruel. It was not a place where you could travel without being constantly on guard. Dangers lurked everywhere. Only the hardy could survive here. Sage was glad he didn't have to survive alone in this harsh place. The Indian Territory he had left was lush in comparison.

On occasions, they saw hunting parties. Pat recognized them by their dress and their decorations. They saw Cheyenne, Pawnee, Kiowa, and Comanche. The Indians made no effort to hide their presence, but they never threatened the wagon train. Information about the outcome of a battle travels fast on the plains. These Indians knew that the men in this wagon train were not the average, and the price they would have to pay for attacking would be high indeed. So they left them alone.

Michael's friendship with the two mountain men was growing into a lifelong friendship. Joe and Bonnie had fallen in love and were talking of getting married. Sage got to know Grant Davis, the wagon master. He was a good and brave man.

On many evenings, Sage and Sally walked together. He told her that he had a mission to fulfill. It was a quest taken on by his father, and he felt responsible to fulfill it. After he had honored his father's pledge, he had to return to the cave of his childhood. He didn't tell her about Evening Star. These obligations had to be met before he would know the path his footsteps would follow. These duties would require several years, and he was not free to make any lifetime commitments until he had completed them. She told him she understood and wished him Godspeed.

At last, they saw the great mountains in the distance. Sage sat and watched the marvelous display of color as the sun set behind them, and he wondered what lay beyond. What would he have to do to fulfill the commitment his father had made to Don Antonio Diego? The following day the trail led up and up until it reached the pass. The pass was just a gap between the peaks of the mountains that made up the Sangre de Cristo Mountain Range. From the top, Michael could see in the distance a large river flowing off to the south. *That would be the Rio Grande*, he thought. *Our destination, Santa Fe, is just a few days ahead.*

CHAPTER 12

▼

GETTING THE LAY
OF THE LAND

Sage called Joe and Pat aside and told them his plans. "No one must know that I am to become half-owner of the Don Diego ranch. I want to look around and get to know the people, the customs, the problems of the ranch, and find out who is causing the problems before I expose my hand. Any information you can get about what is going on at the ranch will be appreciated."

"You can count on us," Pat said. "The wagon people will tell of the three of us coming to their rescue, so everyone will know that we ride together. We can talk freely in public places, but not of the ranch. As far as everyone knows, we are just mountain men waiting to go back into the mountains to trap beaver."

The people were excited as the wagon train wound its way down the well-worn road through the western slopes of the Sangre de Cristo Mountains into the pueblo of Santa Fe, New Mexico. A lodging house large enough to accommodate many people was visible, but the wagon master guided them to a location on the banks of the Santa Fe River where they had access to water. The valley was lush and green, and there was grass for the animals. The travelers set up camp about half hour out of the pueblo, where neither they nor their animals would be cramped or crowded.

The campsite had been used many times; it had corrals for the animals and houses for the people. The houses had been built from straw and mud and looked strange to the newcomers. The houses were not pretty, but they were warm in the winter and cool in the summer. The land belonged to Señor Mendoza. They paid him a fee for the use of the houses. The appearance of the mud houses dismayed the eastern women when they first saw them but they found the dwellings were more than adequate. Fireplaces heated them, and they cooked their food in pots hanging from iron hangers over an open fire, and baked their bread in earthen ovens.

Bread was made of a mixture of cornmeal and flour, the Mexicans called it tortillas. The eastern women had difficulty in adjusting but, in time, they managed quite well. The windows had no glass. They lit their homes with oil lamps or candles. Their children played with the Mexican children in the dirt courtyards and quickly learned to speak the Mexican language. The adults learned the language from their children.

Catholic priests welcomed them to attend religious services, and some of them did. Most of the time, though, they held their own services in their homes. The Mexicans had few opportunities to earn pesos, so their labor was cheap. The people quickly learned to exchange dollars for pesos. Businessmen in Santa Fe had learned to make a profit from these exchanges. Some of the people liked their life in Santa Fe so well that they decided to stay and not continue across the great desert to California.

They were told that the California Trail was arduous, and many travelers died along the rugged trail. It was not a journey for the weak at heart, but the reward was great for those who reached California. The land in the valleys of California was fertile, the climate mild, and life could be wonderful.

Sage and his friends found lodging in Santa Fe and placed their horses in the care of a stable master. The stable was close, so they could get their horses whenever they needed them. Sage paid the stable owner to keep their horses ready. One of Sage's gold coins was exchanged for enough pesos to last all three of them for several months. Pat made the exchange for pesos with a man he knew he could trust— a man who would not divulge the source of the gold.

They purchased the best garments they could find. Sage looked dashing in his new clothes, but he had to adjust to wearing boots. They felt heavy and cumbersome. He changed back to his buckskin and moccasins when he went into the mountains.

Pat and Joe led Sage on exploring trips. They traveled north to the thriving pueblo of Taos, and south to the sleepy little settlement of Albuquerque. They rode wide sweeps through the land both east and west of the Rio Grande. They explored El Rancho Diego, taking care not to allow it to be known why they were riding the range, or to give anyone reason to question their purpose. The Diego ranch covered a large area indeed. The cattle and sheep were in poor condition. It was obvious the ranch was having trouble.

Now that they knew the land and the animals, they would discreetly get to know the people—the ones who managed the ranch, and the ones who worked it. They attended the places where the vaqueros and the miners went to drink. They also went to the high-quality establishments where the owners and managers went to drink and dine.

These places were gaily lighted and decorated, with bands playing Mexican and Spanish music. Attractive young Mexican women sang, danced, and entertained. Sage, Pat, and Joe had no shortage of money, so they dressed to fit the occasions.

*   *   *   *

One night, while they were dining in one of these finer cantinas, three men and two beautiful women came in. The owner escorted them to a special table, and treated them as important guests. The señorita was a woman of astonishing beauty. She was, without a doubt, a woman of high breeding. Her hair was long, straight, and black as the night; the lights of the cantina reflected in its luster. Her nose was high and well shaped. Her eyes were dark brown, large, soft, and expressive. Her breasts were not large, but they were high and full. She wore a black, fitted skirt that accentuated her small waist and round, firm hips. The skirt hung to just below her knees and exposed her long, shapely legs. Her walk was regal. She wore high-topped, shiny boots. She was magnificent. She looked neither left nor right, but Sage was sure that she was seeing everything. Sage took careful notice of the other people in her party.

Pat spoke up, "That's Señorita Juanita Montoya Diego, the grand-daughter of Señor Don Diego, and she's the owner of the largest ranch in New Mexico. Correction, half-owner."

"You mean *that's* my partner," Sage asked, "*that's* the woman Don Diego asked my father to help? I had no idea she was so beautiful. This obligation may not be as troublesome as I thought. But how can I tell her she's only half-owner of her ranch? She's bound to question my motives. Now that I've seen her, I have no idea how tell her who I am, and why I'm here. I'm sure glad I have the letter from her grandfather."

"The tall, thin man on her left is her uncle," Pat continued. "His name is Jose Alvarez. He is the half-brother of Señor Francisco Diego, Juanita's father. Alvarez is a child of Don Antonio Diego's first wife. She was first married to a man named Alvarez in Mexico City; they had one son, Jose Alvarez. His father died when he was about six. Don Antonio married his mother, and Jose has always resented his stepfather. Some say he feels that he should have been the heir to the ranch, which went to Juanita's father, Francisco. Francisco and his wife, Juanita's mother, were killed by Apaches while on a journey to Mexico City. The land then passed on to Juanita. Jose manages the ranch, but he's not managing it well. The bills are piling up, and the señorita is in danger of losing everything."

"He looks like a capable man. Why is he allowing Juanita to lose the ranch?" Sage asked.

"I don't know," Pat answered, "but that's what we've got to find out. The two men with them are the foremen of the ranch. The ranch is engaged in two ventures: one is raising cattle, and the other is mining gold and silver. The older, gray-haired Mexican man is in charge of the cattle operations. I know him. He's a good man. His name is Carlos Viejo, a long-time friend and employee of the Diego family. The other woman is Carlos's wife. The other foreman is Pedro Vacca. He's in charge of the mining. He has a bad reputation. Alvarez brought him here from Mexico. The miners don't like him. They're afraid of him because they say he's cruel and mean. Several miners have died since he's been managing the mines. As you can see, you have your work cut out for you."

Pat continued, "The cattle operation isn't profitable right now, because rustlers are stealing the herd. The ranch doesn't have enough money to hire and maintain enough vaqueros to move the herd to the high meadows in the summer, and then drive them back to the rich grassland along the river in the winter. There have been attempts to kill Carlos Viejo. Someone fired at him from ambush . . . . The miners say they're bringing out some high-grade ore, but the records don't indicate that. The records indicate that they're selling only small amounts of gold and silver."

Sage asked, "Do you think someone might be rat-holing the rest?"

"It's a reasonable conclusion, and it's worth looking into," Pat answered.

Sage studied the faces of the men at the table, and his eyes kept wandering to the black-haired young woman. She sensed him looking at her; their eyes met and held for just an instant, and then she looked away.

"If you're finished with your drinks," Sage said, "let's get outta here." They walked out into the brisk, cool night. "Pat, you seem to know a lot of people. Could you take me to a cantina where I can sit among them? I want to get to know them, and I want to learn their language as quickly as possible."

"Sure. Let's go to Margarita's Cantina. There's always a crowd there. You'll meet the local people, and I think you'll have a good time."

Margarita's Cantina was jumping. Men from all over the frontier were there drinking and talking. Mountain men, miners, cattlemen, Indians, Mexicans, and even people from the wagon train were there. The wagon master was with a Spanish couple. He invited Sage and the two mountain men to join them. Many men wanted to buy drinks for Pat and Joe—everybody seemed to know them.

Grant Davis, the wagon master, introduced them to his friends and asked, "What would you like to drink? Tequila is the drink of choice here."

Margarita, the owner, came by, gave Pat and Joe a big hug, and said, "The first drink is on me. I heard you fellows had a little trouble on the trail."

Joe winked at the wagon master and said, "Nah, just a little skirmish." Looking at Sage, he said, "This young man invited us to a real party. We had enough Indians around to start a new tribe. He invited us to join him under his sagebrush. That's why we call him Sage."

Margarita said, "So this is the wild man I've heard about. He sounds like a good man to have around in a scrap." Looking at Sage, she said, "I'd consider it an honor if you'd let me buy you a drink."

"Thank you, I'll accept," Sage smiled. "I'm not sure I'll know what to do with an alcoholic drink, but I'm willing to learn if the effect is not too sudden."

"We'll keep it slowed down for you," Margarita replied. "We don't get too many beginners in here."

Everybody had a good-natured laugh.

A prospector came staggering up to the table. "Yeah, I've heard about this wild man," he said in a drunken slur. "If he'd stand up, I'd like to introduce him to the place."

Sage started to get up, but Pat put his hand on his shoulder, indicating he wanted Sage to remain seated. "Listen, rooster," Pat said to the drunken miner. "My advice to you is to find yourself a place to hunker down. This young fellow will trim your tail feathers if you mess with him."

The drunk turned around and left. Everyone in the room knew Pat Connors and Joe Martin; no man in his right mind would challenge either of them.

"Thanks, Pat," Sage murmured, "I'm not looking for trouble."

"I know you're not," Pat replied. "I wasn't doing you a favor; I was doing that drunken prospector a favor."

Grant Davis said, "If he ever saw this young man in action, like I saw him in action, he would give him a wide path."

The man with the wagon master smiled. "Now, let's have that drink," he said.

Joe said, "Sage, when you get a reputation, there's always some damn fool who wants to challenge you. If they're drunk, just avoid them. If they're not drunk, put them down hard, and they won't be so anxious to try you next time."

"Sounds like good counsel. I'll remember it in the future."

Sage just sipped his tequila, not knowing what to expect of the drink. He listened carefully to the talk, picking up words and expressions quickly. Everyone was amazed at how fast he was learning the language.

After a couple of hours, Sage had finished his second drink. He said to Pat and Joe, "Let's get back to our hotel; we've got a big day tomorrow."

On the way back, Sage said, "I want to take a look at that mine tomorrow, so I can get the lay of the land. I have a feeling that's where the trouble is coming from. I want to learn as much about that mine as I can, without entering it."

Joe replied, "Okay, the mine is on the west slope of the Sangre de Cristo Range. We can ride out there in a few hours, but they won't let us in unless you tell them you're part owner, and they won't believe you even if you tell them."

"I don't want to go into the mine," Sage explained. "I don't want anyone to know we're there. I just want to get the lay of the land. I want to know what we'll be up against in the future."

✻   ✻   ✻   ✻

They got up early as usual. Sage and Joe had breakfast, and then started up the valley to explore the land around the mine. The morning was cool and crisp, with frost on the grass. In the distance, they could see magnificent mountain peaks, white with snow, silhouetted against a clear, blue sky. It looked as though there had been a quick sweep of an artist's brush across the pale blue sky. The high, thin clouds over the Sangre de Cristo reflected the light of the rising sun leaving streaks of white, pink, and gold. The semiarid land didn't have as many animals and trees as his prairie home, but the magnificence was like a balm to his soul. Sage understood why those who had spent time here were reluctant to leave.

Pat had been to the mine before and didn't go with Sage and Joe. Instead, he wanted to talk to some of the men who worked there, and get a sample of the ore they were taking out. He knew that they were going to have to know the quality of the ore in order to determine if the amount of gold being produced agreed with the quality of the ore. Pat had done some prospecting and had a working knowledge of mining. He went to Margarita's Cantina. She served food as well as drinks. Her husband and Pat had been mountain men together many years ago. When Margarita and her husband got married, her husband became a miner. He was killed in a cave-in, and after he died, Margarita opened the cantina. Her customers come from all over the western range. There wasn't much going on in the Rio Grande Valley that Margarita didn't know about. Since her husband died, she and Pat had become close friends. Pat calls her Maggie.

Pat walked into the cantina and called out, "Maggie, fix me some breakfast; I'm starving."

The cook yelled, "Coming right up."

Maggie called back, "No, Tony, I'll cook for this customer. I know how he likes his eggs."

"I can't compete with that," Tony chuckled.

Maggie brought Pat a breakfast of steak and eggs, tortillas, and coffee, placed it on the table and sat down beside him. "Now, what else do you want? You didn't come in here just for eggs."

Pat smiled and said, "You know me too well, Maggie."

She patted him on the leg closest to her, smiled, and said, "Yeah, I know you, but not as well as I'd like to. Don't you think you should give up climbing those damn mountains and help me keep order in this cantina? It gets a little rowdy in here at times."

"A little rowdy, you say? I think climbing mountains is easier and a damn sight safer." The smile left his face when he asked, "Maggie, what do you know about the Diego mines?"

"I don't really know anything, Pat, I just overhear talk by some of the men who work there. They're wondering why the bullion is being stored in one of the old mineshafts. It seems strange to them. Vacca keeps two armed guards on duty all the time. They say he could save himself some labor costs if he would just sell it down river like they used to. Are you onto something, Pat?"

"Nah, I am just trying to help a friend."

Maggie asked, "Is it that young man of the prairie? I was thinking there was something strange about him. He's not a mountain man, but he sure has the savvy to become one. Is he as good as they say?"

Pat replied, "He's a fine young man, Maggie. And he's damn sure no one to cross if he doesn't want to be crossed."

"He's sure a handsome fellow. All of the girls are competing to see which one can get him in bed first."

"He's a live one, all right, but he's been hurt, Maggie, and getting him in a whore's bed will take some doing. Tell them they'd better not count on it. This young man is from some quality stock."

"That'll just make 'em want him more."

"Well, you tell them good luck. It won't hurt him any, I guess. It might even help him." He chuckled. "Thanks, Maggie, that was a good breakfast. And thanks for the information about what the miners are saying." Looking around, Pat asked, "Do you know if any of these men work at the Diego mine?"

"Yeah, those two over there in the corner work at the Diego."

"Tell them you'll give them free breakfast for a week, if they'll bring you a couple of samples of ore from the mine. Here is $20 to cover the cost of their breakfasts."

Maggie exclaimed, "My goodness, Pat, I could feed them for a month for $20!"

"Will you do it for me?" Pat asked.

"Sure, they'd be glad to bring me samples of ore in exchange for free breakfasts for a week. What if they want to know why I want the ore?"

"Just tell them one of the people from the wagon train wants to see what gold ore looks like, and they're willing to pay for a chance to look at it. If they ask who, tell them the man's name is Grant Davis. I'll set it up with Grant. Tell them you need it by tomorrow morning."

"Okay, you got it. That is a strange request, Pat. Do you want to tell me what this is all about?"

"Nah, I'm just curious."

"But you don't want me to tell anyone how curious, right?"

"Right! Thanks again, Maggie. I'll see you tomorrow morning."

"I'll be looking forward to it. If you ever want more than breakfast, let me know."

"I'm glad I have you for a friend, Maggie, and you never know what time may bring. Ye just never know."

Joe and Sage had ridden for about an hour when Joe said, "The mine is another mile up that canyon on the north side of the draw."

Sage said, "We'd better tie the horses here and walk the rest of the way. Let's go up this side, so we can stay out of sight until I can get close enough to get a good look."

They crept to the top of the ridge and looked down at the mine entrance. Two guards carrying rifles with pistols in their belts were standing near the entrance.

"Isn't it unusual to have armed men guarding the opening to a mine?" Sage commented.

"Well, I've never seen it done before, so yeah, I'd say it's unusual."

"Wonder why they would do that. Who would want to go into a mine, dig ore, and steal it? You would need a wagon to haul enough to make it worthwhile, and then where would you sell it?"

Joe replied, "Yeah, that's kind of unusual all right. What do you make of it?"

"I don't know. It would be difficult getting into that mine without being seen, but I've got to know what is going on. Let's go back to town and talk to Pat. Maybe he's found out something that will help."

When they got back to the hotel, Pat was there talking to Grant Davis. Joe told Pat and Grant about the armed guards at the mine entrance.

"Yeah, that fits with what I've found. They're storing the bullion in the old mineshaft," Pat informed them.

"Why would they do that," Joe questioned, "when they have a ready market for it here in Santa Fe?"

"I don't know, but there's something fishy going on out there. We'd better do some more looking. Let's all have breakfast at Maggie's tomorrow morning," Sage said.

"Okay," Joe said, "but I want to see Bonnie tonight. We have to make plans for our wedding. Her folks are not sure she should be marrying a mountain man."

"I want to start raising some high-quality horses," Sage commented. "Would you go into the horse-raising business with me? I'll pay you well for your help until we can get the herd started, and then the sale of the animals will make it a profitable business."

"That sounds good," Joe said excitedly. "Maybe her folks would feel better if they knew Bonnie and I would be living here in Santa Fe and that I wouldn't be going back into the mountains. That sounds like a good idea, Sage, the beaver pelt business is running out anyway." He turned to Pat. "Pat, we both need to get into something else. Yeah, I think they might feel a little better about me being in the business of raising horses. I'll talk to Bonnie about it tonight and see what she thinks. But I don't want to break up our partnership, Pat; we've been a good pair."

"Don't worry about me, Joe," Pat piped up. "Grant Davis wants me to scout for his wagon trains. That way, I would see you guys every once in a while. I've scouted the California Trail before, and I think I can save some lives, by showing them what I have learned, about traveling through Death Valley. The lady who lost her husband in the Indian raid needs help getting her wagon and her two young sons through to California, and I'd like to help her."

"I think we're beginning to see why the Diego ranch is going broke," Sage said. "We should be able to bring this problem to a conclusion before spring. Then we'll all be ready for something else."

"Okay, Sage," Joe agreed. "I'll talk to Bonnie and see what she thinks. If she likes it, you got a deal!"

Joe rode to the wagon camp that evening to see Bonnie. He was in high spirits, eager to share the news with Bonnie and her parents. Bonnie ran to meet him. She was a delight, so full of life and so beautiful, how could he be so lucky as to have won the heart of such a wonderful girl? He took her hand, and they walked along the Santa Fe River. The light was fading, and shadows were deepening in the valleys.

Joe told Bonnie of the business proposition Sage had made. He told her that they planned to raise high-quality saddle horses, and that he would manage the ranch. They could build their own home, and he would be home each evening. No more trips into the high mountains to trap the beaver, and no more long trips to Saint Louis to market the furs. Bonnie was ecstatic. She was torn between a desire to hurry back to tell her parents, and the desire to spend more time alone with Joe.

They sat on a grassy knoll overlooking the river, watching the sun set behind the mountains to the west silhouetted against the brightly colored sky. To anyone who might have happened to see, they were just two young people in love, contemplating their lives together. Before the darkness settled in, they walked back to the camp to discuss their plans with Bonnie's parents. They were relieved to hear the news and gave their consent. Joe and Bonnie would be married in a few weeks.

*   *   *   *

Sage, the two mountain men, and the wagon master met at Margarita's for breakfast. Maggie helped the cook prepare their breakfast and brought it to them. She sat down with them, and handed Pat a pouch containing ore from the Diego mine.

Pat placed the ore in a container on the table where they could all see it. Even a green horn could see that it was rich gold ore. They all looked at the ore, then at one another, and left.

"Thanks, Maggie," Pat said, as he placed the ore back in the pouched.

When they were out of earshot, Pat said, "I think we have enough information to come to the conclusion that Juanita's uncle and his cohort, Pedro Vacca, are stealing gold from her, and placing her ranch in danger of failing."

"Why would they do that?" Joe asked.

"It fits with other information I've gathered from gossip. Jose is the overseer of the ranch. He doesn't want to be the overseer—he wants to be the owner. If he can convince Juanita that her ranch is failing, she will sell it cheap. It wouldn't look right for him to buy his niece's ranch, which is failing, while he's the manager. However, he can buy it through the name of Pedro Vacca, using the gold they steal from Juanita's mines. Then, as per their agreement, Vacca would then sell the ranch to Alvarez, and it would be in Jose's hands at last."

"What do you know about Pedro Vacca?" Sage asked.

"About seven years ago, Alvarez brought him from Mexico to run the mines. They say he had been running mines in Mexico, where he worked Indian minors to death, disposed their bodies, and then brought in others to replace them. He is from Spain. People who know say he is cruel and ambitious.

"Several years ago, a man brought a message to the señorita from Don Diego while he was still in Spain. The man who delivered the message was killed shortly after delivering it. Juanita was just a child then, but she remembers the message. It said that her grandfather was sending someone to help her. It was so long ago that she had about given up hope. Juanita's uncle told her that Vacca has the money ready, and her uncle is pressuring her to sell. They say he's growing impatient and is considering other methods to force her hand."

Sage said, "Looks like we got here just in time. I'm surprised she has held out this long."

Pat continued, "Those who know her—and not many do—say that she is a strong-minded young woman."

"Why are they trying to kill Carlos?"

"Carlos is loyal to Juanita. It was Carlos who got word to her grandfather that the uncle was plotting to take the ranch. The uncle and Vacca have got to get rid of Carlos before they can complete their takeover. The vaqueros are loyal to Carlos, and they have been protecting him. So far they've been successful."

CHAPTER 13

▼

THE DON DIEGO RANCH

"I think it's time," Sage said, "for me to make myself known to the señorita. It will probably work better if you and Joe remain in the background for now. Who do you know that could introduce me to her?"

"Carlos knows me, and I think he would be glad to introduce you to his mistress," Pat replied.

"Okay, set it up as soon as possible."

"Let's ride out there right now," Pat said. "It's about a two-hour ride to the hacienda."

"Let me take a bath, and get a haircut and a shave," Sage said. "I want to look like someone who has come to help, not someone who has come to seek employment."

Joe smiled and said, "Yeah, I'd clean up a bit, too; she sure is pretty."

Just before midday, they topped a rise on the trail where they could see the collection of buildings that made up the hacienda on the Diego ranch. The site was awesome. There were several barns where animals and their feed were kept. The tools were also kept in separate buildings. An assortment of adobe dwellings housed the workers. The big house, or *La Casa Grande*, as it was called, was the dwelling of the owners. This building consisted of an assortment of adobe rooms with a courtyard between them. The roof was held in place by huge logs. The roof joined all of the rooms into one connected building. Each room was private and separate, except for the large center room, which was in the front center of the structure. This room was connected with the rest by verandas, and an open center space called the patio. Many people could be housed or entertained here.

The ranch was self-sustaining. The workers provided almost everything that they used. They provided the housing, most of the food, water, and fuel for heating and cooking. The workers produced their own blankets and most of their clothing. The ranch had cows, from which they got milk, butter, and cheese. They raised chickens for meat and eggs, pigs for meat and cooking oil. They grew beans, potatoes, tomatoes, peppers, and an assortment of other foodstuff in the large gardens.

In the fields, along the river, they grew corn and other grains to produce flour and meal for making tortillas. These fields provided food for the farm animals, also. They raised herds of sheep and cattle, processed the wool for making blankets and clothing, and then sold the remainder. The ranch sold beef to provide meat and leather for the people who live in the settlements.

The workers lived a short distance from the main house, in adobe dwellings, and the children played in the yards. The ranch was, in reality a small, self-contained, self-governing pueblo.

It took Sage and his friends about an hour from the time they saw the hacienda in the distance, until they reached it. The approach was down a long winding dirt road. The hacienda was on a wide plain with large trees all around to provide shade in the summer and visual beauty all year round. It sat in the Rio Grande valley, with the mountains in the background.

Sage was becoming aware of what he had obtained half-ownership of through his father's agreement with Señor Don Antonio Diego. He felt compelled to fulfill his father's obligation. He was sure that was what his father would have wanted him to do, and now that he had started the task, there was no way he would be distracted from completing it. It was also obvious that a great wrong was being done. He just wanted to make sure he was doing what the señorita wanted before endangering his and his friends' lives in correcting the wrong.

When they first arrived at the hacienda, they didn't see Carlos. The Spanish custom required Sage to be introduced to the Señorita before he spoke to her.

Pat said, "He might be supervising the work of his vaqueros."

Then Carlos, who was working behind the buildings, saw them and came hurrying to greet them. He extended his hand to Pat and said, "*Buenos dias*, Señor Connors. I saw you and your friends at the cantina a few nights ago. It is good to see you are back safe. We heard about your trouble with the Kiowa along the trail. They say these two young men provided a lot of help in the battle. I have not had the pleasure of meeting them, but people tell me you were in good company."

Pat replied, "*Buenos dias*, Señor Viejo, news travels fast here in Santa Fe."

Carlos smiled and said, "Si, Señor, there are few secrets here in the valley of the Rio Grande. How may I help you?"

Pat introduced Carlos to Sage and Joe.

Sage said to Carlos, "I have come seeking your counsel and to ask for your help. I want to purchase a ranch to raise horses. We have been told you would know if there are ranches available."

"Si, Señor, I know of a ranch that is for sale. The owner died, and the señora wishes to sell the ranch and return to Mexico City. I would be pleased to introduce you."

Pat asked, "Where is Señor Alvarez?"

Carlos, with a questioning look, replied, "The ranch manager is at the mines. He and Señor Vacca had business to attend to there today."

Then Pat said, "*Buena*, Carlos, the time is opportune. Perhaps you could introduce Señor McBain to Señorita Diego. He would like to have a private audience with her. He carries a message from her grandfather."

Carlos expression changed to surprise. "This is amazing. When she saw you at the cantina a few nights ago, she told me in confidence that she thought this young man had come to play a role in her life. Women's intuition is remarkable. I will tell the señorita you are here, although I'm sure she already knows. Not much gets by her." He went into the big house. When he returned, he said, "Come, she'll see you on the veranda."

Carlos led them to the veranda, and soon Juanita appeared, wearing black culottes, tight at the hips, with the legs pleated to make it look like a skirt. It was a type of garment oftentimes worn by ranch women who did a lot of riding and didn't want to ride sidesaddle. She was also wearing high-topped boots, a white blouse with a bolero jacket, and her hair was tied back tight against her head with a simple black lace scarf around her neck. Sage sensed that she had been aware of their presence and had dressed for the meeting. *Surely, no one dresses like that just to do chores around the house,* he thought. Whatever she had dressed for, it was effective. She was stunningly beautiful.

Carlos, with a trace of a smile, introduced them all around. When he got to Sage, he said, "Señorita, this is Señor Michael McBain; his friends call him Sage. He has come for a private audience with you."

"Why do they call you Sage?" Juanita asked.

"That's a long story," Sage replied. "I would be pleased to tell you about it at another time. I would like to speak to you in private."

Juanita looked at Carlos and said, "Carlos, please show these men around the hacienda while I talk with Señor McBain."

After they left, Juanita turned to Sage and asked, "May I get you a cool drink?"

"Thank you. That would be nice."

A middle-aged woman, without being called, entered the room carrying a glass of a very refreshing drink, of a type Sage never had tasted before. He wondered how the servant knew to bring the drink, and then realized that the household staff was observing them.

Sage said, "Señorita, would you accompany me? I would like you to show me some grassland I've been told is available nearby." She was pleased to see that he was perceptive and had noticed that she didn't need to ask for a drink to be served—all she had to do was to mention it, and it was done.

"I would be pleased to show you the property." She got her riding crop and her hat, walked to the front of the dwelling, and called out, "Carlos, bring my horse."

"Si, Señorita, *muy pronto.*"

In only minutes, Carlos returned, leading a beautiful white Arabian mare. The mare had been saddled with a small Western-style saddle. Sage was riding his coal-black stallion, which his father had brought west with him. Sage was thinking, *Here is some fine breeding stock for the horse ranching we want to do.* Joe, standing a short distance away, saw what was going through Sage's mind. He looked at Sage with a big smile and nodded. Sage knew that Joe had been thinking the same thing about the two horses. Sage and Juanita rode off in the direction of the river.

They rode until they were out of sight, and then stopped on a knoll overlooking the river. Sage got off and helped Juanita to dismount. When he grasped her waist to help her, he felt her body, soft and supple, with strong muscle fiber underneath the softness. A tingling sensation passed through his fingers, and he was aroused. He sensed that she also experienced a similar stimulation. As he lifted her from the horse, their bodies rubbed together. It seemed the very air around them was charged with the force of the sensation. He stepped back, not wanting to frighten her, and not trusting his own responses. Her eyes were calm and steady. There was no expression of fear. She, too, was fighting her body's response.

Sage tied the reins of their mounts to a branch and took Juanita's hand, leading her under a giant oak tree. The tree's roots spread out like giant gnarled fingers grasping the earth. They sat for a calming moment in silence, observing their surroundings. Sage had spent years training himself to be aware of everything, and he was very aware of Juanita. She was calm to the point of being serene, but he sensed her eagerness to know what he had to say. He hardly knew where to start, so he told her why he and his parents were coming west, including the story of her grandfather dying in their home. On hearing the news of her grandfather's death, she hung her head for an instant, and tears came to her eyes. Sage gave her a moment to regain her composure, then continued. He told her that before her grandfather died, he obtained an oath from his father to help her save her land. Then he told her of the Indian raid, of how his parents were killed in the attack. He told her of his struggle to survive and of his vow to avenge the killings, and that he had brought the vow to a conclusion.

He continued by telling how he rescued the mountain men, and how they became friends, and of their commitment to help him.

She sat in silent awe, then responded, "Almost seven years ago, a man came to me with a message from my grandfather. The message was that Grandfather was sending someone to help me. After delivering the brief message, the messenger was called away by my uncle, and he never returned to complete telling me the details. He never told me who was coming to help me, or who was trying to take my land. The messenger's body was found floating in the river a few days later. No one ever knew what had happened to him, or who he was. I never knew why or by whom the messenger was killed, but his being killed reinforced the truth of what he had told me.

"The only man I can trust is Carlos. I detest and fear Vacca, the mining foreman. He's a cold and cruel man, but he's the friend of my uncle. My uncle employed him, so I don't feel at liberty to discharge him. I'm afraid of making my uncle angry—there's no telling what he might do. He doesn't consider my opinion as worthy when it comes to the running of the ranch.

"I've never gained control of the ranch. My uncle controls the finances and, without money, I'm helpless. It's been almost seven years since I got the message from my grandfather that help was on its way. I haven't heard anything further from him. Nor has anyone come to help me. I know it takes a long time for help to come all the way from Spain. I was about to give up in despair and turn the ranch over to my uncle to sell to Pedro Vacca until I saw you at the cantina a few nights ago. I waited. Then when I didn't hear from you, I was beginning to doubt my own intuition. I had about decided it was just hopeful thinking that you were the one who had come to help me."

Sage explained, "I didn't come right away because I didn't know who was trying to take your ranch, and how they were going to do it. I needed to remain uninvolved in the happenings at the ranch, to enable me to gather information unrestrained. I had to determine who's responsible for your difficulties. We heard of the attempt on Carlos's life, and that started us on a search. It resulted in the conclusion that your uncle and his employee, Pedro Vacca, are trying to undermine the successful operation of the ranch and force you to selling it to Señor Vacca. I believe your uncle and Vacca are stealing the bullion from your mines and storing it, so they can use your own money to pay you for your ranch. We believe they're becoming impatient and are planning to do away with you and Carlos. If you die, your uncle will inherit the ranch, and his problem of obtaining ownership to the ranch will be solved. I believe you and Carlos have reason to fear for your lives."

Sage then gave Juanita the letter written by her grandfather, and also another paper that had been written and signed by him. The paper transferred one-half-ownership of the ranch to Michael's father, if he were able to prevent her from losing the land. Juanita read the letters and recognized her grandfather's handwriting. She said she knew that the papers were authentic. Michael explained that he didn't feel that she was under any obligation to relinquish half ownership of the ranch to him. He was just trying to fulfill his father's obligation.

Juanita said, "Thank you for being candid with me, and for offering to help me so unselfishly. Just last night I was contemplating the complete loss of the ranch. Sage, please tell me what I need to do to help save my land and my home. There are many people whose lives will be affected if the land is transferred to my uncle. The vaqueros don't want to work for Vacca. They know he is cruel and they fear him."

Sage asked, "First we have your safety, and the safety of Carlos, to consider. Does Carlos have the loyalty of his vaqueros?"

"Yes, all of them are loyal. They have their own families to consider."

"Let's ride back to the hacienda. I want to talk to my friends, and I want to talk to Carlos. Perhaps you should prepare to stay at the hotel in Santa Fe until we can solve this problem."

"I'll stay at the hacienda," Juanita replied. "I have people I can trust. If there's anyone I feel I cannot trust, I'll discharge them. Thank you, Sage, for coming to my aid. You don't know how much it means to me, to have someone to depend on and help me. I had about given up—I felt so helpless."

She hugged him. He felt her trembling and was glad he had made the decision to come.

CHAPTER 14

▼

THE SEÑORA CORDOVA RANCH

"Juanita, my desire to buy a ranch is sincere. I want to raise good saddle horses. Riding horses are always in demand, and I have the start of a good herd with this stallion and a mare. I'd like to see the ranch Carlos told me about, if it's not too far, and perhaps you would like to show it to me."

"I would be pleased to introduce you to the señora who owns the ranch. She or one of her vaqueros can show it to us. We can easily ride there and back before dark." She led the way. The trail followed the Rio Grande to the neighbor's hacienda. Señora Cordova greeted them warmly. Juanita explained the purpose of their visit.

"I'm glad to see you for many reasons," the señora replied. "It has been too long since I last saw you. I'm eager to sell my ranch, so I can return to Mexico City to join my family. It has been difficult since my husband died. The vaqueros try, but they need guidance, and I'm unable to provide the guidance they need."

"If I buy the ranch," Sage said, "I'll need help to work it, and I'd be pleased if your vaqueros would stay and work for me. I hope you and I can reach an agreement."

Señora Cordova replied, "That would be wonderful. I was worried about what would happen to my vaqueros if I sell the ranch . . . ." She called out, "Manuel! Bring two horses! We'll be riding for a couple of hours showing the ranch to Señor McBain and Señorita Diego." Then, looking back at Sage, she said, "Manuel is my foreman. This will give you a chance to get to know him and, if you buy the ranch, he would be a good man to have working for you. He has been a capable foreman for my husband and me." Mounting her horse, she said, "Shall we go? You saw a portion of the land as you rode in. To see the rest, we'll need to ride down the river for about an hour, and then take a ride through the foothills. That trail will bring us back to the hacienda."

They rode through fertile river bottom land with grassy meadows, reminding Sage of the meadow across the creek from his cave. Manuel was a friendly Mexican man about thirty-five, with a wife and three children. Sage liked him, and Manuel seemed to like Sage. On their return, they rode through rolling hills with a few small streams. They passed trees that would provide material for corrals and other structures. The ranch consisted of about ten thousand acres. That was considered small at that time and in that location, but it was big enough for what he and Joe needed. He would show it to Joe and Bonnie tomorrow, and if they liked it, as well as he did, he would buy it.

Sage enjoyed the afternoon with Juanita. She was a good rider, at ease on the white Arabian mare. Her movements were graceful and smooth. She talked to the señora as they rode. Juanita had known the señora all her life, and they were good friends. When they returned to Señora Cordova's hacienda, the sun was getting low.

Sage told the señora about Joe Martin, who would be managing the ranch for him. He told her that Joe, and his future bride, Bonnie, would be living at the hacienda and asked if it would be all right to show them the ranch.

Señora said, "Sure, I would like to meet them. I came to the ranch as a bride myself, many years ago when my husband and I were first married."

"I'll see you tomorrow about midmorning," Sage said. "If Joe and Bonnie like the ranch, and I think they will, I'll pay the price you have asked in Spanish gold." Everyone was wearing big smiles.

Juanita said, "I must hurry back to my place. If I don't get back before my uncle does, he'll be angry. He will not approve of me riding alone with Señor McBain."

Señora Cordova replied, "Tell him you were not alone; you were riding with me and Manuel."

"Thank you, Señora; that will help," Juanita said.

On their ride back, Sage told Juanita that he would like for her to ride with them tomorrow, since Joe and Bonnie were going to be her neighbors. "They'll want to meet you, and I think you'll like them."

When they reached the big house, Juanita's uncle met them with a scowl on his face. "Where have you been?" he asked in an angry voice. "Why are you riding alone with this stranger?"

Sage didn't wait for Juanita to reply. Without hesitation, he said, "Señor Alvarez, the señorita was kind enough—at my request—to ride with me and Señora Cordova to see the ranch the señora has for sale."

"I decide who the señorita does and does not ride with!" the uncle retorted.

Sage told him in a very firm but calm voice, "I will return tomorrow morning, to pick up Señorita Diego. If it is her wish, she will ride with me and my friends to see Señora Cordova's ranch again. If there is any indication that trouble has been imposed on her, you and I will discuss that difficulty, and I assure you, you will not like the results of our discussion."

Alvarez replied in a shaky voice, "You do not understand our customs."

"No, but I do understand my customs," Sage answered, "and it is my customs I will observe at this time. I hope I have made myself understood."

Juanita listened to the verbal exchange between Sage and her uncle. She was astonished. She had never heard her uncle addressed in that manner. She was thinking, *Sage's father must have been a very honorable man, because his son turned out the same. He is honoring his father's pledge. Grandfather and I are very lucky to have met such wonderful men.*

The uncle called out, "Throw this man off the ranch!"

A voice from behind them, said, "That will take a little doing, Señor." Sage turned to see his friends, Pat and Joe.

"Juanita," Sage asked, "would you like to come with us? If you feel unsafe, we can provide safe quarters for you for as long as you would like."

Juanita smiled. "No, I'll be safe here, and I'll be looking forward to seeing you with Joe and Bonnie tomorrow." She turned and entered the house.

Sage turned to Señor Alvarez. "We'll return tomorrow midmorning. There had better be no indications of mistreatment on the señorita."

Sage and his friends mounted and rode into Santa Fe. Sage said, "Let's go to Margarita's. This has been an exciting day, and we could all use a drink."

Sage told his friends of his talk with Juanita and of the ride to see the ranch. He said to Joe, "I'll buy if you and Bonnie like it."

"I can't wait to tell Bonnie," Joe exclaimed. "She'll be ecstatic."

Pat and Joe told Sage of their talk with Carlos. Carlos told them that the cattle were being stolen, and that he didn't have enough vaqueros to guard them day and night. The señorita didn't have enough money to hire the men she needed to watch over the cattle, and the men she had were afraid of Vacca and his hired killers. Carlos told them that the situation was getting desperate and that the señorita had held out as long as she could. Sage came just in time; there was no money left to run the ranch.

Sage said, "There's plenty of money in the gold bullion that Vacca and her uncle have stolen from Juanita. We just have to get it back from those two thieves. We'll start getting it back tomorrow."

Pat and Sage went to Margarita's place. It was busy as usual. Joe didn't go; he went to tell Bonnie about the ranch. Maggie prepared a hearty meal of meat, beans, and tortillas, and two containers of tequila. She sat with them while they ate and told them that the news of their trip to the Diego hacienda had spread all over the valley and that everyone in the cantina knew about it. Some men, who had been hired by Alvarez, thought Sage had stepped out of line. She warned them to be careful, that there may be trouble.

Two very pretty girls came to the table to asked Sage if he would like to dance. He answered, "Thank you for the invitation, but the people where I grew up didn't do much dancing, and I don't know how to dance."

One of the girls said, "There are other kinds of entertainment. Come, we'll show you."

Sage smiled and replied, "Perhaps later."

From another table, two men walked up, and one of them snarled, "We hear you want to change the customs here. We know our customs are new to you, but we insist they be observed."

Sage looked at Maggie and asked, "Margarita, are these men friends of yours?"

"Troublemakers are never friends of mine," she said. "These bullies work for Pedro Vacca. They've been mistreating the miners."

Pat looked at Sage and gave ever so slight a nod. Sage rose and asked the larger of the two, "Are you drunk?"

The man replied with a sneer, "No, not that it would make a difference."

Sage said to the ruffian, "A friend told me that if a man challenges you and he is drunk, ignore him. You say you are not drunk, so that changes the rules."

With one quick move, using a technique his father had taught him, Sage threw the man to the floor on his face, and twisted his arm behind his back; a bit more pressure would have broken his arm at the shoulder. Sage then asked him, "Now do you want to continue this conversation?"

The man, with his face showing great pain, shook his head violently in an expression of no. When Sage looked up, Pat had his pistol in the belly of the other man.

Slowly, Sage allowed the man to rise. "You tell Señor Vacca that if he has a message for me, to at least have the courage to bring it himself. You two will remain healthy only if I never see you again." He violently pushed them out the door.

Maggie whispered to Pat, "I see what you mean. It's not wise to rub this one the wrong way."

Pat said, "Nah, he's as gentle as a cat."

"Yeah, a mountain lion," Maggie replied.

Sage said, "Pat, I'm about ready to get some sleep. Are you ready to go? We've got a big day ahead of us tomorrow."

"Let's go. Drinking with you is too exciting for a quiet man."

*   *   *   *

When Joe reached the wagon camp, Bonnie was waiting. He grabbed her by the waist, swung her around, and said, "We have our honeymoon cottage ready for us. Sage and Señorita Diego will show it to us tomorrow and, if we like it, Sage will buy it, and we'll be in the horse-raising business."

The news excited Bonnie so much that she jumped up and down. "I like it already," she said. "I don't even have to see it."

"The hacienda will be our home," Joe said. "I'll be the manager, you'll be the mistress. You'll have servants to help you, but most important, it will be our home. We can have the wedding and the reception at the ranch, and decorate the place for the occasion. We'll invite all the people from the wagon train, the people of the pueblo, and anyone else you might want to invite. We'll have music and dancing."

Bonnie beamed with happiness. "Let's tell Mom and Dad. They've been worried, but now they'll be pleased."

"Maybe they'll be willing to stay here in Santa Fe," Joe said. "The hacienda is probably a big place with many rooms. They could live there and help us run the ranch. We're going to have to hire some help anyway, and who could do it better than your mother and father?"

"I don't know; let's ask them."

Joe, Bonnie, and her parents spent the evening discussing the new ranch.

Frank O'Day, Bonnie's father, said, "We'd better not count our chickens before they hatch. You two look at the ranch, and then tell us what you think tomorrow evening."

✻   ✻   ✻   ✻

Joe picked up Bonnie at the wagon camp early the next morning, and they had breakfast with Sage and Pat, at Maggie's.

Joe introduced Bonnie to Maggie. Maggie said, "I see why they call her Bonnie; she is beautiful. I'm pleased that someone's going to marry this man and keep him off those mountains."

After breakfast Joe said, "Let's go. I want to see that ranch."

"I'll go with you and scout the area," Pat volunteered. "I don't trust Alvarez; he might try to harm you. I'll stay out of sight, but I'll keep a sharp lookout."

"Thank you, Pat," Sage said. "We'll have the girls with us, so that's a good idea. I'll feel better knowing the girls are not in danger."

They got to the Diego ranch at midmorning, as Sage had told Juanita they would. Juanita met them at the front of the big house, dressed for riding, and as usual, she was stunning. Señor Alvarez was nowhere to be seen. Juanita said he had left early, and she had not seen him since he departed. Her uncle had not talked to her, since Sage talked to him, last evening.

"I don't like it, Joe said. "He's up to something."

Bonnie and Juanita hit it off right away. They were chattering in excited voices, talking about the wedding and the prospects of being neighbors.

As they passed a large boulder, Sage told Joe, "That rock marks the boundary between Juanita's ranch and the ranch we're buying. For the next hour and a half, we'll be riding on our own property."

Joe called out to the girls, and they rode back to see what he wanted. Joe repeated what Sage had told him. Bonnie was so excited.

"Isn't it beautiful," Bonnie said. "The river is so clean and clear, with fish jumping and splashing in the water. Juanita and I have seen herds of deer, elk, and antelope in the meadows. The land in the valley is fertile. The snow-capped mountains in the distance are beautiful. It's like a dream."

Sage smelled dust and saw fresh tracks. A horse had crossed the trail. He felt a presence ahead in a grove of trees and asked Joe to remain with the girls while he checked to see who had left the tracks. He rode into the grove, dismounted, and proceeded on foot. He found Pat waiting beside a big cottonwood tree. Pat knew that Sage would become aware of his presence and come to check it out.

"Two men are dogging your trail," Pat said. "So far, they've shown no indication that they're going to do you harm. Would you like for me to get rid of them?"

"Thanks for warning me," Sage replied. "I'll let Joe know. We can handle them since there are only two of them."

Pat rode into a small ravine where he wouldn't be seen. Then Sage waved to Joe and the girls, urging them to come ahead. They rode up, and he told them what Pat had said.

"Do you want me to lie back and deal with them?" Joe asked.

"No," Sage said. "I don't think they mean to harm us. I think Señor Alvarez just wants to know where we're going. I think he has something hidden, and he doesn't want us to find it. If the men following us get too close, you and I will drop back and find out who they are, who has paid them to follow us, and why."

Juanita said, "There are some big canyons west of here where they could hide a herd of stolen cattle. Perhaps that's what they don't want us to see. I am amazed that my own uncle would steal from me. I had no idea he wanted the ranch that much. Thank you for making me aware. He is my uncle, so I don't want him killed."

They rode on, but it was difficult to enjoy the beauty, knowing they were being followed. Around the next turn, Pat appeared beside the trail.

"They've gone back to wherever they came from. I guess they've satisfied their curiosity. I'll wait for you. Now, go do what you came to do. Don't worry about me; I'm at home in these mountains."

When they arrived, Señora Cordova was expecting them. She had lunch ready and served them on the patio overlooking the river. A gentle breeze rippled the new leaves on the poplar trees, making the sound of tiny hands clapping. The señora took them for a tour of the hacienda. The house was large and made of thick adobe walls; the roof was held in place by huge timbers. It was built to accommodate a large number of guests, but its size didn't diminish the feeling of warmth.

"Joe," Bonnie exclaimed, "I don't need to see more; I love it. This will be a wonderful place to raise our family."

"I felt the same way," Señora Cordova said, "when I came here as a bride thirty-five years ago, but after many wonderful years my husband died. Our children live in Mexico City, and I want to be with them."

"Señora," Sage asked, "do you have charts showing the boundaries?"

"I sure do. I have them ready to show you."

Joe and Sage went over the charts, while the women talked about the wedding. Upon examining the charts, Joe estimated the land area to be just over ten thousand acres.

"Let's buy it," Sage said.

Joe nodded. "You're the boss."

"No, Joe," Sage corrected. "This is a partnership. I buy it. You run it, and we share in the profits."

Sage extended his hand and said, "Let's seal the agreement." Joe warmly grasped his hand and a lasting partnership was formed.

Sage said, "Okay, we have our ranch!"

They walked into the drawing room. The señora was showing Juanita and Bonnie the intimate details of the house, and they joined Sage and Joe.

Sage counted out enough gold coins to equal the amount the señora was asking for the ranch, and placed them on a large wooden table. The señora brought out the papers of ownership. She then called her foreman, Manuel, into the room.

"Juanita and Manuel, would you witness the signing?" the señora asked. With tears running down her face, she hugged everyone in the room, and said. "Now, I can go to see my children and grandchildren in Mexico City."

She turned to Manuel. "Manuel, start rounding up the cattle. Leave some good milk cows for Señor Martin and his bride. They will need enough milk and butter to feed the caballeros. Round up only the beef cattle. All the rest will remain the property of the ranch."

"Will you need help to drive the herd?" Sage asked.

"I'll use some of the vaqueros for the drive. When they return, they'll be driving a herd of twenty purebred Arabian horses for you. I'll buy the horses to repay you for the use of your vaqueros."

"Thank you," Sage replied.

"It's a pleasure doing business with good people." She extended her hand to Sage and said, "You now own the ranch."

"Tomorrow," Sage said, "I will take these signed papers to the government offices and register the property in my name." He then turned to Joe and said, "We should get the girls home before dark. Bonnie's parents will be worried."

"Señora, may I bring my mother and father to see the ranch tomorrow?" Bonnie asked.

"You are now the mistress of the *Casa Grande*," the señora laughed. "Do as you wish. I hope you will be as happy here as I have been. *Vaya con Dios.*"

While riding to her ranch, Juanita lingered back with Bonnie and asked, "What do you know about Señor McBain?"

Bonnie thought for a moment and replied, "All I know is that he and his two friends rode in to help our people fight off a band of Kiowa Indians. Their skills as fighters were remarkable. When we first saw Sage, he looked like a wild animal. He didn't look like the handsome young man you now see. He saved the life of one of the girls. Two Indians were attacking her, and she would have been killed if Sage hadn't stepped in. In a display of furiousness no one had ever seen in a man, he killed the Indians with his ax and his knife. The girl he saved cut his hair for the first time in six years. He and the girl became friends. She wanted the relationship to develop into something more, but he held back. The other girls wanted him, too, but he didn't respond to their advances. He is a mystery. Perhaps there's something in his past, I don't know. The men say he's a wonderful friend, or a terrible enemy."

"Thank you, that's much like the story he told me. Let's go join our men."

Bonnie nodded and with a smile said, "Yes, let's join our men. I know you and I are going to be wonderful friends."

When they got to the Diego ranch, the uncle was nowhere to be seen.

"Juanita," Sage asked, "are you comfortable staying here?"

"I'll be all right," Juanita answered. "I can trust my staff."

"Let me know if there's ever a problem; I'll come immediately."

Pat was waiting on the trail. Sage and Pat went to Maggie's, while Joe and Bonnie went to the wagon camp to tell Bonnie's parents that they had bought the ranch.

Thelma was excited; Frank had reservations. He had started for California and didn't want to stop while only halfway. He had heard the

California Trail was long and hard, and that many people had died along the way. He was reluctant to subject his wife to such hardships. What was waiting for them in California was left to be seen. He knew what they had here, and it looked good.

Frank said, "I'll delay my decision until we see the ranch tomorrow."

*   *   *   *

Joe, Bonnie, Thelma, and Frank rode to their new ranch. They didn't go via the Diego ranch; instead, they followed a more direct route, on a well-traveled road, directly to their ranch.

Again Señora Cordova was expecting them and had food and drinks ready. Joe and Frank told the ladies that they would be gone most of the day, riding over the land, taking a good look at what they would be managing.

The women stayed at the hacienda to get acquainted with their new home. The hacienda was what they would be in charge of. Señora Cordova was pleased to show them the home she had been so proud of for so very long. She told them how pleased she was that the home would be in the hands of someone who would love it as she had.

The señora had already packed some of her treasured things. She told Bonnie and her mother that there were many things too bulky to take with her on the long trip. Some of the things were pieces of priceless furniture that had been brought from Spain, some from Mexico City, and some were built right here on the ranch. She told them she would like to leave the pieces she couldn't take with her, and she hoped they could use it. Bonnie and her mother were pleased to have so many beautiful things already in their new home, things that would have been difficult to replace.

Bonnie expressed her gratitude and said she hoped the señora would return for a visit some day, so they might return her hospitality.

The señora replied, "It would be wonderful, if it should be possible, but the distance is long."

CHAPTER 15

▼

THE STOLEN CATTLE

While Joe and Bonnie looked at the new ranch, Pat and Sage rode to the Diego ranch. They wanted Juanita to tell them the location of the canyon where she thought the stolen cattle might be held. They needed to know for sure what was happening to the cattle that were missing. If they could recover them, it would be easier to put the ranch back on a profitable basis. When they asked Juanita to tell them how to get to the large canyon, instead of telling them, she said she would show them. She had ridden there with her father when she was just a little girl. Her father was pleased that his daughter wanted to see the land she would one day own.

"Juanita," Sage said, "perhaps you should not ride with us—the ride will be difficult and dangerous."

Juanita insisted. "It's my cattle that are being stolen, and I want to see for myself if my uncle is betraying me. Don't worry about me; I'm able to make difficult rides, and I have weapons that I'm very capable of using."

"Sage," Pat chuckled, "since there's no way I know of to stop her, I think we should let her show us the way."

"Yeah, I guess you're right," Sage smiled.

"Good," Juanita said. "I'll tell my housekeepers that I'll be gone overnight. We'll not be able to return in one day—the ride is too long. I'll get extra blankets since we'll be spending the nights on the trail, and it gets very cold in the mountains this time of year."

They headed their horses in the direction indicated by Juanita. She was indeed a capable rider—the rough terrain presented no more difficulties for her than it did for either Pat or Sage. The area contained deep canyons, gullies, and arroyos. Steep clefts and butts towered hundreds of feet into the air.

In the late afternoon, Juanita said, "We're getting close."

"Perhaps we should hide the horses here," Pat suggested, "and go the rest of the way on foot. We don't want to take a chance of being seen."

"The rustlers have too much to lose," Juanita replied, "so they'll have guards posted with instructions to shoot on sight."

Continuing on foot for about half an hour, they heard lowing cattle.

"That's cattle, all right!" Sage exclaimed. "You two stay hidden, and I'll take a look. I want to find out where their guards are posted. I'll come back after I've located them."

He returned a little later. "There are four guards—two up on the ridge, one on each rim of the canyon, and two guarding the mouth of the canyon."

"Show me," Juanita said. "I want to see for myself."

Sage led and she followed. Pat held back, wanting to be sure to cover their backs in case there were men that Sage hadn't seen—although he doubted there would be. Sage was so attuned to his environment he didn't miss much.

Sage led Juanita to a spot hidden by boulders and brush, where they could look into the canyon.

After a quick look, she said, "Those are my cattle—what are we going to do?"

"Nothing for now," Sage said. "The cows have grass and water, and they're being looked after. We know where they are, and we can get them anytime. Let's find where they're hiding the gold. When we know that, we'll be ready to take whatever action is needed. They're not going to give up without a fight. You're in danger until you get your property back. You've got to get men you can trust looking after your interests. I believe Carlos is such a man. We're going to get your gold back, then you'll have all the money you need, and you can run the ranch however you want. You don't need your uncle to run it for you. You have Carlos to manage the cattle, and you can choose someone to run the mining operation. You'll need someone to run the hacienda and manage the crops. When you get that, you'll have a successful ranch again. Your people will be happy, and you'll be happy."

Juanita nodded. "This is a terrible thing my uncle is doing, but I still don't want him killed. I just want him forced off the land. He may be past the point of reason, but I hope he won't go any further. I wish he'd go back to either Mexico or Spain, but probably that will not happen."

"Juanita, if that is what you want, then that is what you'll get. But if what we are being told about Pedro Vacca is true, he is a dangerous man, and we should take precautions."

"Yes, I think you're right. He is cruel and ambitious."

Sage knew that Pat was nearby, waiting where he could see in all directions. They found him and walked back to where they had left their horses.

"Let's find a good campsite," Pat said. "Juanita is right. It's going to get cold tonight."

They rode away from the canyon, in the direction of the ranch, for about an hour.

Then, just before dark, Pat said, "This is a good spot. We'll build a fire against the cliff where the rocks will reflect the heat out to us, and hang blankets at our back to keep out the wind. We'll make our beds between the cliff and the blankets and that should keep us warm as toast."

Sage concurred. "You build a fire, and I'll get something to eat." He walked into the brush and disappeared almost immediately.

"How will he get us something to eat?" Juanita asked as she watched him disappear.

"I don't know how he does it, but he'll return with some kind of meat, and it will be cleaned and dressed, ready to be cooked when he gets back. His skills as a hunter are astonishing."

In just a few minutes, Sage returned with two rabbits, cleaned and dressed.

Pat said to Juanita, "Ye see what I mean?" Then he turned to Sage, "While you and Juanita are cooking this, I'll make the beds."

"Okay, this will be ready in about half an hour."

"The beds will be ready in about half an hour," Pat smiled.

"There's a big advantage in camping with mountain men," Juanita said.

"Oh, I'm not a mountain man," corrected Sage. "I'm learning to be a mountain man from Pat, and he's one of the best. He's training me right now by showing me how to get the reflected heat from the cliff while containing it with blankets. He doesn't say he's training me, but he knows I'm watching. Pat's a good friend to us both."

"You're both good friends to me," Juanita agreed. "I've been really blessed that you came to help me, and I'm grateful to you and Joe Martin, also."

The roast rabbit was delicious.

"Sage," Juanita asked, "would you tell us how you get food from the wild so easily?"

"I was alone with no one to teach me," Sage answered. "The only teachers I had were the animals, and they couldn't talk. I had lots of time, so I spent hours watching them to learn how they got their food. There are many kinds of animals, but there are only two basic types:

predators and prey. There are exceptions, but mostly predators eat meat, and the preys eat plants. People are both a predator and prey. We eat both meat and plants.

"The animals taught me that everything in nature has a special place to live and certain things they like to eat. By observing their life habits, I learned at what time, or under what conditions, the animals were vulnerable. Then I caught them at that time. I would never try to catch a prairie chicken in the daytime. It's too fast, and it could fly away. So I wait until night when it's asleep. Everything is like that. I learned how to catch them by watching predators catch them. Many an evening I watched the animals in the meadows across the creek from my cave. I learned to hunt and to hide by watching the way the animals hid when they were being hunted.

"Animals and men are not all that different. Some men are predators, and some are prey." He continued, "We can learn much from animals if we take the time to watch them. Animals are not only more gifted with their senses than we are, they have learned to use them better than we have. Animals can sense the presence of danger and so can we, if we take the time to learn to use all five of our senses at the same time. In nature, there are many things we can learn to recognize by using the senses of seeing, hearing, feeling, smelling, and tasting. Men can develop these senses, the same as the animals can."

Juanita listened intently to this seemingly gentle young man. She was beginning to understand what a remarkable person he really was. She marveled at how he had learned to survive alone in the Indian Territory, and of how his being alone had tuned his senses to everything around him. Now, she understood why they said he was a wonderful friend or a terrible enemy. She watched his handsome face as he was telling his story. It was peaceful and calm, but there was a deep sorrow hidden behind those blue-green eyes. She wondered what it might be, and understood why Bonnie said he was a mystery. She was thinking that perhaps some day she would be able to understand his pain and soothe the sorrow. She wanted to reach out to him, but she knew that now was not the time.

Pat talked of his years as a mountain man, where he also had learned to live alone after his family was killed by the Blackfoot.

Looking at Juanita, Sage said, "Now, let's hear about you."

Juanita told them, "I was born at the hacienda. My father and my grandfather were also born at the hacienda. My grandfather's first wife was the daughter of one of the local ranchers. She died while trying to give birth, and the baby died also. After a time, Grandfather went to Mexico City, where he met Grandmother. She was Señora Alvarez, the widowed wife of Don Alvarez from Spain. She and her first husband had lived in Spain, where their son, Jose, my uncle, was born. They say Grandmother was very beautiful. Grandfather fell in love with her, and they were married in Mexico City. He brought her and her son to the hacienda where she gave birth to another boy. That boy was my father. They named him Francisco. Grandmother died in a riding accident while my father was still very young. Of course, Uncle Jose was a few years older. There was always a conflict between my father and his half-brother. Grandfather tried to treat them both the same, but Jose secretly hated his stepfather, and he was difficult to deal with."

Juanita continued, "When Grandmother died in the riding accident, Grandfather left his two sons in the care of Carlos, and returned to Spain. Grandfather's family has large land holdings in Spain. Carlos raised my father and my uncle. Grandfather wanted grandchildren, but Uncle Jose never wanted Grandfather to arrange a marriage for him saying he would make his own arrangements, so Grandfather never tried.

"But Grandfather wanted an heir, so he arranged a marriage between my father and my mother. My mother was Lolita Montoya, the daughter of a family who also had close ties to the king of Spain. Her father's name was Don Hernando Montoya. Grandfather arranged this marriage while he was on another trip to Spain. Grandfather's family had maintained close ties with the king, who granted this land to my great great-grandfather. Mother was only sixteen when she came to Santa Fe to marry Father. She, too, was very beautiful, and Father fell in love with her right away. They were married in the chapel and lived in the hacienda where I was born, about one year later.

"When I was six, my mother took me to Spain to visit her parents. When we returned, Father took me everywhere he went. He taught me to ride and use firearms. He was preparing me to take over the ranch because it would one day be mine.

"Then, when I was ten, Mother and Father were killed by Apaches while they were on a trip to Mexico City. I had been left at the ranch in the care of Uncle Jose and Carlos. Jose wasn't unkind to me, but he treated me with contempt. He restricted me to the courtyard and kept other young people away, especially young men. Carlos's wife said it was because he didn't want me to marry. Should I marry, the ranch would go to my husband, and Uncle Jose would lose control. Now, thanks to the help of three complete strangers, I'm beginning to understand that my uncle is trying to take the ranch. Thank you."

"That's a fascinating story," Pat said. "Well, it's getting late, so I'll turn in, but before I do, let me show you your beds. I've cut boughs and made three piles, and then placed blankets on them. The boughs will keep you insulated from the cold ground, and the blanket will shield you from the boughs. A buffalo hide or a bearskin would be better, but we don't have them, so these blankets will have to do. Good night, I'll take the bed at this end. You can fight over the other two."

Pat removed his boots and his hat, placed his weapons where he could reach them, and then curled up and was asleep almost immediately.

"I'd like to go for a walk and listen to the sounds of the night," Sage said. "This reminds me of my home on the prairie."

"May I go with you?" Juanita asked. "You can tell me what the sounds mean."

Sage said, "Let's take a few blankets with us to keep us warm . . . . When I was a child, I wanted someone to share the sounds with, but never in my wildest dreams did I dare think that I might some day share it with someone so beautiful."

"You also fulfill a dream for me," Juanita smiled. "There's a chill in the air . . . would you put your arms around me to keep me warm?"

With a little laugh, Sage wrapped her in his arms. "You keep me warm just by being near me."

She cuddled closer saying, "I'm pleased."

He explained the source of every sound and told her what animal, or thing, was making the sound and why. Juanita was amazed by his perception. She realized that she was falling in love. Silently she thanked the Almighty Creator for bringing this wonderful young man to her. She hated to leave to go to sleep. She was wishing she could remain in his arms after going to bed, but she could feel his need for her and knew what she wanted to do. *Sage will be my husband someday*, Juanita thought. *I don't know when, but my heart tells me that we will be together for the rest of our lives.* Juanita wanted to affirm her love for him as she sensed his love for her. Sage lovingly looked at Juanita and knew what she was thinking. He took her in his arms and ran his fingers through her beautiful, soft hair. He kissed her, not with a forceful passion, but slow and ardent. As he ran his hand over her warm and supple body, he could feel her respond to his touch.

"Don't stop, my love. I want you so much," Juanita said.

Sage wanted her, too, but before they made love to each other he knew what they needed to do. Sage helped Juanita to her feet and said, "We will ask the Creator to forever join us. Before the Almighty Creator I swear my love, my life and my heart now and forever."

Juanita looked at Sage, caressed his face with her fingers. With tears rolling down her face, she said, "My love, my heart and soul are yours for the rest of my life. The Creator has blessed us and the land that we love will be our witness."

They were now one. The night was cold, but their lovemaking kept them warm. They didn't want to leave, and they both wished they could stay where they were forever. But they did have to go back for there was much for them to do. They slipped back into camp quietly so they wouldn't wake Pat.

They went to their separate beds, but neither could fall sleep. The stars moved to the center of the sky, telling Sage that the night was half gone. Juanita had at last gone to sleep, so he closed his eyes and was soon asleep.

*   *   *   *

Before his companions awoke, Sage walked out into the hills and brought back three sage hens, and cooked them with the wild vegetables he gathered. He had breakfast ready when Pat and Juanita woke up. He mentioned to Juanita that he had seen a small stream nearby where she could refresh herself. Pat tended the horses making sure they had water and grass. He rubbed them down with dry grass before putting saddles on them.

While having breakfast, they talked of what they should do to regain control of Juanita's ranch.

"Carlos is a staunch and steady ally," Juanita said.

"Yes," Pat said. "I've known Carlos for many years, and I believe him to be a good man, Sage. I know you've just met him, but you need to have a good talk with him. He probably knows more about this than anyone."

"All right," Sage replied. "Let's go talk to him. We met only briefly. I'd like to get better acquainted with him."

They arrived at the hacienda late in the afternoon, and went directly to Carlos's home, but he wasn't there. They met his sons who worked with their father as vaqueros. The sons had their own families and their own homes. Carlos's wife greeted Juanita with the respect due the mistress of *El Casa Grande,* Juanita greeted her as the old and valued friend she was.

Señora Viejo invited them in, but they didn't want to compromise Carlos with his boss, Jose, so they declined the invitation and went in search of Carlos. To Carlos, Juanita's father was like a son, but he had never been able to develop a close relationship with the Jose. Carlos had known for many years that Jose wanted to own the ranch. When he didn't inherit it, Carlos knew that he would stop at nothing to take it from his niece. Carlos learned from Pat that Robert McBain, Sage's father, had rescued Don Diego from the sea and tried to nurse him back to health.

They found Carlos working at the hacienda. Juanita called him to join them. Juanita explained, "Sage is the new owner of the Cordova Ranch, and he will be our neighbor."

"*Buenas tardes*, Señor," he said. "I've heard much about you, and I'm pleased to have a chance to talk with you. The people of Santa Fe are telling stories of the golden-haired young gringo who is making a difference in the Rio Grande valley. Señora Cordova and her *patron*, Manuel, speak highly of you."

"Carlos," Juanita asked, "do you remember the messenger from my grandfather, Don Diego?"

"Yes, but that was long ago."

"It was long ago, but the man mentioned in that message has come at last. He'll tell you why it has taken so long."

"*Buena*, let us all ride down by the river where we can talk in private," Carlos replied.

Sage answered, "Si, Señor, it is better to speak in private."

Carlos was a distinguished Mexican man with hair the color of silver, whose age was hard to determine. He was still strong, his eyes were bright, and when he spoke to Juanita, his face showed his respect and love for her. Sage liked him right away.

They reached the river and dismounted. Sage repeated the story Pat had told Carlos, of how his father had saved Don Diego from the sea. Don Diego didn't tell Sage's father who, or what, was threatening the ranch. Sage then told Carlos of how his parents were killed by Indians and of how he had managed to survive. Sage further explained that, as soon as he became a man, he came to fulfill his father's vow. He mentioned the letter to Juanita, and the paper Señor Diego had signed. He explained that he didn't come for the land. He had bought his own ranch with the money he had gotten from his father.

"Gracias, Señor," Carlos said. "I'm the one who sent the message to Señor Diego. I worked for the Don even before Juanita's father was born. She is like a granddaughter to me. There's nothing I would not do to prevent her from losing her land. I've been aware of her uncle's intent to take the land for many years, but I couldn't tell Juanita because I had no proof. Now that you have proof, and we all understand what is happening, we can take action. Tell me what you would like for me to do."

"How many of your workers can you count on?" Sage asked.

"All of them," Carlos replied. "They do not like Señor Alvarez, and they hate and fear Señor Vacca."

"How about the miners?" Sage asked.

"The miners are not part of the ranch. They are hired from Santa Fe and other pueblos. Vacca brought men from Mexico to supervise the local miners. It is rumored he worked many men to death in Mexico. That is why the local miners hate both Vacca and the men he brought with him. My vaqueros know many of the miners, and they will report to me which ones we can count on."

"We'll have to chase Vacca and his men back to Mexico," Sage said, "before we will be able to restore the mine to Juanita. We must recover the bullion they have stolen, and return the cattle to their pastures. *Gracias*, Señor Viejo, for your friendship and for your offer to help. Can you meet us tomorrow at the Cordova Ranch at noon? We will work out a plan."

"I'll ride with you, Carlos," Juanita spoke up.

Sage could see that Carlos was concerned. "Carlos, there's no need in trying to talk her out of it. Pat and I tried that yesterday; it didn't work."

Carlos smiled. "She is a strong-minded young woman, all right."

"See, Carlos, I told you," Pat said, "you would like this young man. Would you find out how many of the miners we can count on? Tell them they'll be rid of the man they fear, and have a man that will treat them with respect."

"Si, Señor Connors, I will find out. My sons and I will meet you tomorrow at the McBain Ranch."

"Gracias, Señor Viejo, *vaya con Dios,*" Pat replied.

Juanita saw the worry on Sage's face and said, "I'll be all right. Uncle Jose still doesn't know, that I know, that he is trying to do harm to me. My staff will protect me."

Sage nodded. "Then I'll see you tomorrow at noon."

CHAPTER 16

▼

ATTACK ON JUANITA

Joe, Bonnie, and her parents were already at Maggie's when Sage and Pat arrived.

"The señora will be leaving in a few days," Joe announced. "She's eager to be on the trail so they can get through the desert before it gets too hot. Bonnie and I want to get married in two weeks. We will invite the people from the wagon train and anyone else who want to come."

Maggie said, "The musicians from my cantina will provide the music, and I will bring the dancing girls."

"We'll barbecue two steers," Sage suggested. "The other ranchers will be invited. It will give us a chance to meet them. It will be a grand party. Joe and Bonnie can spend their honeymoon at their new hacienda. Frank and Thelma can stay at the wagon camp until after the honeymoon, and then they, too, can move into the hacienda and help Joe and Bonnie run the ranch."

Maggie said, "I knew you'd be hungry so I prepared two of the biggest steaks I could find. I have baked potatoes and beans to go with the steaks."

Maggie brought the food to the table sizzling hot. Sage was thinking, *I wish Juanita were here to help us celebrate.*

Sage told Joe, "We'll meet Carlos and Juanita at the new ranch tomorrow at noon to discuss plans for recovering the Diego ranch."

"Maggie," Pat asked, "do you know that group of men sitting over there in the corner?"

"Yes, they're just a few of the ruffians Vacca brought in from Mexico to oversee the local miners. The local miners used to come in here after work to drink, but they're afraid to now. They say these men make them take unnecessary chances, and a couple of local miners have been killed. I wish these men didn't come here. They're driving my regular customers away."

"They are heavily armed for miners," Pat replied. "They are each carrying two guns and a knife. The guns are specially made, and those aren't the kind of knives you would use to clean your fingernails."

"Perhaps I should get Bonnie and her folks back to the wagon," Joe suggested.

Sage agreed. "Pat and I will go with you. I have an uneasy feeling about that bunch."

"You see what I mean?" Maggie grumbled. "They're driving my best customers away."

"Don't worry, Maggie," Pat laughed. "We'll be back."

With Sage leading, they started for the wagon camp. The night was cold, and they were wearing heavy coats. When they got halfway to the wagon camp, Sage said in a low voice, "We're being followed. I'll drop back to see who is so concerned about us."

Suddenly a shot rang out, and Frank fell from his horse. Joe pulled Bonnie and her mother into the trees beside the trail, hoping the trees would provide cover.

Frank got up. "It's only a shoulder wound; I'll be all right."

"Pat," Joe asked, "would you take Bonnie and her folks to the camp and tend to Frank's wound?" "I have some unfinished business here. Whoever shot at Bonnie will wish they didn't."

"Joe, let's drop back," Sage whispered. "You take that side of the trail, and I'll take this side."

"Okay, ladies, let's go home," Pat said, as he gathered the reins of the horse Frank was riding. "Frank, can you stay on the horse?"

Frank replied with pain, "Yeah, you lead him; I'll hang on."

Sage moved back along one side of the trail, and Joe did the same on the other. Sage heard the men who were following them. A shot rang out, then another. Two hired killers lay dead on the trail, and the other two, knowing Joe had only two pistols and would have to reload, were rushing in on the now unarmed Joe. Sage threw his knife, then his ax. Thud, thud. The other two were down.

"They won't disturb Maggie's customers any more," Joe commented. "Sage, that's the damnedest thing I ever saw. You threw that ax and knife so fast I could hardly see you do it. You saved my hide again tonight."

"Yeah, I had to do something . . . . They were about to spoil the wedding. And by the way, that was some fancy shooting you just did."

"Don't tell anyone. It would just add to my reputation, and I'm trying to live that down."

"I don't think you'll do it that way."

"No, I guess not. What do we do with this carrion on the road?"

"Let's get word to Vacca. These are his men; let him clean up the mess."

"That's a good idea . . . . Let's see how Frank is doing. I just talked him into helping us on the ranch, and I don't want to lose him."

When they reached the camp, Grant was digging the bullet out of Frank's shoulder.

Frank said, "Ah, it's only a flesh wound; I'll be up and around in a few days. What happened to the men who were shooting at us?"

"We spoiled their evening," Joe replied.

"I thought you might," Pat commented.

Bonnie, not completely understanding the conversation, said, "You mean they won't be going back to Maggie's tonight? Maggie will be happy about that."

Sage added, "They may not even go to work tomorrow."

Bonnie, beginning to get the idea, said, "Oh!"

"Well, fellows," Pat said, "I don't know about you, but I'm about ready for some sleep."

✳   ✳   ✳   ✳

They all met at the McBain hacienda the following day, and again Señora Cordova had lunch ready. She and Manuel sat in on the meeting. The group consisted of Joe, Pat, Sage, Carlos, his three sons, and Juanita. Their voices were low and serious. Carlos's sons were all stalwart young men with determined faces. Their lives and the lives of their families depended on the outcome of this meeting.

Ramon, the oldest of the three, said, "I suggest we enlist the aid of the vaqueros of the other ranches. They all have a stake in this, and I know they'll want to help. Two of their friends died in the mines last week. We've got to put a stop to this."

"That's a good idea," Juanita concurred. "Get word to the miners not to show up tomorrow morning. Then we can close in on the mine and send those vermin back to Mexico where they came from."

Joe smiled. "I hate to do that to the good people of old Mexico, but the people of Santa Fe will be glad to get rid of them."

"Carlos," Sage asked, "can you and your sons get word to the local miners? We'll be waiting for the men guarding the mine when they report for work."

"All right, boys," Carlos said. "Let's get the workers notified."

Pat and Joe rode back to Santa Fe.

"Juanita, let's ride down by the river," Sage said.

She was hoping for a chance to be alone with Sage, and was pleased that he wanted to be alone with her. Maybe he wanted to ask her to marry him. She would say "Yes," without hesitation. They followed the river while returning to her ranch. She knew he didn't want her ranch. He had his own ranch, but she would be proud to share her ranch with him as her husband.

They rode without saying a word . . . . She could see that he was troubled. They came to a bend in the river where the banks were lined with cottonwood and poplar. The river was deep and calm. Over on the far side was a cliff; the spot was beautiful and serene.

Sage drew his horse to a halt and dismounted, then took Juanita's hand and helped her from her horse, even though he knew she needed no help. She was pleased by his attentiveness. When she slid down from her horse, she slid into his arms. He held her for a while, and then slowly released her.

Looking into her eyes, he said, "Juanita, I didn't know what to expect when I committed myself to fulfill my father's obligation, but I think I have loved you since the first time we rode together to see Senora Cordova's ranch. I have another obligation to meet. I don't know how long I will be gone. It might be for a few months, or it might be a year."

Juanita waited for him to continue, but he didn't explain, other than to tell her he thought they would be able to restore the ranch to her in a short time. When this was done and after Joe and Bonnie were married, he would be going away.

Juanita drew his face to hers and kissed him. "I'll wait for you, Michael "Sage" McBain, no matter how long it takes. I love you, too, and live for the time when we can be together. Do whatever you feel you must . . . . I'll be waiting."

Holding her closely he kissed her passionately. She could feel his strength and longed for the day when he would take her as his wife. They mounted their horses and were riding back to the hacienda when a shot rang out. A bullet ricocheted off the trunk of a tree near Juanita's head! Sage slid from his saddle, pulled Juanita off her horse, and led her into a ravine where they would have cover. Two more shots rang out, both bullets struck near, but neither he nor Juanita was wounded. Sage had his pistol and powder in his belt, but his rifle was still in the saddle scabbard, and the horses were thirty paces away. Both horses were frightened and unsure of what they should do.

Sage was certain that at least two gunmen were firing, but he wasn't sure where the shots were coming from. It was obvious that Vacca and Jose had decided not to wait any longer to kill Juanita and take the ranch. Juanita had told Sage that if they succeeded in killing her, they would blame the mountain men for the killing.

Sage saw a gully to their right. If he and Juanita could get into it, there would be only one way they could be seen by the gunmen. The gully would force the gunmen to approach from only one direction. He handed Juanita his pistol and told her to hide, with her back to the cliff, forcing the gunman to approach from the open side of the gully. He quickly removed his boots, shirt, and hat, then took his knife from its scabbard and split his hat into two pieces, and then tied the pieces to his feet with strips he cut from his shirt. Without his shirt, his highly muscled back and arms were exposed. Juanita knew she was in the hands of the skilled fighter she had heard about, and she was no longer afraid.

Sage placed his hand to his mouth, indicating silence. His eyes had changed; they now had the look she had seen in the eyes of a mountain lion. He moved into the brush, without making a sound, and disappeared almost immediately. She knew he was stalking the snipers, and his only weapon was his knife.

A shot rang out, followed by another; the bullets struck the cliff behind Juanita but did no harm. The assassins were shooting at shadows. She scooted down tighter against the cliff and moved closer to the bushes.

The shots were what Sage was waiting for. He knew now where they were—that was all he needed. He moved silently with the stealth of the highly trained predator he had become. He spotted a gunman standing against a tree, straining to spot Jaunita. He could easily finish him off by throwing his knife, but if he threw the knife, he would be without a weapon. He moved in on the killer from the other side of the tree. The gunman became aware that he was now the hunted and whirled, bringing his rifle into position to fire, but he was too late. Sage pushed the rifle barrel aside, and in one swift movement with his knife, the gunman was a gunman no more. The only sound the gunman made was his body sliding down the trunk of the tree.

Sage wiped and re-holstered his knife, then took the gunman's rifle and two pistols. Now he was armed with the three guns that had belonged to the killer, and he still had his knife. The pistols were different from any he had ever seen. He knew, by the decorations and by the quality of their weapons, that these gunmen were professional killers.

He moved swiftly in the direction of the other attacker. The second gunman was trying to get into a position for a shot at what he believed to be two waiting victims. The gunman knew Sage was armed, and he had heard of his fighting abilities, so he was moving cautiously.

Juanita knew that the killer was coming, but she didn't know what had happened to Sage. She sat with the pistol ready. Unknown to her, Sage was moving in on the second killer.

The killer had the advantage—he knew where Juanita was, and all he had to do was get into position to fire the bullet that would successfully fulfill his task and earn him the reward he had been promised. That moment was near, and the gunman was closing in with complete confidence. He had only contempt for this wild boy. Why should he fear a boy? He had killed many men. He stepped into the open. He had Juanita in his sights and was raising his rifle to fire the fatal bullet, when he felt a searing pain in his chest. He looked down at the silver-plated handle of the knife that had just ended his career as a killer. He then looked up into the blazing eyes of the wild young man he had held in such contempt. The gunman's lifeless body slumped to the ground. Sage removed his knife and again wiped it clean on the gunman's jacket, rolled the killer onto his face and walked to the trembling Juanita. His eyes were soft and gentle again.

Sage gathered the killers' weapons to show them to Pat and Joe.

"Juanita," Sage said, "there's no way I'm going to allow you to stay at your place tonight. Your uncle and Vacca have reached the point of desperation. Now do you realize your life is in danger? I'm taking you to my ranch. Señora Cordova and her vaqueros will be glad to give you protection. Carlos and his sons will be there to protect you, also."

"I have to go back to the hacienda to get some of my things. I'll need clothes."

"All right. But I'll go with you, and I won't let you out of my sight until I get you to my ranch."

"Señora Cordova is a dear friend, and I know I'll be welcome, but I'll prefer to be in Santa Fe with you. That way, I would know what is happening."

"You can buy new clothes in Santa Fe. There's no reason to expose you to the danger of going back to your place."

When they got to Santa Fe, Sage took Juanita to the same hotel where he and his friends were staying.

When the owner saw Juanita, he bowed low, and said, "Señorita Diego, what a great honor to have you at our hotel. We'll provide you with our finest rooms. I'll personally escort you to your quarters. Please let us know of any service you require. There will be a table waiting for you in our dining room any time you need it."

"I see why you wanted to come to the hotel," Sage smiled. "How much time will you need to buy clothes? Would you do me the great honor of dining with me this evening, and may I bring my friends?"

"It will take me about two hours to get ready. I would be pleased to have dinner with you and your friends. That's why I wanted to stay at the hotel, and perhaps Bonnie could join us."

"I'll pick you up at your room in two hours," Sage said.

When Sage got to his room, both Joe and Pat were waiting. He told them about the two men who tried to kill Juanita and showed them the rifles.

"I have their pistols in my saddlebags," Sage said as he tossed them on the bed. "It seemed wrong to waste such fine weapons. Those men were not miners; they were professional killers. That's obvious by their weapons. These pistols have revolving chambers, and they'll fire six times without reloading."

"I've heard of these guns," Joe said. "There's a man named Samuel Colt who is manufacturing guns like that."

"Yes, I've heard of them, also." Pat mused.

"By the way, we have a date for dinner," Sage said. "We are to meet Señorita Diego in the dining room, in two hours. She asked if Bonnie would join us."

"Sure, I'll go get Bonnie," Joe answered, "but first I want to see those guns. A date with the señorita is important, but those guns are more important. Do you realize what it will mean to us, to have weapons like that in our fight with Vacca?"

They examined the guns carefully.

"These are beautiful guns," Joe exclaimed, "but where can we get cartridges?"

"I have their gun belts—they contain extra cartridges," Sage said. "Perhaps we can buy more at the trading post."

"That's a good idea," said Pat. "A friend of mine is leaving for the fort tomorrow. I'll ask him to buy cartridges for us."

"I'll go get Bonnie. She'll be excited about having dinner with Juanita. She'll want to dress for the occasion, so don't get impatient. I guess I'd better dress up a bit, too."

When it was time for Sage to pick up Juanita, Joe and Bonnie hadn't returned. Pat said, "Sage, you pick up the señorita, and I'll meet you at the restaurant. I want to look around. I don't want to get surprised again tonight like we did last night."

"Thank you, Pat. That will make me feel better, also."

Juanita was not quite ready when Sage called at her door. She called back through the door and said, "I'll meet you in the dining room."

While Sage was waiting in a chair just outside the restaurant door, Pat strolled by. Pat was taking a good look to see if there might be any of Vacca's men lurking around. Joe and Bonnie walked in.

Bonnie's long, red hair curled around her face. Her bright green eyes sparkled with excitement. She wore a white and green dress with ruffles at the shoulders and a low neckline showing off her full bosom. The dress was tight at the waist and hips with a long flowing skirt. Joe was smiling with pride.

He was wearing a tan shirt open at the throat, a leather jacket, and medium-tight brown pants with a large brown leather belt. His Western boots were buffed to a shine, and two pistols hung low. Sage couldn't see a knife, but he knew Joe always carried one. Joe walked smoothly which was unusual for a big man. His body was strong, and his hands were quick. His dark brown hair was combed, and his face was finely chiseled with a high, thin nose and deep-blue eyes. He was an outgoing, friendly man, quick to laugh, and quick to anger. There was something about him that said, "I want to be your friend, but don't mess with me."

When Pat returned, he was wearing highly tailored buckskin with fringed shoulders and arms, loose-fitting pants, a heavy leather belt and suede leather boots. He had a gun and a large knife in a worn, leather scabbard. His handsome face was weather-beaten. One look and you knew he was a mountain man.

As Juanita entered the room, everyone gasped. She was a stunning beauty. Her hair was as black as midnight, extending below her shoulders. Her skin was smooth, with two soft brown eyes. Her teeth were even and white, and her walk was regal. She held her head high, as would be expected of a woman of her aristocratic heritage. She wore a white blouse with a black bolero jacket, a black, tight-fitting skirt, and shiny, high-top, black boots. A white lace scarf caressed her black hair. She was magnificent.

Sage was thinking, *How can I be lucky enough to have a woman like that having dinner with me?* He was dressed completely in black. Nothing shiny. No buttons, no buckles. His boots were buffed black leather, with soft leather soles. He was wore a black shirt with black pants. His black leather jacket extended below his hips. Under the jacket, he carried a pistol and a knife. Both weapons were carried in black scabbards. Even the silver-inlaid knife was covered with black velvet. He always wore black at night; in the daytime, he wore light brown.

Concealment was always a factor in the way he dressed. As a boy, his life had depended upon not being seen. The memory of that had carried over. His black clothes were in contrast to the color of his reddish-blond hair. His face was open and friendly, and he smiled a lot, showing strong, white teeth. He had wide-set blue-green eyes, which looked out from under heavy eyebrows. His arms strong, his shoulders wide, his waist and hips were small. He moved like a giant cat. In a quiet way, he was a strikingly handsome man.

Juanita and Bonnie were a study in contrast. Each was beautiful, and they both knew it. There was no jealousy or competition between them. Because of their respect for each other, they had become good friends.

Bonnie was bright and bubbly, always laughing and smiling. Juanita was quiet and reserved. She was in every way the grand lady of the great house. Her very presence demanded respect, and she received it.

The owner of the hotel led them to the best table in the dining room. He regarded them as important guests. There would be no tequila tonight. Nothing but the best wines and liqueurs would be served. Pat figured this was a little too highfaluting for him, but he would suffer through it.

Joe had no training in social matters, but he saw nothing wrong with whom or what he was, so he felt no need to apologize.

Sage had had no training in etiquette after age twelve, but his mother had taught him well, and he felt at ease.

The meal was wonderful. They ate, drank, laughed, and talked. Anyone watching would think they didn't have a care in the world.

After the meal, Joe said, "I've gotta get Bonnie back to the wagon camp. Frank and Thelma were reluctant to allow her to join us after the trouble last night. They are concerned for her safety."

Looking at Pat and Sage, Juanita said, "Perhaps we should escort them to the wagon camp."

"Juanita, I don't want our evening to end," Sage said, "but I'm concerned for your safety, also."

"Yes, I see what you mean," Juanita commented. "And I agree you should escort Bonnie back to the wagon camp. I'll retire to my room and see you tomorrow morning . . . . What time shall we meet for breakfast?"

"We should get to the mine early," Pat replied, "before they realize that the regular workers won't be coming. Let's meet here at 6 o'clock."

"Sage," Joe said, "Can we get those revolvers? They'll come in handy if we should need them while taking Bonnie back to the camp."

"Yes," Sage agreed. "You can take two of them, and Pat and I will use the other two."

In the room, Joe tried on the cartridge belts. "This fits just fine," he said. "I'll exchange my holsters for these. This way, I will have these extra cartridges with me." He checked the revolving mechanism carefully. "They're in good working order. I think I am going to like these guns."

Sage said, "Pat, these belts are too small for you, and the guns fit my holster just fine. We can use our own holsters and share the cartridges."

"Okay," said Pat. "But I think I'm going to take my muzzle-loading pistol, also. I know how it works, and I'm not sure about these new guns."

The ride to the wagon camp was uneventful. Frank and Thelma were relieved to see Bonnie. Pat checked Frank's wound and said, "This is healing nicely. You'll be good as new in a few days."

When they returned to the hotel, Sage said, "I want to check on Juanita. I'll see you later."

With a smile, Joe said, "Check on her you say?"

Sage knocked on Juanita's door. There was no response, so he went to the lobby to talk to the man on duty. The man at the desk told Sage that after they left to escort Bonnie home, Señor Alvarez and his foreman came to the hotel and took Señorita Diego with them. Señor Alvarez didn't say why he was taking her, or where they were going. Sage knew no one in the hotel would dare ask Jose Alvarez to explain himself.

The hotel employee said, "Before the señorita left, she handed this note to me and asked me to give it to you. She didn't want her uncle to know that she was handing it to me. There's only one word scribbled on the paper. It says, *'mine.'* I don't know what it means." He handed the note to Sage.

CHAPTER 17

▼

THE MINE

Sage read the word *'mine.'* Under his breath, he said, "They've taken her to the mine!"

He dashed to the quarters he shared with the mountain men. They were still examining the new guns.

Sage exclaimed, "They've taken Juanita to the mine. We'd better hurry; they'll kill her for sure!"

They grabbed their weapons as they dashed to their horses.

Alvarez and Vacca had taken Juanita at least a half-hour ago. Pat, Joe, and Sage rode at a full gallop, trying to make up time. There was no chance they could catch them before Alvarez and Vacca reached the mine with Jaunita.

Sage called over his shoulder, "Juanita told me she didn't want her uncle killed, but if he harms her, I *will* kill him. She said nothing about Vacca, so that leaves that rat to our discretion."

"You'll have to hurry," Joe yelled back, "if you're going to get that snake-eyed bastard before I do. Any man who will hire men to shoot at Bonnie and her family from ambush is not worth living, and I'll rid the world of that plague."

Pat said, "We'll have our work cut out for us when we get to that mine. They'll have us outnumbered by at least ten to one."

Just before they got to the mine, they slowed down and moved quietly. They tied their horses back a ways and continued on foot, taking advantage of the cover Sage and Joe had noted when they scouted the mine earlier. They walked to within a hundred paces of the entrance and saw a wagon with two guards stationed there.

Pat said, "That wagon is loaded with bullion, and they're planning to haul it away. They have Juanita in the mine."

"I'll go in after her alone," Sage stated. "If we all go in, we'll be trapped in the mine. You two make a disturbance and, while the guards are distracted, I'll slip past them."

"Do you mean you're going in there alone?" Joe asked.

"Juanita is in there alone with those two killers. I can get in without being seen, and that'll give me an advantage. You just keep these guards busy. I'll handle the ones inside. Don't worry about me."

"Then don't you worry about these scoundrels out here. We'll keep them busy, all right," Pat said.

Sage replied, "Let me get into position on the other side of that mine entrance; then you attract their attention."

"We'll permanently attract their attention with these revolvers," Joe promised. "This will give us good practice."

Pat and Joe got into position, Sage signaled, and they threw some stones in the bushes on the side of the mine away from where Sage was hiding. While the guards were looking for what had caused the noise, Sage slipped into the mine. The mine had torches lighting the tunnel. The torches gave enough light to show the way, but there were areas of shadows where Sage could hide as he moved forward. He had to be sure there were no guards stationed as lookouts. He heard voices. One was Juanita's.

He heard her say, "I'll never sign that paper selling you the mine and blaming my problems on my friends. The community would hunt them down and kill them."

Sage recognized the other voice as Vacca's.

"If you want us to spare your life," Alvarez said, "you'll sign these papers. If you don't sign, we'll dump you down that mineshaft, and no one will ever know what happened to you. I'll inherit the land, and we'll still blame the mountain men and that wild animal they call Sage—the one you have been disgracing your family with when you are seen riding alone with him."

"He is a better, and more honorable man, than either of you could ever hope to be," Juanita retorted.

The uncle glared. "If you sign, I'll send you to Spain where you can live with your grandfather's people. They'll be ashamed of you, but they'll take you in. I am not a part of that family, and they won't take me in. This ranch should have been left to me. I was the older son. It's rightfully mine, and I intend to take it. Eliminating you will be easy." He turned to Pedro and told him to let Juanita look down this mineshaft. "That shaft is more than two hundred feet deep, Juanita. You'll never be found unless we tell everyone where those mountain men have thrown your body. That vein of ore played out years ago, and no one ever goes down there anymore. It'll be easy to just give you a push and down you'll go. Then everything will belong to me . . . . Everything will belong to me!" he repeated with a wild, crazy look. "So, why am I fooling around with you?"

Sage saw them holding Juanita's head over the dank, dark hole and knew that if they became aware of his presence, they would immediately drop her into the open shaft. He had to act quickly. Two guards were between him and Juanita. He picked up a stone and threw it toward the opening of the tunnel.

"What was that?" the guard just ahead of Sage asked.

"You'd better check it out!" the one farther in yelled.

Sage stepped back into the shadows and waited. After the guard passed, he followed him and quietly eliminated him. That guard was no longer an obstacle.

The other guard called out, "What did you find?" No answer. Sage heard him mumble, "What do you suppose could have happened?"

"Well, go find out, you idiot," Vacca retorted.

The second guard rushed back into the tunnel to check on the first guard. As he passed, Sage pulled him into the shadows, and now there were no guards at all.

Pedro said to Juanita, "I'm tired of fooling around with you." He started dragging her to the opening of the mineshaft. Juanita was desperate. She knew Sage would be coming for her, as soon as he found out that she was not at the hotel. She looked back down the tunnel, hoping to see him coming to rescue her. She saw Sage—he was signaling to her, indicating that she should sign the papers.

Juanita knew she must do nothing that would attract the attention of her captors to the fact that Sage was hidden in the tunnel.

"Oh, all right, I'll sign," she said reluctantly.

They dragged her back to the table where they had the papers ready for her signature. As soon as she was away from the danger of being pushed into the mineshaft, Sage jumped into the room and knocked Alvarez unconscious. Juanita broke free from Vacca, and ran to Sage. Vacca was right behind her with a long, thin knife in his hand. Sage drew Juanita behind him and faced the killer.

Pedro glared at Sage and said, "I've heard of your skill with that knife of yours. Now, we'll see just how good you really are. I've killed many men with this knife, and I'm just about to add you to that list." Vacca was advancing slowly, slashing with the long-bladed knife. He had a sadistic sneer on his face.

Sage waited, crouched like a lion. He was again the silent, stealthy warrior, half lion and half man. There was a fury in his eyes that Bonnie had told Juanita about. It was the fury she had seen when the two gunmen tried to kill her in the canyon. And the same fury, the people of the wagon train had seen when he killed the two Indians attacking Sally.

Juanita was so fascinated by this wild young giant that she almost forgot that she was watching a struggle that could end only with the death of one or the other of the men.

Vacca, too, saw this look and he, too, had never seen that look in the eyes of a man. A cold chill ran up his spine. He yelled, "There's no man on earth who can beat me in a knife fight. I'll put an end to this and throw you both down that mineshaft." He laughed wickedly. "And that uncle of yours, too. Who needs a weakling like that? I'll throw him down the shaft with you, and then I'll take over the whole thing."

Vacca was maneuvering, trying to get Sage into a position where he had the open mineshaft at his back.

Sage knew this killer was very strong, very quick, and had lots of experience in knife fighting. Sage remembered the technique he had seen a mountain lion use in overcoming an antelope. The lion had used its paw to trip the running antelope, and before the antelope could get to its feet, the lion was at its throat.

Vacca was slashing and thrusting with his knife. Sage was avoiding the thrusts and slashes, allowing himself to be maneuvered. He wanted the open mineshaft at his back. Then he waited for the rush he knew would be coming. When it did, he dropped to the ground on his side, tripping Vacca with his foot. Vacca's forward movement carried him headlong into the open mineshaft. Sage and Jaunita listened to his fast-descending scream as he plummeted to the bottom of the hole.

Sage ran to Juanita and took her in his arms. She was trembling like a leaf in a violent wind. He held her until she began to recover. She had been through a terrible ordeal. For the past half-hour she had expected to be killed. She knew that signing the paper would not have saved her life. Her uncle just wanted proof that she had willingly relinquished the ownership of her land.

Juanita and Sage heard a groan coming from the uncle. Sage quickly removed a shirt from one of the guards and used it to bind and blindfold Jose. He had to decide what to do with this despicable man.

*   *   *   *

Earlier, when Pat and Joe had watched Sage disappear into the mine, Joe remarked, "I don't feel right letting him go into that mine by himself."

"I don't worry about him," Pat replied, "as much as I feel sorry for anyone in there doing harm to Juanita. I've seen that young man at work on people he doesn't like, and he's a terror to behold."

A bullet ricocheted off a rock near their heads. Vacca's men were coming up the hill in mass.

Pat said, "Looks like we've stirred up a hornet's nest. There are at least twenty of them coming up that hill!"

"We're going to be busy for a while," Joe exclaimed. "Let's duck into these boulders. I'm glad we have these revolvers. With these guns, we will give them a fight. I hope Sage doesn't take too long in there. We may need his help. Keep your eye out for a sage bush. He'll probably crawl out from under it."

Bullets were flying fast and furious. "Wait until they get in range of these revolvers. We'll give them a big surprise," Joe commented.

Soon the men coming up the mountain were in range. With every shot fired by Joe or Pat, one of the attackers was dropping. The miners climbing the hill soon realized what was happening and withdrew out of range of those deadly revolvers. At rifle range, they had the advantage. They had more people, and their weapons were effective at a greater distance. The mountain men had rifles, but they had to reload after every shot.

"We can't wait here!" Joe exclaimed. "As soon as it gets light, they'll pick us off easy!"

They heard gunfire coming from the opening of the mine. At first, they thought the guards in the mine were firing at them. Then they saw Sage standing in the opening of the mine firing at the men with the rifles.

"Pat, let's get into that tunnel with Sage," Joe yelled. "Three of us can hold off an army from inside that mine."

"Well, we'd better do it now before they get any closer. It will be very difficult to get into that mine without getting shot."

Joe motioned to Sage indicating what he and Pat were planning to do. Sage was closer to the riflemen, so his pistols were still in range. He began laying down a cover of fire until both Joe and Pat were inside the mine.

When they got inside, they saw Alvarez trussed up like a chicken. Sage drew them farther inside the tunnel and told them what had happened. Juanita was standing guard over her uncle using Sage's muzzle-loading pistol.

Sage said, "We've got to decide what we're going to do with him."

"I know what I would like to do with him," Joe answered. "Untie him and maybe he'll try to escape and that'll solve our problem."

"No, I promised Juanita we wouldn't kill him."

"After what he tried to do to you, Juanita," Pat said, "do you still feel the same?"

"When I was looking into that mineshaft," she replied, "if I had been holding a gun, I would have killed him myself. But now, I can't do it. We have to find a way to get him out of the country before someone does away with him. That is sure what he deserves."

"We're trapped, you know," Pat pointed out. "They can't get to us, but we can't get to food or water."

"Carlos will be here soon with the local miners and the vaqueros," Sage explained. "They'll deal with Vacca's men. From what I've heard, some of the local miners have a score to settle with the slave drivers Vacca brought in from Mexico. Let's just wait, and give Carlos and his men a chance to settle their score with this bunch of killers. Then, if there are any of Vacca's men left, they'll be glad to skedaddle back to Mexico.

"We've got to decide what to do with these vermin when they give up, and they'll give up when they realize that Vacca is dead and Alvarez is our prisoner. Alvarez can tell them that they are vastly outnumbered. The local miners will want to deal with these men who have been mistreating them, and they'll want to do it in their own way. I think there's a better way. I suggest that we turn this disgusting piece of humanity loose and let him go back to Mexico with the killers he hired. That way, we solve all our problems at the same time."

"That sounds like a good idea," Juanita said. "He gave me an ultimatum. Now I'll give him one. We'll give him enough gold, to get him back to Spain where he can live with his father's people."

"Those bandits will probably steal it from him before he gets to Mexico," Pat said.

"He has a choice," Joe agreed. "He can ride alone and face the Apaches, or he can ride with that bunch of thieves. It seems appropriate to me, thieves stealing from thieves. There's just one problem with that method. What's to stop him from hiring a group of men and coming back?"

"Would you come back," Pat asked, "knowing there are nearly a hundred angry miners wanting to kill you? I wouldn't, and I don't think he will either."

"All right, untie him," Sage said. "Perhaps we can save some bloodshed."

They untied Alvarez and explained the situation to him.

"Uncle Jose," Juanita said tearfully, "we'll give you a horse and a pack mule to carry your supplies. The pack mule will have to carry the bullion we are going to give you. You take the men you and Vacca hired back to Mexico with you. If you're ever seen in New Mexico again, we'll turn you over to the miners you mistreated. Now, call to your men and explain the situation to them."

Pat glared at Jose. "You'd better understand one thing. Sage made a promise to Juanita that he would not kill you. But neither Joe nor I made that kind of promise."

"Yeah," Joe said, "your killers shot Bonnie's father, and there's nothing that would make me happier than for you to try to run."

"How much gold can I take?" Alvarez asked.

"A pack mule can carry up to a hundred pounds," Pat replied. "If you're smart, you'll use part of that carrying capacity for carrying food and water. In the desert, both of those things are more valuable than gold. If you load your mule too heavily, you'll kill him, and you'll end up carrying the load on your own back. That's your limitation. You decide."

Alvarez stepped to the entrance of the mine and called out, "Vacca is dead. I am their prisoner. More than a hundred miners and vaqueros will be here in less than one hour. These people will give us horses. If we go now, we can go back to Mexico. If we don't go now, we'll be killed when the other miners and vaqueros get here. I suggest we take them up on their offer."

Sage stepped out to where the miners coming up the hill could see him, and yelled, "If you agree, lay down your guns, and put your hands in the air. Any man who tries to escape or use a concealed weapon will be killed. If you understand, then start walking forward, but make no mistake, one false move, and you'll be shot."

Sage turned to Alvarez. "You better explain it to them. My Spanish is not that good, and I don't want them, or you, to misunderstand."

Alvarez repeated Sage's words and added, "Don't try anything foolish. They are just looking for a reason to kill us."

The men came forward and stood in a bunch just outside the entrance to the mine. Sages sensed danger and saw one of the imported miners with a knife in his hand step forward and try to grab Juanita. She slipped from his grasp, and in the blink of an eye, the killer looked down at the silver-plated handle of a knife protruding from the center of his chest.

Joe, with his hands poised over his revolvers, said, "All right, is there anyone else who would like to try that? Try it, and die."

They heard a yell. It was Carlos and his men coming up the hill. The mistreated miners were looking to settle the score. It seemed a shame to deny them their revenge, but Sage had agreed to let the prisoners go.

Sage stepped forward and called out, "Carlos, I gave my word that they wouldn't be harmed if they surrendered. Will you and your men return with them to their camp? Let them pick up their horses and their things. Make them walk for three days, then leave them, and let them deal with the Apaches and the desert if they can." Pointing to Alvarez, he said, "Take this snake and his pack mule with you."

"Carlos, old friend," Pat said, "if you'll come with me, we'll go with the miners and vaqueros. I want to see that this is well done. We have a promise to keep, and we must drive this vermin out of the country."

Carlos said, "Me and my sons will be happy to go with you. *Gracias*, Señor."

Sage asked Juanita, "What do you want to do with this wagonload of gold and silver bullion? There's at least a ton of it here."

"After my uncle has taken what he was promised," Juanita replied, "I suggest that we take the rest to the hacienda and store it there until we can take it to either Saint Louis or Mexico City."

Sage said to Pat, "Joe and I, with the vaqueros and the local miners, will escort Juanita and the bullion back to the Diego ranch. If you walk these hired killers south for three days, you'll be able to return on horseback in two days, so we'll see you at the ranch in five days. If you haven't returned in six days, Joe and I will lead a group of men to find you."

Carlos said, "Don't worry about us; we'll do just fine. *Hasta luego*."

Juanita told the local miners, "There'll be no working at the mine today. Before you return to work, you will select the man who will be in charge. I suggest you select the man who was in charge before Vacca took over. He was a good foreman, and you know what to expect from him, and he knows what to expect from you. You'll all receive full pay for helping to eliminate this bad influence out of our country."

"Si, Señorita. It's an honor to be working for the Diego family again."

Pat went to Sage and Juanita and said, "We have them ready to start walking south." He turned to Joe. "Look what I found in their quarters: cartons of cartridges for the revolvers. They were prepared for war. We don't need to get cartridges from the trading post. Here are two boxes for you. I'll keep what I need and put the rest in the wagon." Pat then said to the vaqueros, "Let's get 'em started south!"

One of the vaqueros drove the wagon, and Joe rode with him trailing his horse behind. Juanita and Sage, with other vaqueros and miners, followed. The bright winter sun streamed through the tall pine trees, and the horses stirred up little puffs of dust as they trotted. Herds of antelope grazed in the meadows. One would never have guessed that a life-and-death struggle had just occurred only moments ago, and a great wrong had been righted. Sage was feeling good; he had fulfilled his obligation to his father and to Don Diego.

Under his breath, he asked, "Father, are you pleased?" Almost as if in answer to his question a flock of quail flew up, sunlight glistened off their wings. Sage imagined his father's voice saying, "Yes, son, you have done well."

Juanita reached from her horse and placed her hand on his arm, and said, "Thank you, Michael. Words are not sufficient to express my gratitude. I know my father and grandfather would be pleased to have me share the ranch with one so worthy. You are now legally half-owner and manager of the hacienda and all its lands. What a relief it is to have it in such capable hands."

With admiration, she gazed upon the face of the man she loved. She was sure of his love and knew he had other duties to perform before he could make a final commitment to her. She would wait, hoping the wait wouldn't be too long or his duties too difficult. When they reached Santa Fe, the miners began dropping off as they passed their dwellings. Their wives and children were eagerly waiting, but before they left they each came to Sage and Juanita and expressed their gratitude.

At last, Sage, Joe, and Juanita reached the hacienda, and placed the bullion in the big house. Pat was helping to escort the bad men south. Joe was going home to Bonnie. Juanita was again safe in her home with people she had known all her life. For the first time in almost a year, Sage was alone. He was uncertain about what to do next.

"This is your home," Juanita said. "Stay here at *El Casa Grande*."

"No," Sage replied. "It would be torture for me to be sleeping so near to you and not be able to have you. I'll wait. I'll go back to the hotel, get my things and live for a time in the mountains. I'll ride the lands I am to manage. I'll use the charts you have shown me as a guide."

"I'll go with you," Juanita said. "Father showed me the land when I was ten, but I remember it well."

"Thank you, Juanita. There's nothing I would like better than to share a ride like that with you. One day you and I will take the ride together when we can do it without compromising your reputation. We were fortunate to have that time alone up in the canyon. There was no one to see our lovemaking except our Creator, and I know the heavens smiled upon us that night. You are well known, and too important to me and this whole community to place you and your name in jeopardy."

"You are right," Juanita said, "but don't forget, you are to meet Pat and the vaqueros in five days."

"Don't worry, I'll be back," Sage said.

CHAPTER 18

▼

TAKING OVER THE MANAGEMENT

For five days, Sage rode every river, creek, draw, hill, and valley. He rode through canyons, meadows, and mountains, and he saw places where nothing indicated that men had ever been. Animals were so tame they let him touch them. The land was beautiful and wild. He understood the fascination that mountain men felt for this place. The Diego ranch contained so much land it seemed wrong for one man to own it all, but as its new manager, it was his duty to preserve and protect it, and he would do his best.

This wasn't like the great prairie where he had lived alone for six years. This land was not as fertile, nor was the vegetation so bountiful, or the wild fruit and nuts so plentiful, but it had another kind of beauty. The peace and quiet soothed his soul, and his mind wandered back to Evening Star. She was the wife of another man now, but he had told her he would return to see their child. He would keep that promise. This was a promise he made to himself and to Evening Star. If he has a child, he wanted to see the child. He had an obligation to that child, and he must meet that obligation.

*   *   *   *

At noon on the fifth day, Sage rode into the courtyard of *La Casa Grande*. Juanita saw him coming and ran to greet him. He bounded from his horse to hold her in his arms; she felt wonderful. He had missed her so much. He had seen the land and had come to grips with what he must do.

Pat, Joe, and their friends were waiting, also. A feast was prepared. They ate, they drank, they talked, and they laughed. Everyone was there and they all wanted to meet the new manager. The women and children were laughing and playing around him. Juanita was constantly at his side holding his hand and lifting her face to be kissed. He had never before experienced anything like this. He had come home. For the first time since he was a child, he knew the meaning of family and friends.

*   *   *   *

Pat reported on his trip south to escort Alvarez and his cohorts out of the area.

"Before we released them," he said, "we again reminded them of the consequences of returning. Alvarez and his band of thieves were already arguing about the gold. Their trip to old Mexico is going to be an eventful journey. No one felt sorry for them. They brought their problems on themselves with their greed."

Carlos and his family were happy. They were again at home in the hacienda where they had lived all their lives. Their work, their homes, and their lives were now safe and secure. Repeatedly, they expressed their gratitude to Sage and Juanita. They had been saying thank you to Joe for days, and to Pat ever since he returned from escorting the bad men out of the country.

Frank announced that his daughter, Bonnie, would be marrying Joe Martin in one week, and everybody was invited. It would be the biggest wedding celebration the valley has seen for years.

Juanita had been helping Bonnie prepare for the wedding. Joe and Bonnie had been decorating their home, preparing it to receive the many guests who would be attending the wedding. They would serve the finest food and drinks the area could produce for this was the happiest time of their lives and they wanted to share that happiness with everyone.

The wagon train would depart on the second leg of its journey to California the day after the wedding. They would follow the Old Spanish Trail, with Grant Davis as the wagon master and Pat Connors as their scout. It would be a hard and terrible journey, but the people couldn't have two better men leading them. Both Grant and Pat had made the journey before.

Sage was getting acquainted with the people with whom he would be working while managing the ranch. He spent a few hours alone each day honing his skills with the new revolver. If he were going to carry a gun, he had to be able to draw quickly and shoot accurately. He wanted to be the very best.

Juanita rode with Sage, acquainting him with the land and the people. She continued to teach him the Mexican language. His proficiency improved every day. He discussed the policies and practices he wanted to introduce to the running of the ranch. Juanita was excited and enthusiastic and suggested they call the people together so he could tell them of his ideas.

Sage and Juanita asked Carlos to leave a few vaqueros to watch over the animals and call all the rest, including their wives, together in the courtyard. Sage wanted to talk to them. Carlos called the meeting for early in the evening. Food and drinks were served. The mood was festive. After the meal, Sage asked Juanita to stand with him to help convey his plans to the people.

When they all were listening, he said, "We want this hacienda to be a good place for everyone to live and work. This is your home as much as it is ours. We want all of our homes to be happy, healthy, and prosperous." A cheer went up from the people.

"Here is what I propose. Everything we need, we will produce. If there is anything you need, and we do not have it, let either me or Juanita know, and we as a group will provide it.

"The ranch must be self-sustaining. We'll build a school where the children will receive the finest education. If you, or a member of your family, get sick, a doctor from Santa Fe will be provided.

"Juanita and I will provide the tools, animals, and the land. You must provide the labor to make it happen. The work will be divided among everyone. Each of you will be responsible to perform his or her task to the benefit of everyone.

"One person will be in charge of each operation. One will care for the cows; another will be in charge of the sheep. Others will be in charge of the fields, where the food is grown. Someone will be in charge of keeping the place clean and attractive. Someone else will care for *El Casa Grande*. Another will be in charge of preparing the food and entertaining the guests.

"Each person will have an assigned task, and each person will be responsible for doing the task well. If any of you need help, let us know, and we'll provide that help.

"Our chief foreman will be Carlos Viejo. He will assign the tasks and work with you to get your work done. If there's a problem, take that problem to Carlos. If you and Carlos cannot find a solution, then bring the problem to Juanita or me. We'll work with you. If you have a suggestion on how to handle a problem, please let us know, and we'll see if your idea is something we can use. Together, we can make this the best ranch in all of New Mexico. It will be a wonderful place for all of us. Does everybody understand? Are there any questions?"

They were smiling, but they were quiet. They had never heard of a ranch being run by the people, so no one spoke.

Juanita said, "You may volunteer for any of these specific tasks if you wish. Think about it tonight and tell us tomorrow morning when we meet to assign the tasks."

One of the women spoke up and said, "I could do the weaving, if I can get some of the other women to help me."

"I can work leather," a man said. "I'll make boots, saddles, and harnesses."

"I'll do the gardening," another said.

Soon most of the tasks were assigned. Everyone was talking excitedly about who would help, and who would be in charge.

"Thank you for volunteering," Sage said. "We'll begin our tasks tomorrow morning. Juanita, Carlos, and I will work with you to help you get started. Thank you for coming. Tomorrow we'll begin a new day at this ranch."

Turning to Carlos, he said, "Carlos, could you please stay for a little while? Juanita and I want to discuss something with you." After the others departed, Sage said, "Carlos, the first thing I want to do is to deal with the problem the women have of carrying water from the river to their homes. It is too far. I want to bring the water closer. We'll dig a catch basin far enough upriver to hold a supply of water, so that we'll have good gravity flow. Then we'll dig a trench, so that the water will flow through the village. We'll plant trees and flowers along the stream and use the running water to irrigate them and add beauty to the hacienda.

"We'll start tomorrow morning. If we need more laborers, we'll hire them from the workers in Santa Fe. I'd like to complete this job as soon as possible. Then I want to start improving the homes for the workers. After the homes have been repaired, we'll start on the big house."

Carlos was amazed. "Are you are going to repair the houses of the workers before you repair the house of the owners?"

"Yes, Carlos. This is going to be a better place for all of the people of the hacienda."

"That's a wonderful idea," Juanita said. "Uncle Jose let everything run down for years. What can I do to help?"

Sage suggested, "You and the wives of the workers could bring food and refreshments to the workers. Your presence will be an incentive for both the workers and me, to do our work better. To improve the appearance of the hacienda, we'll mix lime and whitewash the buildings and the walls of the courtyard. Then we'll plant more trees and flowers. I want to make this place beautiful for you. When we get this done, Joe and I will do the same for his place. That will be our wedding present to the newlyweds.

"I must go now. I want to ride to my ranch to see when Señora Cordova will start the cattle drive. Summer is coming, and they must start soon, if they're going to complete the drive before the summer heat comes to the desert.

"Juanita, will you have dinner with me tomorrow evening? We haven't had time alone for such a long time."

"Yes, oh, yes," Juanita gleamed. "I'll look forward to it, Sage."

"Then, I'll see you tomorrow morning when we begin work on the stream."

*   *   *   *

When Sage arrived at the McBain ranch, both Joe and Pat were helping Señora Cordova make final preparations. Their journey would begin tomorrow morning. The snow in the mountains was melting, and the flow in the Rio Grande was up. The señora would be able to float down the river in a flat-bottom boat to Matamoras. They would be stopping at the missions along the way, to rest and refresh themselves. The señora planned to sell some of her cattle to the missions. The missions needed beef, and it would reduce the number of cattle the vaqueros would have to manage. She would drive the rest of the herd to Matamoras, ship them to Vera Cruz, and then drive them overland to Mexico City. People who had just returned from Mexico said the price for cattle was good. Mexico City was growing fast, and there was a big demand for fresh beef.

Joe greeted Sage saying, "I've been getting acquainted with our foreman. He's a good man; I like him. The biggest problem he'll have on the drive will be getting the animals past the bandits along the Texas and Mexican border. I've seen to it that he and his vaqueros are well mounted and well armed. He's confident that they can get through without too much trouble."

"Perhaps I should go with them?" Sage asked.

"No! You can't go," Joe said anxiously. "You're to be best man at my wedding."

"The wagon train will be leaving right after the wedding," Pat said. "The wagons have to get through the desert also. I've crossed Death Valley, and it's always difficult. Both Grant and I have crossed it before, so we know what we have to do. With a little luck, we will make it just fine. Grant and I will see you next winter, on our way back to Missouri, where we'll pick up our next wagon train to guide through." With a big smile, Pat said, "When I come back, I want to see both of you married and your wives pregnant."

"If it doesn't happen, it won't be for lack of trying," Joe laughed.

Sage said, "I've got a lot to do, before I'll know what the future holds for me. Only time will tell. Every time I look at Juanita, I tell myself that I'm the luckiest man in the world to have a woman like that promise to wait for me."

Pat advised, "Don't make her wait too long. There is a beautiful woman going to waste there."

"Well," Joe said, "we'd better get started. I've got to get my things together, and I have a ranch to run. Sage, why don't you move your stuff here? There's plenty of room. Bonnie has enough help. One more room to keep clean and one more person to feed will be no trouble for them. They've heard stories about you, and they're all looking forward to serving you. I've told them that most of the stories are exaggerated," Joe said with a chuckle.

Sage replied, "No, Juanita and I must go to the people who extended her credit during the time she was experiencing financial difficulties. We must clear up all of her obligations, and transfer the accounts into her and my names. We will arrange it so either she, or I, can deal with whatever problems the ranch might encounter. Then I'll register and transfer the title of the Cordova Ranch into my name before the señora leaves, should there be any questions."

Sage continued, "I'll stay at the hotel in Santa Fe until after your honeymoon. Then I'll stay at one of the rooms at *El Rancho Diego*. I'll be going back to Indian Territory as soon as I get the ranch back in good running order. With the help of Carlos and his sons, Juanita will run it until I get back."

"You mean you're going back among those Comanche and Kiowa by yourself?" Joe asked.

"I'll be going with one of the mule trains, as far as the Cimarron Junction, and then I'll go to my cave. I was safe when I lived there as a child, and I'll be safe there again. I've got to know what happened to Evening Star. I promised her I'd return, and I have to keep my promise."

"What about Juanita?" Joe asked.

"You know how I feel about Juanita, but I don't know what's going to happen between us until I do what I have to do in Indian Territory. Only time will tell what our future will be."

"How long will you be gone?"

"I don't know for sure; probably about a year."

"A year is a long time."

"Yes, I know. Juanita has said she will wait so regardless of what happens in Indian Territory, I'll be back. I'm hoping you and Bonnie will watch over Juanita for me while I'm gone."

"You know we will. Bonnie and Juanita have become good friends. You don't have to worry about this ranch. Frank and Thelma will be here to help Bonnie and me. Together we'll be able to take care of just about anything that might come up. We'll be available to help Juanita anytime she calls on us."

"I'm not worried," Sage nodded. "I know you'll do a good job, and I'll leave my Arabian stallion here for you to get a herd started. Then Manuel will be bringing a herd back from Mexico City when he and your vaqueros return. That will take at least six months. Some of the vaqueros are staying here, and Carlos could let you have some of his men to help, should you need them."

"I hate to see you going to Indian Territory alone," Pat said, "but I understand. To do what you need to do, you must go alone. If anyone on earth can do it, you can. I'll be expecting to see you here when I return from California. All three of us have big jobs cut out for us, so let's get them done. The lady who lost her husband in the Indian raid needs help getting her wagon and her two boys to California. You know, I lost my boys, and those two of hers are about the same age mine would be if they hadn't been killed by the Blackfoot."

"What are you going to do about Maggie?" Joe asked.

"Maggie can take care of herself until I get back," Pat replied. "Say, since we're going to Santa Fe, let's drop by Maggie's and have a couple of drinks. We have a victory to celebrate."

"That's a good idea; let's go." Joe said.

"I'll buy the drinks and anything else you want," Sage said. "I owe you two a very great favor. Anything you ever want from me is yours just for the asking. I hope that one day I'll be able to repay you for helping me get Juanita's ranch back in her control. You've made it possible for me to fulfill my father's promise. Thank you."

"You've already repaid me," Joe responded. "Helping me to get a start with Bonnie at the new ranch is more than I could have done by myself. I didn't help you for a reward. Don't forget, we owe you our lives. Our bacon was sure in the fire when you came to our aid from under that sagebrush. You were a strange-looking sight waving to us from under that bush."

"I couldn't believe my eyes," Pat laughed. "I still find it hard to believe." They all laughed at the recollection.

"Well, don't tell anyone," Sage smiled. "I want to keep my cave a secret. But if you ever need to use it, you know where it is. There's still a large store of dried fruit and nuts in that cave. My parents' things are still there. I want to bring them back with me when I return. That's all I have to remind me of my mother and father. I want to bring back my mother's Bible and books. There are some pictures and my father's tools. Those things are important to me. I'll need a pack mule to carry all the things on the list. That's why I want to go with Becknell's mule train. I want him to haul a load of silver bullion to Saint Louis for me. Then I'll meet his train on their way back to Santa Fe."

"You've given this a lot of thought," Pat said. "That could be a little difficult knowing just when to meet Becknell on the trail. They won't know for sure when they'll be coming back and, since you don't know for sure when you'll be able to meet them, you may have to camp on the trail for quite a while. You're going to be exposed to all sorts of things waiting out there on that prairie. You might be better off to just follow the trail we used when we left the Comanche village and come back alone. At least you know what to expect."

"Yes, you're right, and I'll make that decision when the time comes. I'll buy a couple of those revolvers from Bent's Trading Post before I go. Joe, will you teach me to use them?"

"It doesn't look to me like you need a lot of teaching," Joe replied. "You're one of the best I've ever seen."

"Thanks," Sage said, "why do you go so far north on the California Trail when Los Angeles is southwest? Wouldn't you save a lot of time by going southwest?"

"A few men have tried that way. They say the terrain is easier on the wagons, and it's shorter, but there are long stretches where there's no water for the animals. The country to the north is beautiful, but it is hell to get wagons through that rough terrain. There's plenty of water until you get to Death Valley. The rivers run through deep canyons, and it's hard to get to the water at times. Death Valley is aptly named. There've been many people who didn't make it across that stretch of desert. Both Grant and I have been across there, and we plan on taking two extra wagons loaded with nothing but water.

"Each of the other wagons will be loaded light with personal belongings, and they, too, will be carrying an extra barrel of water. That should give us the reserve of water we'll need. If we don't have bad luck, we'll make it just fine. On the way back, Grant and I will bring an extra pack mule loaded with water. We'll scout a southern route. If we can find a way through the desert south of the Grand Canyon, we could cut two months off the travel time to California."

"That sounds like an interesting trip," Sage mused. "I wish I could go with you."

"Yeah, I wish you were going with us, too. We could sure use your skills on this trip." Pat smiled. "But you have your work cut out for you here, so I'll be seeing you when we come back through."

*   *   *   *

Margarita's was crowded. Greetings came from every corner of the cantina. Maggie took them to a table and sat with them.

She said, "*Mi amigos*, everyone in Santa Fe has heard of what you've done. Whatever you want, food, drink, girls, just name it, and it's yours."

Pat hugged Maggie and said, "Maggie, we came here for food and drinks. We would enjoy listening to the music and watching your girls dance. We accept your offer of a drink, and then we want to buy a round of drinks for everybody in the cantina. So, bring us three tequilas and three of your best steaks!"

Two miners came over and said, "*Gracias*, Señor. We owe you a very great debt. We no longer work in fear."

"Si, Señor," Sage smiled, "but you owe me no debt. I'm pleased to have your friendship. Tomorrow you'll be working in the sunlight.

Tell the miners, all of them who would like to work, to come to *El Rancho Diego* tomorrow morning and bring their tools. We'll be rerouting part of the river to run it through the grounds of the hacienda."

The miners replied, "We'll be there, Señor."

* * * *

Men from all over the area were at the cantina. Mountain men, most of whom were friends of Pat and Joe, were there. Grant Davis and a few of the men from the wagon train were seated at a table nearby, as well as vaqueros from many of the other ranches, and some from the Diego ranch and from the ranch now being managed by Joe.

In one corner was a group of men who had come west to prospect for gold. Many men were moving west now, some for adventure, some for the riches they had heard were to be had. Most were good men, but a few were looking to take from others what they themselves did not want to work for.

Four such men came from the corner table, and one of them said to Sage, "We've heard of this wild man from the plains. We heard you've killed many men. I want to see if you're really that tough."

"I came here to have a drink with my friends," Sage replied. "I would like to be your friend. Would you have a drink with me?"

"We don't drink with cowards," the belligerent stranger said.

Grant and three of the men from the wagon train stood up. "We owe these men a great debt," Grant said. "If you come against them, you'll have to deal with us. And I can tell you right now, there is not a coward among them."

The other mountain men stood up, and one of them said, "If this man is a friend of Pat Connors, he's a friend of ours. You'll have to deal with us, also."

The miners stood. The vaqueros stood. One of the vaqueros said, "Señor, this man has earned, or bought, everything he has; he has taken nothing, or anything, from anybody. The men he killed were trying to kill either him or someone he had sworn to protect."

Joe agreed. "I owe this man my life, and I can tell you with absolute certainty, he's no coward. You have a choice: you can drink, or you can die. You decide, and you'd better decide right now."

"I want to be your friend," Sage repeated. "Will you have a drink?"

The spokesman for the belligerents said, with a sneer on his face, "Well, fellows, I'm going to enjoy that drink; how about you?"

"Maggie," Pat asked, "please send drinks to their table."

Maggie muttered, "It is a waste of good tequila, but I'll take the drinks myself." She took the tequila to their table and told them, "This is my cantina. Now drink, then leave, and don't come back. Señor McBain may want to be your friend, but I don't. Men like you cost me too much business. There are other cantinas in Santa Fe. When you go to them, you'll drive their business to me." She then returned to tell Pat, "They enjoyed their drinks so much they decided to move to another cantina where they can have another."

Pat laughed. "Maggie, I'm surprised at you, running off good customers like that."

"They'll bring me more business by going to another cantina," Maggie replied.

Sage laughed and said, "I don't think they'll be missed."

CHAPTER 19

▼

PREPARING FOR THE RETURN TO INDIAN TERRITORY

"Pat, I have silver bullion to sell—where do I sell it?" Sage asked.

"There are men here in Santa Fe who'll buy it," Pat replied, "but you could get twice as much for it in Saint Louis. The men who own the mule train will haul it for you. Of course, they'll charge you a lot to haul it, and there's no guarantee it will get to Saint Louis. There's always a chance you'll lose it to the Indians or to bandits along the way, but if you get it there, it will bring a good price."

"It looks like I may have to take it to Saint Louis myself. I could hire drivers and ride scout, and we'll go along as part of the mule train. That way, we'll strengthen their train, and they'll give us cover."

"Sounds like a good idea. I think they'll go for it. We could talk to them and see."

"Thank you, Pat. I'll talk to Becknell. I want to see Bent's Trading Post, anyway."

"I'll go with you. I want to buy supplies for the journey to California. Could we leave tomorrow morning? It's a two-day journey each way."

"No, I can't go tomorrow. I have to be at the ranch with Juanita and Carlos, but we could leave day after tomorrow. I'll bring a couple of pack mules and two handlers to haul the things we want to buy. Will that be enough?"

"Yeah, that'll be enough. Grant might want to come along. He could bring his own mules. He'll probably want some things, also."

"Good, we'll have plenty of men in case we run into trouble. I'll see you here, day after tomorrow. I'll bring two mules and two handlers. I'm going to get some sleep. I've got to be at the hacienda early to help get the men started digging. We're channeling water through the grounds of the hacienda."

"Hmm, that sounds like quite a job," Joe said. "I've got to see Frank. He'll want to be with me when we get started at the ranch. I'd like to buy more Arabian stock, to go with the two you brought with us. You'll have to choose another mount if I am going to use that stallion for breeding."

"All right," Sage agreed. "Pick out the best mustang we have on the ranch in exchange for the stallion. The horse you pick must be either brown or black. I don't want my horse to attract attention, in case I want to remain hidden. White horses are pretty, but it isn't smart to ride one in Indian country. They're too easy to see. I'll bring the stallion by and make the exchange tomorrow night, after I have dinner with Juanita."

*　　*　　*　　*

Sage arrived at the hacienda just after sunrise. Juanita had breakfast ready. She said, "I knew you would be early, and I wanted to serve your breakfast. I missed you last night."

"I thought of you last night, too. Thinking of you keeps me awake most every night," Sage said as he embraced Juanita. "I've got something I want to talk to you about before we start diverting the stream. I want to take the silver to Saint Louis and trade it for gold coins. We can get twice as much for the silver in Saint Louis as we can get for it here. I'm going to Indian Territory anyway, and if I go with the wagons, I can make sure the bullion gets to Saint Louis."

"That's a wonderful idea. We could make the exchange from dollars to pesos any time. We'll have all the money we need. We could take the bullion to Mexico City, but it takes too long to make that journey. This way, we'll have both American and Mexican money." Juanita looked at Sage with concern. "There's trouble brewing between the United States and Mexico. We should be prepared for whatever happens. It's good we have the land registered in both our names. There are more and more *gringos* coming into Santa Fe all the time. With my Mexican citizenship and your US citizenship, we should be able to protect the ranch no matter which way the trouble goes."

Sage was amazed—he had no idea she was that aware of what was going on outside the ranch. He was so proud of her; not only was she beautiful, she was also very smart.

The miners were just gathering for their day's work, and Carlos was giving them instructions. After that was done, Carlos came to Sage and said, "*Buenos dias*, Señor, Señorita."

"*Buenos dias*, Carlos," Sage replied.

Carlos rode with him and Juanita to where they would begin diverting the stream. They would take only a small portion of the water from the river. They planned to build a holding pond from which to draw water, so that the amount of water running through the diversionary stream would remain constant under all conditions. Then they laid out the path the stream would follow, and then dug the trench on through the hacienda to where it would irrigate the fields before it re-entered the river.

The women were thrilled that they wouldn't have to go so far to get water, and the children could play along the stream. By irrigating the plants in the courtyard, it would make the place more beautiful. The miners were glad to be working in the open instead of working in the dark mine. They were good at moving dirt, and the work proceeded rapidly. All Carlos had to do was tell them what he wanted. They knew how to do it. The project would be completed in less time than Sage had estimated.

The workers lined the streambed with rocks to prevent erosion. It would be good to have flowers, trees, and shrubs growing along the new stream. The women brought food and drinks. Everyone was looking forward to getting the work done so they could see the finished project.

At the end of the day, Sage went to the river, bathed, and changed into fresh clothes. He wanted to look good, for he was having dinner with Juanita. This would be the first dinner together at *El Casa Grande*. The ladies doing the cooking and serving were excited. They knew this was an important occasion for everyone concerned. Juanita wanted it to be attractive to the man she loved, and Sage wanted time alone with her.

Juanita chose the patio as the place for their dinner. The patio was where the Diego family had dined for three generations. There were memories here. The hacienda was as she remembered it before her mother and father had been killed by the Apaches. But it had not been a happy place since her uncle took over the management of the ranch.

Sage and Juanita heard men playing guitars, the women were dancing, and the children playing. Juanita had about lost hope that it would ever be this happy again. She was grateful to Sage and his friends for making it possible.

The ladies served veal, with wine, and dessert. They lit the table with candles and graced it with flowers. The food was served with the finest Spanish silverware. No king and queen ever dined more elegantly.

After dinner, Sage and Juanita strolled through the grounds. The men serenaded them, the ladies curtsied, and the children came to hold their hands.

Juanita's skirt swirled around her long shapely legs and the candle light sparkled in her soft brown eyes. She was the most beautiful woman Sage had ever seen. They strolled back to the privacy of the veranda where he took her in his arms and kissed her with a passion that took her breath away. She returned the kiss with an eagerness that pleased him. She loved to feel his strength as she nestled closer into his arms. He looked at her amorously. She slowly shook her head and said, "*Mañana*. There are too many people around us right now. Whenever we make love has to be special."

Sage held her close, nodded his head, and repeated, "*Mañana*. Thank you for a wonderful evening. I'll see you when I return from the trading post. I'll be back in time for Joe and Bonnie's wedding."

Juanita said, "*Vaya con Dios.*"

Sage mounted his Arabian stallion and rode to his ranch, to exchange horses.

＊　　　＊　　　＊　　　＊

Everything was quiet at the McBain ranch. Most of the vaqueros had gone with Señora Cordova to Mexico. Bonnie's family had moved into the big house to help Joe get the horse ranch going; Thelma was helping Bonnie get ready for the wedding.

It took four people working full-time to care for the big house: one doing the cooking, one the cleaning and keeping of the house, another woman and her husband taking care of the courtyard and doing the repairs that were needed.

Bonnie—the lady of the house—managed the people and assigned their duties. The system worked well indeed. It was a big responsibility for the lady of the house, for she had to greet and care for the guests, as well as make sure the duties were performed well. Being kind and helpful to those who served the household was an important part of the job. Bonnie was well suited for the task; she was naturally kind and caring. Sage commented to Joe, "Bonnie will make a great lady of the house; everybody loves her."

The wedding was only one week away. Sage and Pat would be gone for three days, maybe four, on their journey to Bent's Fort. They would be back in time, but Bonnie was nervous. The wagon train would leave only two days after the wedding.

It seemed that everything was happening at once. New lives were being started. Old friends were parting for a lifetime. It was a sad time, but it was also a happy time. There was little chance that the people who were going on to California would ever see again the people they were leaving. The distance to California was too great.

Sage stayed in one of the guest rooms. He would be gone before sunup with the mules and the drivers to meet Pat at Maggie's.

Sage and his men arrived at Maggie's as the sun was breaking the horizon. Pat was already there. Maggie fixed everyone a hearty breakfast. Grant was there with trading goods on mules to trade for the things the travelers of the wagon train wanted. The westward travelers had seen the new six-shot revolvers and wanted them. They remembered the Indian raids and wanted to be prepared should it happen again. Grant told them, this time their problem would be with the desert, and the difficult mountain trails, but the new guns would come in handy should they encounter trouble.

The small group of men with the four mules traveled northeast through the semiarid foothills to the Sangre de Cristo Mountains. The morning was bright and crisp, with the sun shining on snow-capped peaks. Herds of antelope and elk grazed in the meadows. The hillsides were covered with tall pines. There was a majesty about the whole scene. Everything seemed so peaceful.

"Don't be fooled by this peaceful feeling," Pat remarked. "This can be a harsh land."

Sage was wearing buckskins. The horse Joe had chosen for him was strong and bred to the mountains. Sage liked his horse—it was half-mustang, and eager for the journey. The mustang had a soft brown color that blended well with the terrain. Sage felt good about being out in the wild again; he was at home here. All of his old senses were awakened, and he felt alive and a part of it. He thought the mules would be slow, but they weren't. They were better on the mountain trails than the horses. At times, they were stubborn, but their handlers were up to the task, and they, too, were enjoying the trip.

They had packed food for the journey. They stopped in a glen by a mountain stream to eat their midday meal, and allow the animals to rest and graze. Sage sensed that Pat, too, was feeling at home in the mountains, and again he saw by watching him why he was called a mountain man. He was equally at home here or in Santa Fe.

Early in the afternoon, they saw a party of ten Indians. Sage sensed that they meant no harm.

Pat said, "They're an Arapaho hunting party."

The Indians were wary of the white men, and stopped a short distance away. Pat signaled to them and then said to Sage, "Come with me." They went to the Indians, and Pat told them why he and his companions were passing through their hunting grounds.

Sage remembered some of the words the Arapaho were using. They were words he had learned when he was with Evening Star. He asked them about the tribe of Arapaho he had known in Indian Territory. They said that they knew of the tribe, but they knew very little about them other than that their chief was called Chief Long Knife. They had heard that the tribe was still having difficulty with the Comanche and the Kiowa. Pat gave them tobacco and salt. The Indians gave Pat blue stones called "turquoise," like the ones they wore as ornaments. The Indians raised their hands in a salutation and rode away.

Sage was impressed by how well Pat spoke their language.

"I lived among them for a time several years ago," Pat explained. "Most of the time they want to be friendly. If you know them, you can tell when they are not friendly or when they want to take what you have. They always want wool blankets and metal tools. They like salt and tobacco, but they prefer knives and axes. Guns are not much use to them because they have no powder or shot. That may change, now that they can use cartridges, like the ones in the new guns. It would be bad for white men if Indians ever get guns."

Pat found a sheltered spot for the night, near running water, with plenty of grass for the animals and a supply of wood for their campfire.

While the others were setting up camp, Sage moved off into the hills and returned with a deer ready to be cooked. Both Pat and Grant were aware of Sage's skill at hunting, but the mule handlers were not. They had not heard a gun fired and was amazed that Sage could come back so soon with a fully dressed animal without firing his gun.

Pat smiled and explained, "He's had lots of practice, and can get food anytime he wants."

After they tended the animals, they sat around the fire talking. Pat told stories of his adventures in the mountains. He told them about living with the Indians and learning to speak five Indian languages. Grant told about his life on the trail with wagon trains. He said that handling the problems which arise among the people can be just about as difficult as handling the problems with the Indians or the terrain.

"Men and women can find the damnedest things to argue about," Grant chuckled, "when they're restrained for long periods of time. Even though the wagon train is traveling through wide-open spaces, the people are still confined in a group."

After the storytelling, each man retired to his bedroll and to his own thoughts while he waited for sleep to overtake him. Each looked at the sky with the whole universe in display. It was a time to think and reflect on your life. Sage thought about where he came from, and where he wanted his life to go.

*   *   *   *

Next morning, they went through the pass. Bent's Fort was only a few hours' ride from the pass. They arrived at the trading post before dark. People were there from all over the area. There were mountain men, hunters, trappers, adventurers, prospectors, and people from other wagon trains on their way west. Grant knew the wagon masters, and Pat knew many of the mountain men. They drank and swapped stories.

White women were rare in the West, and they were attracting a lot of attention. The fathers and husbands of the women were nervous, but the women were enjoying the attention while pretending to be indifferent to it. It was always an explosive situation, having women around men who had not seen a woman for a long time. Most men were shy, but some were bold. And that always caused trouble. Fathers of the young unmarried women didn't want their daughters getting involved with these men. They were not good prospects as husbands, and they sure didn't want their women getting pregnant as a result of an encounter with one of these men.

The trading post was surprisingly well stocked. It had goods for mountain men and the travelers alike. Grant and Pat bought the things they needed. Sage was in luck. Becknell was at the trading post buying the trade goods for his next mule train to Saint Louis. Grant introduced Sage to him. Sage told Becknell he would like to join his train eastbound and that he would be hauling a load of silver bullion to Saint Louis.

"I'll buy it from you here," Becknell said, "or I'll haul it for you. I'll guarantee that I'll try to get your silver to the market, but I can't guarantee I'll get it there. That's why the price I pay for it here is much less than you could get for it in Saint Louis. If you want to bring your own wagon and driver, I'll be glad to have you along for the added guns to protect my goods as well as yours. You'll be responsible for your own wagon and animals. I suggest you bring an extra pair of mules and a couple of extra wheels for your wagon. Wagons do break down, and we can't take the time to repair them on the trail. You can't leave a load of silver bullion lying out on the plains; it might not be there when you get back."

Grant told Becknell, "This young man has experience on the trail, and he will be a good man to have along in case of trouble. I'll see to it that he has all the tools and supplies he'll need for the journey."

"Then be here in two weeks," Becknell said. "That's when we'll be leaving."

"I'll be here with my wagon and drivers, thank you," Sage replied. Then he turned to Pat and said, "Well, fellows, as soon as I can buy a ring for Juanita, I'll be ready to get back for Joe and Bonnie's wedding."

"Sounds good," Pat responded. "We'll camp on the trail. The mules will be loaded, so the journey back will take a little longer, although after we go through the pass, it's downhill all the way."

Sage was happy with the mustang Joe had selected for him—he was strong, fast, and sure-footed. He was eager and manageable. Sage trained him to come when he whistled and named him, "Rambler." A rider needs to be friends with his horse. The horse and rider are a team, each looks out for the other. The mustang was not as showy as the Arabian stallion, but he was dependable because he had been bred to the rugged West.

Sage said, "I'll have to remember to thank Joe, for making a good selection. Rambler is the right horse for this rough country."

The trip back was easy, and Sage was eager to see Juanita. He knew what he needed to do, to get ready to take the load of silver to market. He would go all the way to Saint Louis, sell the silver, in exchange for gold coins. Then his men would return with the coins to Santa Fe. He would accompany the train until it reached the point closest to his cave. There, he would leave the train and go on alone to keep his promise to Evening Star. He would go to his cave first. It would be like going home. Sometimes he missed the evenings watching his little animal friends playing in the meadow.

When Sage arrived back at *El Casa Grande*, Juanita was expecting him and came running to greet him. She wanted to show him the results of the four days' work on diverting the stream. One more day and they would be ready to start the water flowing. The water would run through the courtyard, and everyone was excited. Juanita told him how wonderful it was to have the people working together again.

One of the vaqueros came to get Sage's horse. Sage said, "Take good care of the horse; Rambler's been a good mount for the journey." When Sage was sure the horse would be well tended, he went into the big house with Juanita. The housekeepers had a meal prepared. Sage told Juanita about the trip and his plans for taking the bullion to Saint Louis. Juanita was pleased that they would get twice as much for the silver this way. That was equal to a year's work for all their miners. She hated to see him go, but it was a trip worth making.

After the meal, they went for a walk in the twilight. Sage gave her the ring as a pledge that he would return. With tears in her eyes, she accepted the ring and promised to wear it in memory of this time, and to wait for his return. Sage told her that when he returned, they would plan for their marriage, if she would consider sharing her life with him.

"You are the man I want for my husband." Juanita whispered. "I'll wait for you no matter how long it takes. But please hurry back. My life will be empty until you return."

She continued, "I've been working with Bonnie, helping her get ready for their wedding. A protestant minister will marry them in the little chapel in Santa Fe. There'll be a wedding reception at the McBain Ranch. Many of the ranch owners and many of the business people of Santa Fe will be there.

"Everyone will get a chance to meet the new bride and groom, and get acquainted with the new manager of the McBain Ranch. They're also looking forward to meeting the new owner. They've heard much about you. I'm so proud of you. You must be tired. Will you sleep in one of the guest rooms? We have a room ready."

"Yes, I'm tired, and I'll sleep here tonight. Tomorrow I want to see the work you've done. I want to be here for the opening of the stream and watch with the water make its first run through the grounds. I want to thank you and all of the workers for working so hard and getting it done so quickly. Then I have to prepare the wagon and get the supplies ready for the trip to Saint Louis. There's much to be done, and we have only a few days to do it.

"I'll prepare the wagon so it can be defended from either bandits or Indians. We'll be hauling valuable cargo, so I'll make the wagon into a rolling fortress. Men will be able to stand inside it and defend it against all attackers. We'll build sideboards of heavy wood that can be quickly put into place. The defenders will be able to remove the sideboards and store them under the wagon when they're not in use. There'll be a false bottom in the wagon to hide the gold coins we'll be hauling back from Saint Louis. The wagon will look like just another freight wagon loaded with trade goods. Should anyone look for the gold, they won't find it."

"That's a wonderful idea. The workers will be glad to help you fortify the wagon and prepare it for the journey. I'll feel better knowing you're prepared in the event of trouble. It's such a long and dangerous trip, and I fear for you. Yes, I know you're capable of handling yourself, but still, I'll worry."

"Please tell the ladies that I'm an early riser, and I'll want breakfast at sunrise. If that's too early for you, then I'll see you when you get up."

"No, I want to have breakfast with you. Then I want to show you what we did while you were gone."

Sage took her in his arms and said, "I'd better not hold you like this very long; I won't be able to sleep. Good night, I'll see you at breakfast tomorrow morning."

The guest room was spacious. The bed was made of heavy wood with a mattress of linen stuffed with cotton. It had linen sheets with pillows. The room was furnished with a table made from hand-cut wood and two stuffed leather chairs. The bathtub was filled with hot water; soap and towels lay nearby. The room was lit by candles. This was better than his room at the hotel.

One of the ladies knocked on the door and told him to leave his clothes outside his door, so they could be washed and ironed.

"They'll be ready when you wake up tomorrow morning," she said.

I could learn to like this," Sage thought. *It'll take me a while to adjust, but I could learn to like having someone attend to my needs.* For Sage to go from having no human companionship at all, to having someone serving his every need was almost too much. He was used to doing things for himself, and it made him uneasy having others doing things for him.

Before he went to sleep, he wondered where Juanita was sleeping. He thought, *"I better not think about her, or I won't get any sleep."*

When he awoke, his clothes were impeccably done. He washed his face and shaved, then went to the dining room. Two ladies were there, ready to serve him. They asked him what he wanted for breakfast. He told them he would like two scrambled eggs, with bacon, coffee, and bread.

Then he said, "Please wait to prepare it until Juanita arrives. I want to have breakfast with her." They brought him a cup of coffee while he waited. He didn't have to wait long; she soon appeared, beautiful in her bright, shiny boots with a dark skirt and white blouse; her hair was combed back, showing her fine profile.

She smiled and greeted him with a kiss on the cheek and asked, "How did you sleep?"

"I slept well." Turning to the housekeepers he said, "And thank you, ladies, for the nice bed and for having my bath ready. Also, thank you for washing my clothes."

Juanita smiled, "I'll have whatever Sage is having." The ladies smiled and brought the food. Juanita told Sage about all the exciting things that had been happening. After breakfast, she took his hand to show him the work that they had done on the streambed.

"All that's left to do," she said, "is to complete the leaching fields and the filtering system, so the water will be cleaned before it re-enters the river. Then we'll open the dam at the head of the stream, and the water will begin flowing through the grounds."

Everyone was up early to see this happen.

At first, the running water picked up the dirt in the channel, but soon the dirt was washed away, and the stream ran clean and clear. Each lady wanted to be the first to get water from the new stream.

"Now we must do the same thing for Joe and Bonnie," Juanita suggested.

The workers agreed. "We're ready to start."

"We'll have to wait until after the wedding," Sage said. "We don't want to interfere with their wedding plans. As soon as the wedding is over, we'll begin the work."

The man whom the miners had selected as their foreman said, "If we can't do the new channel, let's go back to work at the mines."

"The first thing you must do," Sage said, "is to fill that old mineshaft. It's too dangerous to leave it open."

The workers were glad to erase all traces of the hated Vacca from the mine forever.

"We'll do that today," the foreman replied. "Bring your tools, men, let's go."

Sage called out, "I need two carpenters and one blacksmith to work with me today." Three men stepped forward.

Sage showed them what he wanted done, and showed them how he wanted metal brackets attached to the sides of the wagon to hold sideboards that could be quickly assembled or disassembled. When the sideboards were assembled, eight men could stand behind them and fire through openings cut into the boards without exposing themselves to attackers. Then he had the workers build a false bottom in the wagon for hauling concealed cargo. The workers were surprised; the idea was so simple yet so effective.

"Why had it never been done before?" they asked.

"It has been done," Sage said. "I learned to do it from my father."

They made a container to hold an extra supply of water for the animals. The wagon was rigged to carry two extra wheels. They installed two more racks for barrels: one for salt pork, and the other for flour and meal. They made containers to carry coffee and other necessities. Sage made sure he had a bucket of grease for the wheels.

After this was done, the wagon was ready. Sage talked to Grant and Pat, both experienced men, in what a wagon would need. He wanted to be sure that he hadn't forgotten anything.

When he showed the wagon to Juanita, she said, "I don't know much about fighting Indians, but it looks to me like eight men could stand off a whole tribe of Indians from inside that wagon."

"That's the idea. We can use this wagon for future deliveries of our bullion to the best markets available, without having to sell the bullion for less than it is worth. I'm ready, and now I can concentrate on running the ranch and being the best man for Joe, at his wedding. I would like to have a meeting with you and Carlos. Let's see if Carlos can talk with us for a while."

Juanita asked one of the workers to find Carlos and have him meet them in the big house. Juanita and Sage waited for Carlos, while the men working on the wagon put the finishing touches to it. When Carlos arrived, they sat in the master room.

Sage said, "I want the ranch to be completely self-sustaining. We must produce everything we need. I want the valley land planted in corn, beans, potatoes, tomatoes, onions, peppers, sugar beets, and whatever else we may need. We'll produce our own sugar from sugar beets. Sugar will provide a tasty addition to our diet.

"We have cows for milk, cheese, and butter; chickens for eggs and meat; pigs for meat and cooking oil. Sheep will provide wool from which we can make clothes and blankets. About the only things we can't provide for ourselves are things like cooking spices. We have a wagon going to Saint Louis, so make a list of what each of you need. Perhaps we should buy a plow for tilling the fields. We could bring back things like vanilla, cinnamon, black pepper, and salt, just to name a few things that will make our lives more interesting."

"That's a wonderful idea," Juanita said. "I'll make a list. Maybe you could buy books for the children. If we're going to teach them to read and write, they'll need books."

Carlos, normally a calm man, was excited. "The plows are a good idea. We'll need extra plow shears. I'll make a list, also. We could use the water from the diverted stream to irrigate the fields."

"Carlos, work with Juanita," Sage suggested. "The two of you will run the ranch while I'm gone. Juanita, you can rely on Joe and Bonnie for help. They'll be glad to work with you in any way you might need. The wagon will be back this summer, and I'll be back no later than this fall. Carlos, would you select two good, reliable men to drive the mules? I want to train them to use guns. Single men would be best. I don't want to put the fathers of children at risk on such a dangerous journey. Please send them to me tomorrow morning. I'll begin their training."

"Si, Señor, I know two young men who will be glad to make the journey."

"Good. Also," Sage continued, "I need four good mules for pulling the wagon. We'll be leaving in a few days. We have to meet the mule train in ten days. Now I have to meet with Joe and Frank to arrange for them to begin the work on their ranch. Juanita, would you like to ride with me? You could visit with Bonnie while I talk to Joe and Frank."

"Yes, I'll be ready in a few minutes," Juanita answered.

"Carlos, I'll see you tomorrow. I'll get your list and meet the young men."

"Si, Señor, *mañana*."

The ride along the river was pleasant. It was an early spring day. Flowers were just beginning to bloom. It was a wonderful time for two young people in love. They talked of the things they wanted to do with the ranch. They were both thinking of their life together, but neither wanted to talk about it until Sage returned.

When they arrived at the McBain Ranch, they found everyone preparing for the wedding, which was only two days away. Juanita went to Bonnie and Thelma and offered her help. They were preparing to receive guests.

Sage found Joe; he wanted to talk to both him and Frank. Joe called his prospective father-in-law, and they sat down with Sage. Sage told them about the diversionary stream and suggested they do the same.

"You can use the water for irrigation, and the plants in the fields will filter the water before it flows back into the river," Sage explained.

They both liked the idea. Then Sage asked if they had enough money to operate the ranch until they could build up a herd of horses to make it profitable. They thought they had enough, but it might get a little tight down the road a ways. Sage told them to use some of the gold coins that were left to him by his father. This would allow them to develop the ranch at a more rapid pace until they could get horses ready to sell.

He then suggested that they grow crops to make their ranch and its people self-sufficient, like they were doing at Juanita's ranch. The excess crops could be sold in Santa Fe to get extra cash for operating the ranch. They immediately saw the advantage of doing it that way.

Sage said, "I'll be bringing plows back from Saint Louis for the Diego ranch. I could bring plows for you also. I can buy another wagon if more space is needed. There'll be plenty of men in Saint Louis who'll be willing to drive the mules."

Joe and Frank were pleased and said they would make a list. Everything necessary to succeed had been taken care of.

Sage told Joe how pleased he was with the horse he had selected in exchange for the stallion. He mentioned that a cross between the Arabian and mustang would produce a horse that would have both size and stamina. Such an animal would have the advantage of both breeds. He suggested they round up as many wild horses they could, and select only the best for breeding purposes. In that way, they would have a herd in no time. They could sell the animals that weren't good enough for breeding purposes. Both Joe and Frank agreed and were eager to start rounding up wild horses.

"Now, let's get back to helping the ladies," Sage said. When they were again in the company of the women, he mentioned that he had to get the clothes he would be wearing as best man.

"Juanita is going to be the maid of honor, and she'll want to get everything ready, also. Juanita and I will ride into Santa Fe tomorrow morning, but tonight we'll need a place to sleep."

Joe said, "We can prepare rooms for you here at the main house. There's plenty of room."

"That's a splendid idea," Bonnie replied. "Sage and Juanita will be my first guests. We can talk of what we'll need for the wedding."

Sage said, "Then it's all set. As soon as we get our clothes, we'll be ready. We can lay out the plans for diverting the stream. I would like to get that done, so it can be completed right away. The miners have done one stream, and they'll be able to do this one even more quickly."

"Thank you," Frank said. "That will solve several problems all at once."

Bonnie told the ladies to prepare a special meal for their first guests and to prepare two of the guest rooms for Juanita and Sage.

After dinner, they talked well into the night. Bonnie was glad to have Juanita to advise her on how to make guests comfortable.

When Sage told Juanita that he wanted to go to Santa Fe to get the things he would need to wear, she told him that she already had her dress, but she would help him select a tailor to sew his special clothes. Sage was pleased to have her help him. It was something he had no experience in doing. The girls were discussing the suit Sage would wear. Sage could see that all he had to do was be there, and everything would be taken care of.

Sage and Juanita rode into Santa Fe the following morning to get his suit made. The tailor Juanita chose was the best in town. When the tailor was told what the suit was for, he put everything else aside to work on this order. He had to complete it today because the wedding was going to be tomorrow. After the tailor took his measurements, he asked Sage to be back in two hours, and the suit would be ready for a final fitting. He and Juanita went to the hotel for breakfast, and when they returned, Sage tried on the beautifully tailored suit. All it needed were a few adjustments. For the first time, Juanita saw the man she loved dressed in the manner in which she was accustomed. Sage had donned the formal garment of Spanish aristocracy and she was pleased. He was bigger than the men she had seen before, but he looked great in his new outfit.

When Sage and Juanita returned to the ranch, the two young men were waiting. Sage took two boxes of cartridges, and began their training. They proved to be adept students, and in a few hours they were able to fire the guns with a high degree of accuracy.

Sage showed them the wagon and taught them how to install the barricades to make the wagon a rolling fortress. They would leave in three days. In the meantime, they had to learn to harness the mules and care for the wagon. Sage checked with them to make sure they were proficient. They were strong young men and eager to begin the journey.

*   *   *   *

The next morning, Sage, Juanita, and many of their people rode to the McBain Ranch for the wedding. Joe and Bonnie decided to hold their wedding at the ranch in a grove of large trees beside the river. The ride to and from the chapel was too far, and not all of the people who wanted to attend would fit in the chapel.

The grove was decorated with flowers and brightly colored ribbons. The musicians played. The place was lovely, and there was plenty of room for their guests.

Joe, dressed in black and white, was a handsome bridegroom.

When Bonnie came down the aisle on her father's arm, she was like a dream come true. She was dressed in white silk and Spanish lace, her red hair shining in the early morning sun. She was beaming with happiness.

"Sage," Joe said softly while waiting for the girls, "I've faced many men with guns, and I've never been so nervous. Is it possible that a guy like me is being married to a girl so beautiful? Thank you for all you have done for me, and thank you for being my best man. Now, don't you let me stumble and make a fool of myself."

Juanita, as maid of honor, was glowing, also. She presented a quiet elegance that left no doubt that she was the descendant of nobility. Sage couldn't take his eyes off her. She glanced at him, gave him a little smile and a wink.

The grove was as quiet as a chapel while the wedding vows were being exchanged. When it was over, a cheer went up, and the newlyweds greeted their guests. The wine and the food were delicious. The ranch owners, the people from Santa Fe, and the people from the wagon train were all there. Maggie brought her musicians with her, and they played while the dancing girls performed and the guests celebrated.

As the evening wore on, the guests started leaving. Some had to ride for hours to make the return journey to their ranches. After a time, there were only a few close friends and members of the family remaining. Sage sat quietly on a bench under the big tree near the veranda. It was a lovely old ranch house. There had been many celebrations in this house, and there would be many more.

Juanita came and sat beside him and held his hand. It felt good to be sitting there with the woman he loved and with his friends around him. The changes in his life had been profound. He thought of his parents and wished they could be here. He would have liked for them to meet Juanita.

Juanita whispered in his ear and said, "We must go now and leave the newlyweds alone." He nodded and called for a wagon to take them back to their place. They tied the reins of their horses to the tailgate. Sage lifted Juanita up on the back of the wagon, and they rode along with their feet hanging over the end, discussing the things that needed to be done before Sage could leave with the wagonload of bullion.

"I'm leaving," Sage said, "but never doubt, I will return. You're the most important thing in my life, and you always will be."

CHAPTER 20

▼

THE MULE TRAIN
TO SAINT LOUIS

"Juanita, I'll be taking only the silver bullion to Saint Louis, and leave the gold here. Carlos is the only other person who knows where we hid it. No one else needs to know. I'll bring the gold coins back, hidden in the false bottom of the wagon. You and I will be the only persons who know that the coins are there. Not even the drivers will know. When the wagons return, if I'm not here, get Carlos to help you store the gold. I'll be back as soon as I can complete what I have to do."

Juanita snuggled in his arms and said, "I'll live only for your return. We'll share the ranch and have a wonderful life."

*　　　*　　　*　　　*

Sage awoke early and spent his time going over everything, making sure nothing was overlooked. He rode to the wagon camp to bid farewell to the people leaving for California. When he arrived, Sally came to him and again thanked him for saving her life.

She said, "I'll always remember you and wish you well."

"Have a good life in California," Sage said, "and perhaps some day our trails will cross again."

Then Sage returned to the hacienda and asked Carlos to help load the bullion. He placed two armed guards at the wagon and then went to Juanita. He wanted to spend as much time with her as he could before leaving. Everything was working well at the ranch, and there was no reason to believe that it wouldn't continue that way until he returned.

The following morning, after breakfast, Sage and Juanita went to the wagon. The drivers were saying goodbye to their families. Sage dressed in buckskins, the same as when he first came to Santa Fe. He was once again a man of the Great Plains. He carried his ax under his arm and his knife in its scabbard. The only difference was that he now carried a revolver in a holster at his waist.

Sage and his drivers began the journey to Bent's Fort. They arrived one day before the mule train was to leave. The leader of the mule train was named McFarland. They called him "Mac." Sage took Mac to look at the wagon, and showed him how the barriers fit, making the wagon into a fort, to stand off an attack.

Mac said, "Eight men with guns could stand off a whole tribe of Indians in that wagon. I don't know why I never thought of it."

The bullion was intentionally open to view. Sage didn't want anyone to know about the false bottom. It was made in a way that it was almost impossible to detect. Yet, you could store a ton of bullion it.

While waiting to depart, two men came into the fort and said, "The Arapahos are on the prod. They're looking for four men who raped and killed some of their women. If the Indians can find the men, they'll kill them, and those four lousy bastards need to be killed. You'd better be on the lookout for both the Indians and the four men."

"Thank you for the information and your concern," Mac said. And then he finished securing the packs of beaver pelts and otter skins to the mules, and headed out. The trip east didn't hold the feeling of adventure that the trip west held, but it was just as difficult and just as dangerous.

The trail followed the Arkansas and the Missouri rivers. It would take several months, and every mile was fraught with hardships and danger.

The mule train consisted of 28 mules led by seven riders on horse-back. Each rider was responsible for four mules. Sage scouted for the mule train and his Mexican drivers.

Pack mules walked where the wagon couldn't go, so Sage had to look for a route for the wagon. At times, the wagon would be miles from the mule train. Everyone met at night and shared the same camp-site. When the wagon was alone, it was vulnerable to attack. Sage was constantly on the lookout for trouble. That trouble could be Indians, bandits, bad weather, or difficult river crossings. As scout, he had many things to watch for other than Indians. He had to be concerned about food and water for the people and the animals. Every night, when Sage returned to camp, he came with fresh meat and knowledge of condi-tions ahead that Mac could use while planning the next day's journey.

At night, the drivers taught Sage the Mexican language, and he taught them English.

One day, Sage came upon two Arapaho warriors. They were ready to attack until he gave the sign of peace, then they allowed him to approach. Sage told them that his people knew why they were looking for the bad men. If his people found them, he would let the Arapaho know, and allow them to deal with the bad men in their own way.

Sage asked them if they knew of Chief Long Knife and his sub-chief Black Crow. They said they had heard of Chief Long Knife, but they had not seen him for many years. They told Sage that the southern Arapaho were talking of moving back to their ancestral hunting grounds in Colorado. The Comanche and the Kiowa were banding together to drive the Arapaho out. The warriors didn't know about Black Crow or Evening Star. They told Sage they would not bother the mule train, and that they would check with him farther down the trail, to see if he had encountered the men they were looking for.

At last, the mule train passed north of Indian Territory. Sage could have ridden to the cave in a few days, but first he had to make sure that the bullion got to Saint Louis safely, then purchase the things on the list.

He had so many things to bring back that he would probably need to buy another wagon. If he bought another wagon, he would have to hire two more drivers and mules to pull the wagon. He would accompany the wagons to this spot on the return trip, and then go to his cave.

The next day, the mule train came upon a gruesome scene—somebody had slain a group of Osage Indians—women, children, and old men. The women had been ravaged; the children and old men had been wantonly slain. This was not the work of Indians. This was the work of deranged white men. These men must be found and dealt with.

Sage left camp early the next morning, long before the mule train was ready to go. A few miles out, he came across the tracks of four horses that were being ridden at a gallop westbound. Now, why would the four riders be going west in such a hurry? Suddenly it occurred to him that they were after the bullion! The people at the trading post knew that he would be hauling bullion. The riders had somehow gotten word of it and were here to steal it!

Shortly after his drivers broke camp, a wheel came off. The pin holding the locking nut had fallen out. Sage's men told Mac that they had a spare wheel and could handle the problem. They would just put the wheel back on, and be on the trail in no time.

The train continued, with the understanding that the wagon would rejoin them when they stopped for lunch. But since the wagon didn't show up, Mac sent one of his drivers back to see what had happened.

The four men who were going to steal Sage's bullion saw the man Mac had sent back. They lay in ambush and shot him off his horse.

The men in the wagon heard the shot, put up the barricades, and waited to see who had fired the shots. In a short time, the thieves showed up, expecting an easy time of killing the two drivers. When they attacked, the drivers hid behind the barricade and put up a strong resistance. Afraid the mules would be killed, one of the drivers released them to allow them to run away. The drivers knew they could retrieve them once the problem with the robbers had been dealt with. While the driver was trying to get back into the wagon, he was shot in the shoulder. He could still fire his revolver, but the wound was painful.

The thieves realized they couldn't drive the defenders from the wagon and decided to burn them out, if they could drag brush under the wagon and set it on fire. The fire would drive the defenders out into the open. The bullion wouldn't burn, and they could take all their horses could carry.

Sage heard gunfire and proceeded carefully. His drivers would be able to make a stand until he could get behind the bandits and eliminate them one at a time.

Sage saw one of the men trying to pull up a dead bush. He hit him over the head with the butt of his pistol, gagged him, and tied him up with his arms and legs around a tree. He then continued looking until he spotted the leader who was watching the others gather dry brush.

When the one Sage had tied didn't return, the leader called out, "Deet, what's holding you up? Get that wood over here. We've got to get out of here before people in that mule train show up. I hope that wild man shows up. I still want to see if he's as tough as they say. I'll beat him with my fists, then putting a bullet through him . . . . Carl, go see what's holding Deet up."

Sage stepped back and waited for Carl. When Carl saw his companion tied up, he looked around, but it was too late. The blunt end of a knife hit him between the eyes with a thud. He, too, was soon tied up. Now, Sage had only two more to deal with.

When the firing stopped, the drivers wondered what had happened. They could see the leader, but he too far away to get a shot at, so they just waited, knowing that Sage would show up soon.

"Skinner," the leader of the four said to the man near him, "bring your wood on over here, and let's get this fire started. I want to get out of here."

Before Skinner could move, Sage hit him on the head. Then Sage threw his knife and pinned the leader's gun arm to the tree he was standing beside. The ruffian's startled look was frozen. He hadn't heard or seen anything, before he felt the knife pin his arm to the tree.

Sage walked to him and said, "Now, at long last, you're going to find out just how wild a wild man can be. I tried to be your friend. You rejected my offer. You raped and killed Arapaho women, and then killed a group of friendly Osage Indians. You raped their women, and killed their old men and children. You have killed one of our men, and you're trying to steal something that doesn't belong to you. I'm going to turn you and your men over to the Arapaho warriors. You have broken their law and killed their people. You will stand trial by their law and face their justice."

The mule drivers saw Sage take control of the robbers, so they came out, got the mules, and hooked them back to the wagon.

"Tie these men to those trees," Sage said. "Tie them with their hands and feet around the trees. If they even try to get away, shoot them. I know where those Arapaho warriors are, and I'll be back with them in a couple of hours. One of you, go see what you can do for the man Mac sent to help you."

When Sage returned with the warriors, Mac and some of his men were at the wagon. The drivers had told Mac what had happened.

"Sage," Mac asked, "are you going to turn these men over to those warriors? Do you have any idea what they'll do to them?"

Sage replied, "These thieves killed one of your men. You can take any one of them, to deal with as you wish for that killing. They killed two Arapaho women. The Arapaho men could deal with two of them as they wish for that crime. Then I will take the other one to the Osage to deal with for killing their women, children, and old men. Does that seem fair to you?"

Mac, seeing the logic of Sage's thinking, said, "Yes, it does."

Sage then explained the proposal to the warriors. They, too, felt that would be fair, and they accepted the arrangement.

Sage said to Mac, "Okay, pick your man, but be prepared to explain to the dead man's family what you did to the man who killed their loved one."

"I couldn't do that," Mac said. "I wouldn't know which one to pick."

"Okay, let's give them a trial. Ask them who killed your man."

Each of the thieves blamed the killing on the others. They were all shouting, and saying that they didn't know who had killed the man Mac had sent.

"Who raped the women?" Sage asked.

They each accused the other. They all raped the women, the warriors said.

"Who killed the old men and children, and who raped the Osage women?" Mac asked.

They had all participated in the killing and the rapes.

Sage asked, "Now what should we do? Do you want to let them go free to continue killing and raping?"

"No!" No one wanted to let them go free.

"Now, who wants to kill them?" Sage asked.

"Why don't we just leave them tied to the trees and let the animals take care of them?" Mac suggested.

"I promised these warriors that we would let them deal with these horrible creatures. I'll keep my promise," Sage replied.

Mac said, "Okay, I'll go along with that."

Sage then asked the warriors what they wanted to do with the men. The warriors talked together for a while, and then the leader said, "Strip them of their clothes and all their tools, then leave them to survive like the animals of the prairie. They're no better than animals, so they should live as the animals do."

Everyone thought that was a good idea. The robbers were relieved that their lives had been saved, so that was what was done. They were stripped of everything, and turned loose on the Great Plains completely naked, to see if they could survive. Everyone watched the killers stumble away, and then the Arapaho and the people in the mule train went their separate ways.

Mother Nature has a way of dealing with those who break her rules, Sage thought.

The train moved on following the south side of the Arkansas. One afternoon, they saw a dark cloud in the west. A storm was on the way. Because of the difficult terrain on the south side, they had to cross the river, and they had to do it before the storm caused it to rise so much that they were unable to cross.

The crossing was downstream, so they hurried to reach it. Sage and his men tied two logs to the sides of the wagon, to make it float. Sage rode his horse across the river and tied a rope to a tree on the other side. Then he had the drivers tie the other end of the rope to the wagon and push it into the river. The moving water swung the floating wagon to the other side just like it was on a pendulum. The drivers swam alongside the wagon, and drove the mules out of the river just as it began to rise out of control.

A funnel-type formation extended from the dark cloud! Sage had seen these storms before and knew that they could be very destructive. He and his men unhooked the mules and used heavy ropes to tie the wagon to large boulders because this kind of wind could rip even the largest trees from the ground. They finished tying the ropes just as chunks of hail as large as hen eggs began falling.

They got under the wagon seeking protection from the hail. The wind grew stronger and stronger until it looked like the ropes might break. The heavy wagon bounced up and down against the ropes, as the men hung on. Branches flew through the air, and some of the men were hit and injured. At last, the wind stopped, just as suddenly as it had started.

No one knew what to do so they waited. Soon the river began to flood, and they had to hurry and get out of the valley before the swirling water swept them away. They hitched the mules and dragged the wagon to safety.

"I think we'd better camp here," Mac said, "and take stock of our damage. Tomorrow morning will be plenty early for us to continue."

The men gathered their scattered mules and horses. It was getting dark before they found them all. Tonight, they would be without warm food; perhaps tomorrow, Sage could provide meat for their breakfast.

The farther east the mule train traveled, the more vegetation was evident, and the more rolling the terrain became. The trees were larger, and the streams were larger. Sage was enjoying the fruit and berries he remembered.

Days passed and the mule train entered areas that had been settled by farmers and ranchers. Children were playing in the yards, bridges crossed the streams, people waved to them as they passed. They had reached civilization!

Saint Louis, with all its houses and buildings, seemed crowded—people were everywhere. Sage was more lost here than he had ever been on the Great Plains or in the high mountains; it was uncomfortable.

"Mac," Sage asked, "why are they looking at me in such a strange way?"

"It's because of the way you're dressed. They're not used to seeing men dressed completely in skins."

"Well, I guess I'd better change into my other clothes, but where do I go to change?"

Mac laughed. "Scary isn't it? Makes you wish you were back on the prairie. We'd better sell this cargo, and then get a hotel room. I don't know about you, but I'd like to have a drink. My men are in a hurry to find whiskey and women. I've got to sell these furs before I can pay the men. Let's trade that silver bullion for gold coins. Then you can put your wagon and mules in a stable. They'll care for them until you're ready to return.

"There's a man I know who'll buy your silver, and he won't cheat you. He'll pay in gold, and hold the gold until you're ready to go back. There are many men here who'll try to steal it from you, and you couldn't use your ax and knife to defend yourself, the way you do out on the plains. You'll get in a lot of trouble doing that here."

"Then how do you defend yourself?"

"You don't. The law is supposed to take care of that for you."

"But what if they don't?"

"Then you have to go to court, to settle the disagreement."

"How long does that take?"

"Sometimes it takes months, even years. Oftentimes the thieves are in cahoots with the law, and you never get your money back. It's called civilization."

"Does it work?"

"Oh, yeah, it works just fine, for the men who run the system, but it doesn't work worth a damn for the rest of the people."

"Why do the people put up with such a system?"

"How are they going to change it? The men who control the system make all the rules. It's like sitting in on a poker game where your opponent is the dealer. He decides what game you play; he deals the cards, and he gets all the trumps. If you object to the way the game is played, you're called a troublemaker, and the dealer has the law haul you off to the jail. Then, while you're in jail, the crook takes all your money. If you object, he has you thrown back in jail. If you think I'm kidding, just look around you. There are only a few big houses in this system, and all the rest are slums where the workers live. That's the way it works . . . . Nothing we can do about it . . . . Now, let's sell that silver. Just follow my lead."

The man who purchased the silver told them he would hold the gold until they were ready, just like Mac had said.

"How do we know he'll give us the gold if we can't force him to give it to us?" Sage asked as they walked away.

"He's in the silver-trading business. If he doesn't give us our gold, then we won't bring him any more silver, and he'll be out of business. He gives us a piece of paper that says he'll give us the gold when we come after it. It's called civilization."

"But what if he doesn't?"

"Then you take him to court, and he has all the lawyers, and often-times the court is on his side. If you're lucky, you might get part of it. Again, it is called civilization."

"I'm not so sure I like this civilization. I think our method is better."

"I agree. That's why I live in the West, where men are judged by their courage, not by how well they follow other men's rules." Mac turned the corner, and said, "Now, come with me while I sell my furs. Then we'll find a place for these animals. And after we've done that, we'll find a place where we can stay."

The fur traders were down by the river. The trading of furs was more complex than the trading of silver and gold. The buyer had to examine each bundle, one bundle at a time, and then decide what he would pay. It took a long time, but finally the trading was done. The fur trader said he would hold the payment until Mac was ready to go back to Bent's Fort.

"That's quite a system they have," Sage noted.

Mac smiled. "In the big cities back east, I understand they have places called banks, where the bank keeps your money, charges you for keeping it safe, and then charge you again for taking it out. We'd better thank God we live in a place where words like honesty, decency, and integrity still have meaning, because those words lose all meaning in this system. Let's work to keep meaning in those words as long as we can. Civilization is coming all too fast."

＊   ＊   ＊   ＊

Saint Louis was bustling. Traffic was going up and down the Missis-sippi and the Ohio rivers. Wagon trains were forming for trips west. It was an exciting place. Sage walked around watching all the goings on. He spent three days purchasing the things on the lists, then made a special purchase of gifts for Juanita and Bonnie. He bought books, pencils, and paper for the children. He bought a hundred pounds of candy since there was no way to get candy in Santa Fe.

He bought plows for tilling, and seeds for planting. He had to buy another wagon with mules to pull it and two more drivers. The men would have to be armed and supplied. He had no trouble finding men, many of them from Europe. He hired two young immigrants from Ire-land who were eager to make the journey. After three days of prepar-ing, Sage was ready for the return trip.

The night before the train was to leave, Sage loaded the gold in the false bottom and slept in the wagon to guard them. No one else would know what the wagon was carrying. It looked like just another load of freight for the trading post.

Mac bought and loaded the supplies he would be taking back to the trading post. He then had to re-organize his mule train. Some of his men were staying in Saint Louis, so he had to hire more muleskinners. Most of the new men had to be trained. When the time came to begin the trip, even the animals seemed eager to get going. The animals had been well cared for, but the fresh water and grass on the trail was bet-ter.

The men from Ireland were having difficulty communicating with the Mexicans. Each was trying to learn the other's language, and all were better off for the experience.

After two weeks, things settled down. The new men began to under-stand how to do the things necessary for life on the trail. Life consisted of days and weeks of plodding along, following the rivers, and the sun.

There were always problems to face and difficulties to overcome. In the evenings, Sage instructed the new men to use their weapons, and told them what to expect in the event of an Indian attack.

The mule train was loaded with things the Indians would like to have, and there was a pretty good chance they would try to take it. Fourteen heavily armed men guarded the mule train, and only a very large or very foolish band of Indians would dare to attack. They traveled two months on the open plains and saw thousands of buffalo. Sage had no trouble providing meat.

It was summer and the evenings were warm. The men had just completed setting up camp and were cooking their food when Sage heard a lone coyote howl. The howl came from the trees down by the river. Then he heard up on the prairie a howl in reply. The howling of a coyote was not unusual, but Sage knew that this howl was very unusual. He had sat in the evenings by his cave listening to the sounds of the night too long to be fooled by an Indian, imitating the howl of a coyote. He sprang to his feet.

"Mac," he yelled, "get the mules bunched in that little draw and have the men tie them together and form a circle! We're going to be attacked by Indians!"

"What makes you think we're going to be attacked?" Mac asked.

"Please don't argue with me; just do as I say, and hurry."

Sage told his men, "Move the wagons into the mouth of that draw and get into the fortified wagon. Make sure you have plenty of ammunition and water. We're going to be attacked by Indians."

The men were astonished, but they knew better than to questions, so they quickly did as they were instructed. Sage then tied his horse between the two wagons.

"Mac," he yelled, "give me three of your best men to fire from the fortified wagon!"

"Sam! Luke! Wes!" Mac called out. "Get into that wagon with plenty of ammo! The rest of you men get under the wagons. That way, we'll have a heavily armed and concentrated fortress against the attack."

Just in time, the men reached the cover of the wagons. Out of the darkness arrows began to fly, and two of the men were hit by arrows. If it had been one moment later, it would have been too late.

"Sage," Mac asked, "how many of them do you reckon are out there?"

"I don't know, but there's probably a bunch, or they'd never dare to attack a group of this many armed men. One thing I know for sure, it's going to be a long night, so keep your eyes open. They'll be crawling in to pick us off as soon as it gets a little darker. Each man, choose a partner so you can cover each other's back."

Sage heard a man cry out and knew that one of the men had been hit with an arrow. He called to the man who had been wounded earlier, and asked, "Sam, can you still fire a gun?"

"Yeah," Sam replied, "they just got me in the leg."

"Well, get up here in the wagon and take my place. I can do more good out there in the dark."

"You sure won't have to ask me more than once. Here I come."

Sage slid silently out of the wagon and disappeared into the night. He had his knife, his ax, and his revolver. As the darkness closed around him, he became a part of the night itself. The brush and the tall grass were thick. The darkness was like a physical thing, engulfing everything. The threat of death hung in the air like a fog. Sage would rely on his highly trained five senses. His sense of smell told him that he was near to an enemy. Sage was lying completely still, taking shallow breaths to prevent being heard. His opponent was also a man of great stealth. Sage knew that the first man to move would be the first man to die. Time passed. Then just to his right, Sage felt the grass move.

Now, he knew where his enemy was. He continued to wait; he had to know where to strike. The strike must be silent, because there were probably more than one Indian hiding close by. Sage felt, more than heard, soft breathing. Then, quick as a striking rattler, his knife slashed out, and he severed the throat of his unsuspecting enemy. Sage rolled quickly out of the arch of a smashing tomahawk in the hands of another warrior. Sage's ax found its mark, and the second Indian lay permanently silenced.

Sage heard movement. He moved ever so slightly ahead and to his right and then waited, listening to determine what this new adversary would do. The new threat moved in the direction Sage had moved. The Indian could not imagine that a white man could beat him at his own game, so he made the mistake of believing he could move with less caution. That error in judgment cost him his life.

Through the night, many shots rang out, sometimes followed by the moan of wounded or dying men. The attackers were taking advantage of the darkness and attempting to kill as many of the defenders as they could, hoping to drive them into panic.

The attackers wanted to steal the animals, and as much freight as they could, hoping to do it with no loss to themselves. They didn't count on someone in the mule train coming out and attacking them on their own ground. They knew that this white warrior was there, but they couldn't find him. Finally, they realized he was decimating their numbers and decided the price they were paying was too high, so they withdrew into the night.

When darkness gave way to the coming light, the area was strewn with the bodies of dead Indians. The men in and under the wagons couldn't believe what they saw. The Indians who survived had just disappeared into the vastness of the Great Plains. No one would ever know how many of them there had been.

Sage was nowhere to be seen. No one knew what had happened to him or which way they should go to look for him. They were busy treating the wounded and burying their dead. By tying the mules together, they had prevented the Indians from stealing them. Two Indians had been killed by the muleskinners while they were trying to untie the mules. Not a single mule had been taken.

Just as they were getting the camp back in order, Sage came over the ridge with a fully dressed deer over his shoulders. Every man in the train was dumfounded. Sage had gone to the river, bathed, cleaned his clothes and weapons, killed and dressed a deer!

The train's losses had been two men dead, and two men wounded. There would have been more if Sage had not alerted them. The story of that night would be told around campfires for years to come.

After breakfast, Sage thanked his men for standing firm, then told them that he would be leaving to complete a personal journey. They would be under the guidance of Mac until they reached Bent's Fort. Then they would be on their own, for the rest of the trip to Santa Fe. Sage was sure they'd get the wagons through, now that they had experience fighting Indians, and they would know what to do should another attack occur.

Sage said to the Irish drivers, "After you get to Bent's Fort, the two Mexicans will be in charge. They know the way, and they'll be responsible for getting the wagons back to the hacienda. Here's a note to give to Joe Martin, the manager of my ranch. Joe will pay you for your services and perhaps hire you to work for him on the ranch."

CHAPTER 21

▼

THE RETURN TO EVENING STAR

"Thank you for your help, Mac," Sage said. "Here's the money for your services. I'll be leaving the train in the morning."

"We're in Comanche territory!" Mac exclaimed. "You just saw what's out there. Are you sure you want to ride out into that country alone?"

"I've spent many years alone in this territory," Sage replied. "Don't worry about me. I'll be all right."

Mac shook his head. "All right, it's your hair. If any man on earth can do it, you can, but we're going to miss you."

*   *   *   *

At first light, Sage rode southbound, leading a pack mule. He was alone again on the great prairie. A tingling of excitement ran through him knowing that in a few days he would be in his cave. He hoped to see Evening Star, and fulfill the promise he had made. His mind was in turmoil. He didn't know what he was going to find, or what he should do. He may be the father of a baby and if he is, he has an obligation to the child. He must not shirk from that obligation, but his heart is in Santa Fe.

He was again the man who had grown up alone and was as wild as the land. Sage rode southbound all day and made camp beside a small stream. There was plenty of water for his animals, so he let them graze and rest. He needed to get in touch with his past, and try to figure out what to do when he saw Evening Star. She was a very important part of his past, and he looked forward to seeing her, but his destiny now lay with another woman.

What should he do to fulfill his responsibility to Evening Star and to the child? He needed time to think. The only way to find the answer was to find out what Evening Star wanted. He had to know if her life was in danger, or was she happy as the wife of Black Crow?

He picketed his animals where they could get to water and grass, then walked away to where he would spend the night. If anyone were tracking the animals, they would find only the animals. He would be where his followers couldn't find him, but he would be able to see them. He found the right place on a knoll a short distance away. Lying on his blanket looking at the starry sky, he was at peace, being completely alone in so vast a land.

Clouds filled the sky to the east. He knew that there was little chance it would rain where he was camped. When weather comes to the plains, it comes from the north or west. He heard distant thunder coming from the clouds and knew that under those clouds it would be raining hard. He didn't have to worry about the streams flooding because all the streams on the plains ran to the southeast, and the water from that rain would flow away from him.

He watched the flashes of lightning and waited to hear the rumble of the thunder. The time between his seeing the lightning, and hearing the thunder, told him that the clouds were a long way off. The sky to the west was blue; the dwindling sun painted the sky with brilliant colors. He sat alone and listened to the sounds of the day, changing to the sounds of the night. The land was like a giant animal settling down to sleep.

A feeling of peace settled over him as he listened as the sounds of day becoming muted, while the sounds of the night were becoming more and more dominant. He heard buffalo grunting and bellowing in the distance. Coyotes were yelping and howling as they called to one another—he wondered what they were saying. A whippoorwill called from down by the creek. Once again he was in communication with, and a part of the greater scheme of all there was, in the universe.

He thought, *I'm just a part of something much, much bigger than any single part of the whole. This is something lost to all but a few, who live in cities and towns. They get so busy dealing with their personal problems that their sense of the creator's universe is lost to them.*

He saw in the twilight two riders approaching. They were following the tracks of his animals. He waited silently and watched. When they came over the rise, they saw his horses. They dismounted and began creeping upon, what they believed, would be a camp of the man or men riding the animals. They were confused by what they saw. There were no campfire, no men sitting around, and no bedrolls. All they saw were the animals. They thought that perhaps they had walked into what might be a trap set for them. This was different from anything they had ever experienced in the past. Hoping they had not been seen, they hurried to their horses, mounted, and quickly rode away.

Sage was pleased. A confrontation had been avoided. If the Indians had tried to steal his animals, he would have had to kill them. The Indians would talk of this strange event as they sat around their campfires. Each would tell the other what he would have done. The men who had ridden away had made the right decision. The price for making the wrong decision could sometimes be your life when you're dealing with things where the only rule is the survival of the fittest.

Sage watched the stars move slowly across the sky, pondering his many conflicting thoughts. His mind cleared, and he soon fell asleep. When dawn came, he continued southbound across the undulating prairie. He crossed small creeks and ravines until, in the distance, he saw the Cimarron River. He recognized the terrain as being the same as that which his family and the other two wagons had crossed. The erosion of time had long ago erased all traces of the wagons having passed this way.

He then followed the south side of the Cimarron, looking for the spot where their wagon train had turned south. He found it just as it was getting dark. Again, he tethered the animals and ate cold meat. He gathered wild fruit to supplement his diet and then spent the night upon a knoll overlooking the river where he could keep an eye on his animals and not be seen.

Before sunrise, he moved on. A great sadness rose as he remembered waking up to the sounds of horses running and seeing his father take an arrow through his chest and the two Comanche warriors fighting with his mother.

At midmorning, he came to the place where the wagon had overturned and pinned him under it. He found his father's grave. It was good that he had marked it with stones placed in the shape of a cross. Without the stones, he would never have been able to find it. Nature had a way of erasing all past deeds.

Sage sat down beside his father's grave and told him all that had happened. He told him that his promise to Don Diego had been kept. He sat remembering what a fine and honorable man his father was.

He then rode to his mother's grave. The flowers were still growing from the seeds they produce each year. The color reminded him of his mother's hair. He told his mother about Juanita and wished that she could meet her. He thanked her for loving and caring for him. He remembered her sweet, gentle ways and the smile she always had for him. He watched a pair of birds flying to their nest. He felt so connected to the memory of the past and understood how the past and the future all fit together.

When he got to his cave, he put his animals in the blind canyon, and he got another log to block the mouth of the canyon because the one he had used before had decayed. He then walked to the opening of his cave, being careful not to leave a trace of his passing.

He carried a piece of salt pork for cooking oil. He would have fresh meat tonight. He sat beside his cave and watched the animals playing in the meadow. The memory of the lonely days and nights he spent here brought tears to his eyes.

His cave was unchanged. His things were still there. The only difference was some drawings on the wall showing a man with long hair and beard fighting a pack of wolves attacking two women. Beside it was a drawing of a young woman holding a baby up for the man to see. Evening Star had been in the cave, and she had had a baby!

Sage had brought a bag of coins back with him. He lit one of the pine torches, placed the bag in a spot he remembered, and covered it with stones, completely hiding it. No one would ever find the bag unless they knew where to look. He remembered the coins his father had left for him and the difference it had made in his life. He wanted to leave the same for his child should he or she ever need money. Then he left a knife, an ax, and the spear in the main room of the cave. These would be the weapons for his child, the same weapons he had, that helped him. Other than the spear, he had made before he left the cave, these weapons were things Sage had brought from Saint Louis.

After eating a meal of fried rabbit and taking a bath in the waterfall, he sat on the limestone ledge listening to the night and watching the stars. The six years he had spent here had been terrible, lonely years. However, as he sat contemplating his life during that time, he realized he had many fond memories. His life in that cave had taught him that in life there are predators and there are preys, and that men are not really different from animals.

There is no way to judge the right or wrong of it, because there *is* no right or wrong. That is just the way everything in the universe works. Is it wrong for an eagle to kill a rabbit to feed its young? For one to live, the other must die. Is it better to be a hawk than a dove? Even a dove, which is one of the creator's most gentle things, must consume life if it is to live.

The Indians had a saying—only the rocks live forever. But the Indians were wrong about that. In time, even the rocks crumble to dust and return to the elements from which they came. Then the elements will, in time, return to the source. They are just energy, the same energy the entire universe is made of. Any man who can sit completely alone for long periods of time under the dome of heaven, and not contemplate the meaning of life, isn't really alive.

Sage was faced with one of the most important decisions he would ever be called upon to make. He needed this time alone before he went to see Evening Star. When his mind was at ease, he went inside the cave and fell asleep.

Next morning, when the darkness was yielding to the light, he set out for the Arapaho village. He carried some of the candy that he had brought from Saint Louis. Candy would be a treat for Evening Star, who had never tasted candy and didn't even know such a thing existed.

He spent the night hidden among trees just outside the Arapaho camp looking for Evening Star, but he didn't see her. He knew she would be going to the river to bathe the next morning. He would wait and find a way to talk to her.

As expected, she came early, and he could see she was with child. She was no longer a girl. She was a woman now. He called to her from the cover of vegetation. She recognized his call and looked in his direction. He beckoned for her. She ran to him, knowing they were concealed, and threw herself into his arms. She was so excited to see him that it was hard to control her emotions. She asked him to wait near a spot they both knew. She said she would come as soon as she had attended the needs of their baby and fed her husband, Black Crow. He would be angry if she were late coming back from her bath because he would be waiting for his morning meal. Evening Star looked well fed and well cared for. Sage told her he would wait until she came.

About two hours passed; then he saw her coming. She was with the girl that Sage remembered. Evening Star was carrying a baby. Her friend, Little Calf, was pregnant, also.

Evening Star handed the baby to Sage and said with great pride, "This is your son."

He was a handsome baby, big and strong. His eyes were dark, but his hair and skin were a little too light for an Indian. He had strong features, and his eyes searched everywhere. He was a curious child, interested in everything. He didn't cry when Sage took him in his arms. Sage had mixed feelings, knowing he was holding his son. He wanted to take Evening Star and the baby with him, leave the village, and make a life together. They could go to his cave and then figure out what they should do next. He still had a shipbuilding business in Virginia—he could take them there. *But how could I take her away? Her life is here,* Sage thought. And at that moment, he knew his life and his love were waiting for him back in Santa Fe.

"I cannot go," Evening Star said. "My husband is Black Crow. Little Calf will take care of the baby so we can talk."

Little Calf took the baby and withdrew to pick berries. That is what they had told the people they would be doing.

Sage asked, "Evening Star, what name did you give the baby?"

She said, "The village named the baby Puma Son of Mountain Lion."

"That's a lotta name for a baby."

"Yes, it is, but it's a good name for an Indian boy. Someday he'll be a great chief."

They sat, each looking very carefully at the other. It had been a long time, and they both had changed. Evening Star had never seen Sage without his long hair and flowing beard. She was pleased with how handsome he looked. Indian men had very little facial hair, and Michael looked better without the long hair and beard.

Evening Star's face was more round; she had lost that little-girl look and was now a woman. She was still pretty and had not lost her gentleness and reminded Sage of a little bird about to take flight. She looked searchingly into his eyes when she told him that she was pregnant again, this time with the child of Black Crow. She didn't love Black Crow the way she loved Sage, she said, but he was a good husband. He took care of her and her mother. There was food in their lodge now and, as the wife of a sub-chief, she had a strong standing in the tribe. Other women looked to her for guidance.

Sage had mixed feelings. He was happy that she was well, and that she was being taken care of, but what about their son? The baby was too young to be taken from his mother.

"How will Puma ever know of his father?" Sage asked. "Who will raise him? Who will teach him the things he will need to know, to grow up to be a good man?"

"The whole village loves this baby," Evening Star said. "They'll teach him, and I'll tell him about his father. They are grateful to you for killing the four warriors who had killed so many of our people. The Arapaho are still at war with the Comanche, but they no longer fear them. The Comanche tell stories of the great half-man—half-mountain lion who came into their village in the night and killed four of their greatest warriors . . . all by himself. They say he was so great a warrior that no man could stand against him. Yes, your son will hear plenty of stories about his father."

Sage then told her that he had left presents in his cave for their son. He told her what the gifts were, and why he had left them. He then told her about the gold coins, and where they were hidden. He asked her not to give the gifts to Puma until he had become a man. She must never reveal the secret of the cave to anyone other than their son, and not even to him until he had became a man.

She promised to keep his secret, and thanked him for returning so she could show him their son.

"If you or the baby ever needs my help, leave a message at Bent's Fort, and I'll come right away."

Evening Star held him close, told him goodbye, and then walked back to her life in the village. He watched her walk away and said goodbye to a chapter in his life, wondering if he would ever see her, or his son again. Perhaps some day, when Puma Son of Mountain Lion, became a man, they would meet again.

CHAPTER 22

▼

BACK TO SANTA FE AND JUANITA

When Evening Star returned to Black Crow, Sage returned to his cave, gathered his mother and father's things, prepared to load onto the pack mule, so he would be ready to leave in the morning. He had kept his promise. He had done all he could do for his son and Evening Star. Now he would return to Santa Fe and Juanita. He wanted to be back earlier than planned. He would like to get there before the wagons containing the gifts and gold coins arrived, so he could give the presents he had bought in Saint Louis to the people.

Sage cleaned his cave, one last time, and replaced the now decayed sagebrush at the top of his cave with a large jagged stone that would conceal the opening, without blocking the ventilation. He took one last look, to make sure everything was as it should be, and then departed. He had a sense of urgency about getting back. He didn't know why, but he had a feeling he was needed at the ranch.

He traveled steadily following the route he and his friends had taken. He knew the way and knew what to expect. He wanted to get to his destination as quickly as possible without overstressing his animals.

He rode from before sunrise until after sunset. He gathered food along the way, ate it when he stopped for the night. He always slept away from his animals.

He saw a few Indians, but by taking great care, they didn't see him. When he arrived in Santa Fe, the wagons had arrived just before him, and the drivers were at Maggie's getting something to eat. Sage went directly to Maggie's. Someone told her they had seen him ride in, so she had food ready. He sat at the table with his drivers and ate. He told them he was going to the hotel to get cleaned up, get a haircut and shave. He suggested they do the same and meet him at the stable in two hours, for the final trip home.

It was a beautiful late summer morning. The journey had been successful. He had purchased all the supplies on the list, and he had special presents for Juanita and Bonnie. Sage's spirits were high, and he was looking forward to seeing Juanita.

*   *   *   *

As the hacienda came into view, Sage was surprised. He could see no one at the compound, not even children playing in the courtyard. He signaled for the wagons to stop. Something was wrong! They watched for a while. The hacienda was too quiet.

"Men," Sage said to the drivers, "when we get to the ranch, pull the wagons into the barn, unhook the mules, and turn them loose in the pasture. Keep your horses saddled and ready, then wait with the wagons, and stay ready with your guns. If I don't come right back, go to my ranch and have Joe bring his vaqueros. Don't allow yourselves to be taken."

Sage knew he was walking into a trap, but he was concerned about Juanita. There was only one possibility. Jose Alvarez had returned and he was desperate, which meant he would be dangerous. He wouldn't hesitate in killing Juanita to get what he wanted. Sage had to go to her at all costs.

As he stepped into the courtyard, two men stepped from behind the gate with guns pointing at him. He allowed himself to be disarmed. When his captors pushed him into the main room, he saw Jose. Juanita was nowhere to be seen. They kept his guns and placed his knife and ax on the table out of his reach. They didn't know of his skill with that knife or they wouldn't have left it where he could get his hands on it. He might have a chance after all.

"Where is Juanita?" Sage asked.

Jose said in a loud and demanding voice, "I'll ask the questions. Where's the money you got for the gold and silver?"

This question told Sage that Juanita had told her uncle that he had taken all the bullion to Saint Louis to sell. That meant that they were holding Juanita until they found out what happened to the money. Sage heaved a sigh of relief.

"I'll tell you nothing until I see Juanita," Sage replied.

Jose said to one of his men, "Okay, bring her in."

Two men dragged Juanita into the room. One look and Sage knew she was under a lot of stress, but she was unhurt. Her eyes told him that she was relieved to see him.

Sage gave Juanita one quick reassuring look, then looked back at Alvarez. "You want to know what I did with the money. I left it with the silver dealer in Saint Louis for safekeeping. I brought this sack of coins back with me." He threw the sack on the table. "The wagon train goes back and forth twice a year and trades gold and silver bullion with the dealer in Saint Louis. I've arranged for the dealer to hold our money in safekeeping until we need it. We can draw money anytime from Bent's Fort."

"Don't give me that. You wouldn't leave all that money with someone in Saint Louis. Where's the money?"

"Well, you can see I don't have it on me. My saddlebags are on my horse in the barn. I have a pack mule out there. You could take a look, but you won't find any money."

"What's in those wagons?"

"They're loaded with freight that I brought back for the ranch. There's no gold there, either, but you're welcome to look."

"What happened to your drivers?"

"They had done their jobs, so I told them to release the mules and go home to their families. You could send one of your men to Bent's Fort to check for yourself. But they won't give you any money unless I go with the man to verify that the money is for me, and I won't do that unless you release Juanita in the care of the people at my ranch."

"Why should I release Juanita in your care?"

"It's the only way you're going to get any money from me. You have to release Juanita first."

Alvarez snarled. "No, there's another way. If I do away with both of you, the ranch will belong to me. Don Diego should have left it to me instead of leaving it to Juanita's father. There's still plenty of gold in that mine. Can you think of a reason I shouldn't just kill both of you, here and now?"

"Well, for one thing, if you kill us, how will you get the money for that gold? They won't give it to you just because you say you own the ranch."

Frustrated, Jose yelled at his men, "Lock them in that room until we can look in that wagon and check his saddlebags! I need time to think this out!"

Juanita was standing beside the table where the man had put Sage's knife. Sage caught Juanita's eye and indicated that he wanted her to look behind her. When she looked, she saw his knife and realized what he wanted. With her back to the table, she picked up the knife and concealed it in the folds of her dress. Then she went with Sage as they were escorted into the adjoining room.

As soon as the guard left, Juanita gave the knife to Sage who instantly hid it on top of one of the rafters out of sight to anyone who might be looking for it. However, it would be within his easy reach when the time came for him to use it. Then he turned to Juanita and took her in his arms.

Tears of relief ran down her cheeks. She clung to him and cried, "Oh, thank God you're here. I didn't expect you for another month or more. What are we going to do?"

"We're going to play for time until Joe can get here with his vaqueros. My drivers went to get him. He'll be here in about three hours. We've got to stall your uncle until then. Joe will let me know when he gets here. Then I'll use this knife to get my guns back. If I had my guns, we could hold out in this room until Joe's men can get here."

"Is the money in the wagon?" Juanita asked.

"The money is in the wagon, all right, but they won't find it. It's stored in the false bottom, remember?"

"Yes, I do remember."

"Only Carlos and the two carpenters who built it know that the wagon has a false bottom. Even the drivers don't know where the money is hidden."

"Carlos is wounded, and his youngest son has been killed," Juanita explained. "That's how they took me captive. They were threatening to kill more of our people if I didn't turn the ranch over to my uncle. He knows that the people of Santa Fe wouldn't let him just take the ranch, but if he could show them that he had bought it, they wouldn't try to stop him. He wanted me to sign the ranch over to him as though he had bought it, and I wouldn't do that. If he killed me, he couldn't get my signature. He doesn't know that you now own half of the ranch. He's willing to take the money you got for the bullion and go back to Mexico, but if he doesn't get the money, he's going to be furious and no telling what he might do."

"We gave him money, and gave him a chance to go to Mexico and start a new life. Now he has come back wanting more. I don't think we should give him anything. He won't stop with wounding Carlos and killing his son. He won't quit until you are dead. We're going to stall him until Joe gets here with his men, then we'll have a chance to get this situation under control again. You look tired. Why don't you lie down and get some rest? You're going to need all your strength. I'll watch over you until Joe gets here. We're going to have a fight on our hands.

"I'll put my hat on this windowsill where Joe will see it, and he'll know where we are. I'm hoping he'll let us know when he gets here, and then we can give him a helping hand."

When the mule drivers saw Sage being taken with a gun at his back, they went into action. One of the Mexicans went with the Irish men to tell Joe what had happened. The other Mexican went to get to Carlos.

Joe quickly figured out that Alvarez had returned and was trying to take over the ranch. Alvarez was a dangerous man and had to be stopped. Joe noticed that the three drivers were armed with two revolvers each, and asked if Sage had trained them to use the guns. They answered yes and were quite competent with them. That gave them four sets of revolvers and each had a rifle. That made a formidable fighting force. He armed ten more of his vaqueros with rifles. That gave him fourteen fighting men, against what he figured would be an opposing force of approximately twenty men. Joe was counting on the element of surprise, and that would have to be enough. He knew that the other driver had gone to Carlos, and his vaqueros would help in overcoming these villains.

When the driver got to Carlos's home, he found that Carlos had been wounded and one of his sons had been killed. The others were eager to help in any way they could. Carlos's oldest son, Ramon, took the lead and armed as many of the vaqueros as he could, and led them to the hacienda. They got there just as Joe and his men were arriving.

Joe had no idea where Sage and Juanita were, and the light was fading fast. He walked around the house, staying out of gun range, looking for some indication of where Sage and Juanita were being held. When he saw Sage's hat in the window, he knew that was a signal from Sage. He waited for darkness to give him cover, then carefully worked his way to the window and gave a low night-bird call.

Sage came to the window and called out in a quiet voice, "We're all right. I'm unarmed, but I think I can get my guns. If I can, I'll hold them off until you can get Alvarez out of the house."

"We'll be attacking before daylight," Joe said. "Just hang on. Don't try to come out. We'll shoot anybody who tries to escape. Keep that bedroom door locked and barred."

When Joe got back to his men, he found Ramon and his vaqueros waiting for instructions.

Joe told the vaqueros, "Stand guard over every exit and don't let anyone escape."

"I hope Alvarez tries to escape," Ramon said. "I have a score to settle with him. He killed my brother and wounded my father. There's no way he's going to leave that house alive, if I have anything to say about it. He has been a source of misery for me and my family for more than seven years. He had his chance to live, and he threw it away when he came back here. Now he's going to have to pay the price."

Sage called out to the guard in the other room and asked him to open the door to let Juanita go to the bathroom. When the guard came to unlock the door, Sage noticed that the guard was wearing his guns. He grabbed him from behind, dragged him into the room, and knocked him unconscious. He then retrieved his guns and put them on. Now he was armed and ready for whatever might happen. Sage called out through the window.

"Joe," he said, "I've got my guns. I can hold out however long it might take."

Joe yelled to Alvarez's men. "The house is surrounded! Give up and come out with your hands over your heads. You will then be allowed to return to Mexico City unharmed. But if you don't give up, you will be shot!"

Joe's intention was to cause the men to rise up against Alvarez. Alvarez saw what Joe was trying to do, and decided to go after Sage and Juanita, to use as hostages to force Joe to release him and his men.

"Men!" Alvarez barked. "Get those two out of that room!"

The men were hesitant, knowing Sage had two revolvers and plenty of ammunition.

Alvarez yelled, "Pick up that table and smash the door!"

When Sage heard all of this going on in the next room, he went to the window and called out to Joe's men outside, "Someone, come to this window . . . . I need to talk to you."

"Yeah, what do you want?" someone answered.

"I want to get Juanita out of here. This is going to get downright sticky in here in about a minute. I'm sending her out this window, and I don't want you to shoot her as she's coming out. I want you to take her somewhere out of gunshot range."

"Send her out," Joe called out. "In fact, why don't you both come on out while we keep them busy?"

"The window is too small and too high. It's too small for me. It will be difficult for Juanita to crawl through. I'll help from here, you pull her through."

Alvarez's men were about to get through the door, so Sage had to direct his attention to defending the room. He fired a couple of shots through the shattered door. That stopped them long enough for Juanita to escape, but it didn't leave Sage enough time to try to get his much larger frame through the small window. Sage placed his back against the wall of the room. The door was located where the men in the other room couldn't see him with his back to the wall. They knew that for them to come through that door was an invitation to be shot, and no one wanted to do that.

Even though the door was shattered, they were in a standoff. Sage knew it was only a matter of time before Alvarez forced his men to risk their lives to get into the room.

Sage called, "Joe, knock a hole in the outside of this end wall, while I hold them off!"

Two of Alvarez's men stuck their heads through the door. Sage fired through the door, and they fell in the doorway. While the other attackers were getting out of range, he grabbed the weapons from the bodies of the two he had shot and left them lying in the doorway as a reminder to the rest of the men of the price they would pay for trying to come through that door.

Jose's men were trying to knock a hole in the end wall. It was about two feet thick and difficult to break through. At the same time, Sage could hear Alvarez's men in the other room trying to knock a hole through the inside wall between the two rooms. It was a race to see who would get through first.

Alvarez knew he had to have a hostage if he were going to have a chance to get out of the house alive. He was becoming desperate. Someone stuck his hand through the door to fire at Sage. Sage used his ax to knock the gun out of his hand. The attacker screamed; he wouldn't be using that hand for a while. Sage was slowly but surely cutting the attacking party down to size. Each time he eliminated one, he made the others a little more reluctant to try. Alvarez was urging his men to intensify the attack. Sage could see the wall beginning to break. When they got the hole through the wall, they would have two openings through which to mount an attack, and it would be difficult to hold out very long. Joe's men were cutting away at the outside wall, but it was much thicker, and it was going to take more time.

Sage stood between the smashed door and the hole in the wall. He fired a couple of shots through the small hole and heard someone yell. He had scored a hit. He had to slow them down until Joe's men could break through,

"Sage," Joe called out, "I can see the door between the two rooms by looking through this window, and whoever tries to come through that door is going to get one hell of a surprise."

Now Sage had only the opening in the wall to defend. He heard a shot fired through the window and then heard a moan in the other room. He knew, with the skill of the gunfighter firing the shots, there was one less attacker trying to knock a hole in the wall.

Alvarez's men were beginning to see that they were not going to win this race, and they were becoming more afraid of Joe's men than they were of Alvarez. It was only a matter of time until they turned on Alvarez. That's what Joe wanted.

Alvarez realized that he was losing and decided to make a break for it. He ran through the front door, intent on escaping. He made it to a horse, mounted, and quickly rode away. It all happened so fast that he caught Joe's men by surprise. Ramon saw what was happening and was instantly on a horse in hot pursuit. Alvarez disappeared into the night with Ramon right behind him. Ramon was determined to settle the score with Alvarez.

With Alvarez gone, the attackers called out, "We're ready to give up. We're coming out empty-handed. Don't shoot!"

"All right, men," Joe yelled, "take their guns and tie them up. We'll turn them over to the authorities in Santa Fe."

Sage came out right behind Alvarez's men making sure none of them had concealed weapons. When he got outside, he called out, "Joe, I'm going after Alvarez. I want to make sure he doesn't get away, and I also want to make sure Ramon doesn't get hurt by that madman."

"I'm going with you," Joe shouted. "I want to make sure we don't have any more trouble with that scoundrel. I still owe him one for shooting at Bonnie."

Sage and Joe rode into the night, following Alvarez and Ramon. After a short ride, they found where Alvarez's horse had stumbled and Alvarez had been thrown. Ramon's horse was standing nearby unattended. They knew Ramon had gone after Alvarez on foot and was stalking him like a hunter after a vicious animal. Ramon had grown up under the thumb of this cruel man, and he wanted to settle their differences in his own way. Neither Joe nor Sage wanted to interfere. This was something personal to Ramon; however, they realized that Ramon was outmatched. Alvarez had trained to fight in whatever manner it took to win—dirty and sneaky tactics were his specialties.

Sage and Joe dismounted, tied the reins of their horses to some bushes, and moved cautiously into the brush looking for Ramon and

Alvarez. Sage was once again in his element. Hunting a vicious animal in the night was not new to him. He was sure Alvarez would be waiting for Ramon to show himself. Sage moved through the boulders, silent as a shadow. He made no sound and moved no branches. His senses told him he was getting close. He saw Alvarez about twenty paces away, hiding in wait, behind a boulder. Sage saw Ramon moving forward about fifty paces from Alvarez. Alvarez was aware that Ramon was approaching and was just waiting until he could get a good shot.

Sage knew that he must make Ramon aware that Alvarez was waiting in ambush. Ramon would be killed if he kept going in the direction he was now going. Sage threw a rock into the brush near Alvarez. The rock startled Alvarez, and he fired in Ramon's direction, but because he was startled and fired in haste, he missed. Now Ramon knew where Alvarez was waiting and that gave him an even chance.

Each was now stalking the other. Sage watched and waited to see how it would play out. Soon they clashed hand-to-hand. Alvarez was larger and stronger, but Ramon was quicker and armed with anger. The fight lasted only seconds. Ramon stepped back. He had a knife cut on his arm, but Alvarez would never cause anyone trouble again. Sage moved away into the night, never allowing Ramon to know that he had witnessed the struggle. Sage saw Joe hiding behind him. Joe, too, had seen the fight. Neither man spoke, but each knew what the other was thinking. They went to their horses and rode back in silence. Now that the fight was over, Sage wanted to see Juanita.

She was the first to see them coming, and she ran to make sure Sage was all right. He told her that he was unharmed and stepped down from his horse to take her in his arms. She was outwardly calm, but he could feel her trembling. He realized what an ordeal she had been through and how much she meant to him.

"Did you find Ramon and my uncle?" Juanita asked.

"No," Sage lied. "Your uncle had disappeared into the night." That was the truth. It was not the complete truth, but Sage felt it was all Juanita needed to know.

Joe heard and nodded his head. "Yeah, he's gone for sure this time."

"Do you think he'll ever come back?" she asked.

"No, he'll leave us alone from now on." Sage replied.

Joe said, "I'll go with the vaqueros and turn Alvarez's men over to the Mexican army. They'll know what to do with them. I just want to wash my hands of this whole mess."

"Thanks, Joe," Sage said gratefully, shaking his hand. "I'll see you tomorrow, and I'll tell you about our times on the trail. I want to know how things are going at the ranch. I want to see Bonnie and her folks. We have a lot of catching up to do, but I'll spend the night here. Juanita and I have a lot of catching up to do, also, and it can't wait until tomorrow."

"Okay," Joe replied. "I'll see you at our place. Anytime tomorrow will be just fine. I can see that you have more important things to do right now."

Joe and his men tied the prisoners securely, loaded them into an empty wagon and hauled them to Santa Fe. Joe sent one of his men back to his place, to let Bonnie and her folks know that everything was all right, and he would be home in a few hours.

While Joe and Sage were talking to Juanita, Ramon rode up. Sage went to him and explained, "We told Juanita that her uncle had gotten away in the night. That's what happened, isn't it?"

"Si, Señor, he got away permanently this time. I don't think we'll hear from him again." Ramon now realized that Sage knew what had happened, and why Alvarez fired that wild shot at him in the dark. A very understanding man had probably saved his life tonight. Ramon was thinking, *This is the kind of man that should be running this ranch. We're lucky to have him as our manager.*

"Ramon," Sage said, "thank you for your help. Take your men home and get some sleep. I'll be at your place tomorrow to see how Carlos is doing. I'm sorry about your brother."

"Thank you, Señor, *hasta mañana.*"

Sage turned to Juanita and said, "Now, maybe there's some time for us. Do you think the ladies could fix us something to eat? I'm hungry."

"They'll be pleased to fix us something," Juanita replied. "I'll have to call them. They've been hiding in the homes of some of their friends while all this trouble was going on. I'm hungry, too, and I sure want to hear about your journey."

"I need a bath and a change of clothes," Sage said. "I've got to take care of my horse, and I want to check on the wagon to make sure Alvarez's men didn't damage the things I brought back from Saint Louis."

Juanita replied, "I'll have the women get your room and bath ready. There's so much I want to show you and tell you about what we've been doing while you were gone."

"I want to hear all about it. We'll talk while we have dinner, and tomorrow morning you can show me around the ranch."

When Sage returned from taking care of his horse, both his room and bath were ready, and the ladies were cooking. Juanita was in her quarters getting dressed for dinner.

After his bath, Sage went to the big room to wait for Juanita. The big room was still a mess from the struggle they just had with Alvarez. The staff would clean it tomorrow.

When Juanita came into the room, she was beautiful. No one could tell, by looking at her, that she had gone through two days of being held hostage. She had to be exhausted, but it didn't show. She was regal as always.

Hand in hand they went into the dining room. The ladies had prepared a wonderful meal in a short time. Sage and Juanita sat down to a candlelit table with fine food and wine. He told her the story of his journey and about trading the silver for gold coins. He then told her that he had set his mind at ease, with the problem he had gone back to deal with, and now he was ready to get on with his life.

Juanita's face was beaming. This was the part of the story she was most interested. Sage wanted to ask her to marry him, but he felt the timing was wrong. He thought it would be better to wait for a happy time, when they were both rested and feeling good.

"Everything turned out so well." Juanita remarked. "I'm very pleased."

"I have gifts for everyone," Sage said, "and I'll give them out tomorrow night. We'll celebrate the journey and the hacienda returning to normal."

"Oh, that's a wonderful idea; everyone will be delighted. Could we announce our wedding at the same time?"

Sage was surprised and pleased by her question. He walked around the table, took her in his arms, and asked, "Will you marry me?"

"Of course I will. Everyone has known, for a long time that we're going to be married. The announcement will confirm what we've both known from the first day we met at the restaurant in Santa Fe, when you first came to town, don't you remember? Bonnie and I have been discussing it for a long time now. Joe talks to Bonnie you know."

"Yes," Sage said. "I fell in love with you the first time I saw you in the restaurant. I didn't know you were even aware of my presence." He took her hand, and they walked into the courtyard, neither saying anything, just enjoying the night and being together.

After a time Juanita reached up and kissed him and whispered, "*Mañana.*"

He walked her to her room and kissed her longingly. They clung to each other. And he said softly, "*Mañana.*"

*   *   *   *

They met for breakfast, and went to see how Carlos was doing. His wounds were painful but not life threatening. Carlos and his family were celebrating the return of the hacienda to the rightful owners and, at the same time, mourning the loss of their son and brother. Carlos said he would be back on the job in a few weeks. In the meantime, Ramon would be in charge. Sage told them of the celebration they were going to have that evening and that he had gifts for everyone. They said they would all help in getting ready for the fiesta.

Sage asked Ramon to have his men unload the wagon and placed the contents in the courtyard, ready for the celebration. He didn't tell him about the gold coins in the false bottom. He and Juanita would have to unload the coins after the party. They didn't want anyone to know about the gold. There was no one for them to be concerned about, but it was a precaution against possible attempts at stealing the gold in the future. The fewer people who knew about it, the better it was for everyone.

Juanita took Sage for a tour of the hacienda. She wanted him to see the results of irrigating the crops. They had produced a bumper crop of everything. There was plenty of food for everyone and plenty of food for the animals, also. The women had been making blankets and clothes, the men had been busy building and repairing the adobe houses. They had made the houses bigger and better. The women were pleased to have water so near.

Now they were ready to improve the big house. They would have to repair the holes created in the struggle with Alvarez.

*   *   *   *

It was time for the fiesta, and everyone was invited. They ate, drank, sang, and danced. Joe and Bonnie were there with Frank and Thelma. After the meal, Sage handed out presents to everyone. He had toys and candy for the children, cloth for dresses, brightly colored jewelry for the women, and tools for the men. Everyone was pleased. Then Sage showed them the plows and seeds for the growing of next year's crops. The tools would make work easier and more productive. He gave Bonnie and Juanita jewelry and dresses.

Then he called to get everyone's attention, and said, "Juanita and I have an announcement to make. We want to confirm what you already know. We will soon be wed."

A cheer went up, and they danced the night away. The next day was a day of rest. Happy times had come again to *El Casa Grande.*

978-0-595-48625-0
0-595-48625-8

CPSIA information can be obtained at www.ICGtesting.com
Printed in the USA
LVOW082127270912

300674LV00002B/74/P